THE HORSEA MARINA MURDERS

A gripping crime thriller full of twists

PAULINE ROWSON

The Solent Murder Mysteries book 3

Originally published as
The Suffocating Sea

Revised edition 2022
Joffe Books, London
www.joffebooks.com

First published by Severn House Publishers Ltd.
in Great Britain in 2009 as *The Suffocating Sea*

This paperback edition was first published
in Great Britain in 2022

© Pauline Rowson 2009, 2022

This book is a work of fiction. Names, characters,
businesses, organizations, places and events are either
the product of the author's imagination or are used
fictitiously. Any resemblance to actual persons, living
or dead, events or locales is entirely coincidental.
The spelling used is British English except where fidelity
to the author's rendering of accent or dialect supersedes
this. The right of Pauline Rowson to be identified as author
of this work has been asserted in accordance with the
Copyright, Designs and Patents Act 1988.

Cover art by Dee Dee Book Covers

ISBN: 978-1-80405-225-9

For my Mum and Dad

NOTE TO THE READER

Please note this book is set in the early 2000s, when technology was somewhat different.

ONE

Wednesday, 17 December, 7.45 p.m.

The blue pulsating lights of the fire engines radiated out of the dense freezing fog like revolving spotlights on a stage as Sergeant Cantelli swung into the car park at Horsea Marina. Inspector Andy Horton shivered. A cold, clammy feeling fingered its way up his spine. He'd been to hundreds of fires in his career, and had seen burnt and shrivelled corpses before. This was no different, he told himself, yet instinctively he knew it was.

The fog and smoke curled together like a snake and seemed to ooze their way inside the car, bringing with them the smell of danger and death. They clawed at his throat, making it hard for him to catch his breath. A premonition so strong that it was almost urging him to turn back and leave this to others, but it was too late for that. Cantelli was already drawing to a halt in front of the police vehicle straddling the fire engines. Beyond, somewhere on the pontoon, thought Horton, was a burning boat and inside it a charred corpse. He shuddered as Barney Cantelli said, 'Quite a crowd for a night cold enough to freeze the whatsits off a brass monkey.'

Horton surveyed the spectators' gawping features. There were about twenty of them, but thankfully no journalists that he could spot, though for a moment he thought he recognized a dark-haired woman in her mid-thirties dressed in a smart trouser suit and three quarter-length raincoat. As their eyes connected, she stepped away from the crowd and hurried towards a car. He couldn't see which one because a middle-aged woman, wearing a felt hat shaped like a flowerpot pushed low over her forehead, blocked his view.

Cantelli said, 'You'd think they'd have better things to do with Christmas looming.'

Christmas. Horton grasped at the thought like a drowning man clutching a lifebelt. Not because he liked the season. On the contrary, he hated it, but there was one bright spot in the festive calendar: he was going to spend Christmas Eve with his daughter, Emma. A whole day, and the first since his marital split in April. He half expected and dreaded that Catherine would have second thoughts by next Wednesday and deny him access. But his solicitor, Frances Greywell, said that Catherine *couldn't* change her mind. You wanna bet, he thought, stepping out of the car as PC Seaton came hurrying towards him.

'The boat's called *Enterprise*, sir,' Seaton said excitedly. 'You know, like the star ship . . .'

'I am acquainted with *Star Trek*,' Horton replied, striding past the fire engines, noting that his curt tone didn't extinguish Seaton's grin. It seemed totally out of place in the circumstances, but Horton told himself that Seaton was young, keen and ambitious, and he probably didn't have any hang-ups over seeing shrivelled corpses. Of all the deaths Horton feared in his job, with the exception of children, the one caused by fire was his worst. It was that rictus smile, so grotesque, inhuman and mocking, and the smell of roasted flesh which was exactly reminiscent of fried bacon or roast pork. He wouldn't be able to look at that kind of meat, or be within sniffing distance of it for days, weeks even, without recalling what he was about to see here.

'The boat went up like the clappers,' Seaton enthused. 'The fire investigation officer called us because he thinks it's a suspicious death.'

Horton drew up in front of the bridgehead. He could see the firefighters reeling in the hoses on the pontoon, but the boat, or what was left of it, was hidden by the thick fog. He hesitated and silently cursed himself for his foolish fears and uncharacteristic indecisiveness. Hoping he wasn't betraying what he was feeling, Horton glanced at Cantelli who was chewing gum and frowning at the sight of the fire. Perhaps he should confide in the sergeant. Cantelli, with his more intuitive nature and half Italian blood, would understand about premonitions. But what the devil could he confide? A feeling? It sounded crazy and weak.

His new boss, DCI Lorraine Bliss, would put him on sick leave if she knew what he was thinking. Either that or have him sectioned. And maybe she would like that. She was taking some getting used to and they hadn't exactly started off on the right foot. Horton could still recall her reaction when he'd questioned her efficiency on the case where their paths had crossed before her promotion.

'Have you seen the victim?' he asked Seaton.

'The fire officer wouldn't let me on board. He said it wasn't safe.'

He looked so disappointed that Horton felt like admonishing him, but he held his tongue. Instead he asked, 'What about an ID?'

Seaton began to look uncomfortable. 'I haven't had the chance to check it out at the marina office, and WPC Somerfield is asking around for anyone who witnessed the explosion.'

Something inside Horton snapped. Enthusiasm was all very well, but when it got in the way of procedure then it was sloppiness. He heard himself say, 'Your first priority, Constable, is to control this crowd, secure the scene, and ascertain the identity of the victim, not jigger up and down as if you've wet your pants at finding some poor bastard burnt to a crisp.'

'Sir,' Seaton snapped to attention, staring straight ahead.

Horton could feel the young constable's disappointment and it irked him that he'd been so harsh because he recalled his own sense of excitement at a high-level incident when he was a young PC. He knew that Seaton's enthusiasm was only natural. He also knew that he was a fine one to talk; procedure could, and often did, go the way of the dodo if Horton thought he was on to something.

'Secure the area, and get Somerfield cataloguing everyone who goes on to the bridgehead. See that no one gets within spitting distance of those fire appliances except those who are authorized to do so, and if you're not sure who that is then you'd better go back to basic training,' he said stiffly.

Seaton scurried off like a scalded cat and Horton caught Cantelli looking at him mildly surprised. 'Seaton won't be so chipper after he's seen the body,' Horton grumbled, heading towards the security gate that led on to the pontoon.

Damn it. Why was he feeling and behaving like this? Perhaps he'd been working too hard. He'd had a traumatic year after being charged and subsequently cleared of rape. That, and fighting to gain access to his daughter against a wife who was out to prevent him from doing so at every opportunity just to spite him, was enough to make any man break, he consoled himself. But even as he did so he despised the excuses. *Concentrate on the facts. You're a policeman; so damn well act like one.*

He peered at the security gate that led from the bridgehead on to the pontoons. It was wedged open for the firefighters, but normally admittance would only be allowed after tapping a security code on to the digital keypad, and that code was regularly changed.

Horton examined the opening mechanism. 'There's no sign of a forced entry, which means that if it is a suspicious death, our killer must either have known the victim, be a boat owner or a member of the marina staff. Either that or he slipped in behind another boat owner.'

'Perhaps the fire investigation officer is wrong and this is an accident,' Cantelli said, unravelling another piece of gum and popping it in his mouth.

'Let's hope so, for all our sakes. We're enough officers down already with this flu bug, and with only a week to Christmas, managing a murder investigation will be a nightmare.'

'Yeah, but not yours, Andy,' Cantelli said quietly.

Horton glared at him. 'Thanks for reminding me that I failed to get into the major crime team, or get promoted. For a moment I'd almost forgotten.' But Horton couldn't take offence; he'd known Cantelli too long for that and respected and valued him as a friend. Besides, he knew what Barney was doing. He took a breath trying to release some of his tension. 'Let's get on with it.'

Mentally he began to prepare himself for what he was about to see, but he couldn't shake off the feeling that this was going to be no ordinary victim and no ordinary case. The fog didn't help to dispel his jitters either. Its freezing tendrils rolled up from the sea, as dense as a featherbed, and wrapping itself around them like a cloak that smelt as though it had been doused in diesel, plastic, wood and salt. It was suffocating and evil.

Above the booming foghorns he could hear the throb of the fire-engine pump, but the rest was just silence. Not even the sound of laughter and music from the restaurants on the board-walk penetrated the thick grey blanket. It was as if they were suspended in time and place.

Cantelli broke the silence. 'This reminds me of a scene from *The Ghost Breakers*. Paulette Goddard inherits this West Indian mansion haunted by ghosts and zombies and surrounded by foggy water.'

Horton didn't think they'd meet any zombies, though he could name a few coppers down at the station that bore a remarkable resemblance to the species: DI Tony Dennings for one. No, that was unfair of him. He was just piqued because Dennings had become Uckfield's DI on the major crime team when Uckfield had promised him the job previously.

And ghosts . . . Horton felt as if they were all around him, which was ridiculous because he didn't even believe in them! As they drew nearer to the boat, he saw Cantelli shiver. His body tensed and Horton knew that he too had finally caught the scent of danger.

A tall man with a balding head and a round jolly face greeted them. 'Jim Maidment, Fire Investigation Officer.'

Horton bristled at his cheerful tone, which was so out of place given the circumstances, but he shook hands and did the introductions. Then he stared at the remains of what had once been a very large and no doubt very expensive motorboat. There was nothing supernatural about that. The tangibility of it made him feel better and once more in control. There wasn't much left of it, but Horton could see by its shape that it was a traditional trawler yacht rather than one of the sleek powerboat models. He guessed it was a Grand Banks.

Maidment said, 'We managed to get to it before it sank, and thankfully there were no boats either side, otherwise the fire could easily have spread. He's over here.'

As Horton followed Maidment further down the pontoon he felt the anxious tightening in his stomach that always heralded the viewing of a corpse, only this time it was stronger than usual. He slowed his breathing and tried to relax his facial muscles. Glancing at Cantelli he knew he felt the same and was steeling himself to face the ordeal. At their feet was a small bundle covered by a grey blanket.

Horton didn't want the blanket removed. He sensed it as a defining moment. There's still time. Turn back, the silent voice urged him, but he had never ducked responsibility before or run away from danger, and he wasn't about to start now.

He nodded and Maidment drew back the blanket. Horton took a breath and stared at the leering, empty grin and hollow sockets of the roasted face, willing the contents of his stomach to stay in place. The smell of burnt flesh was overwhelming and sickening. The body had taken up a pugilistic attitude where the heat of the fire had contracted the muscles. It looked grotesque, like some evil goblin sent to ridicule him.

'Poor blighter,' Cantelli said quietly.

Maidment pointed to the right-hand side of the victim's head and, despite not wanting to look closer, Horton knew he had to. 'See here,' Maidment said, 'his skull's caved in. It looks to me as if he's been struck. We found him lying face down. His buttocks and the lower half of his back aren't quite so badly burnt because a cupboard fell on him and covered them from the worst of the flames.'

'How did the fire start?' asked Horton, nodding at Maidment to cover the victim. The blackened, contorted face disappeared from sight, but not from Horton's mind. He heard Cantelli let out a long slow breath and felt like doing the same himself but didn't want to appear relieved in any way in front of Maidment. As they stepped away from the corpse, Cantelli once again resumed chewing his gum.

'It's difficult to tell without further investigation,' Maidment said, frowning and scratching his nose. 'It could have been a leaking gas cooker pipe and when he lit a match the whole thing blew, or gas could have built up in the bilges, and he went to light the cooker for his supper and bang, got blown off his feet and struck his head. But, with that hole in his skull, my guess is he was knocked out and someone threw a lighted match on to the boat to ignite the gas, having made sure the gas pipe was loosened beforehand.'

It wasn't a very nice way to go, except for the fact the poor man wouldn't have known much about it. If this was murder then whoever had done it was a very nasty piece of work.

Horton had already ruled out juveniles. Although they were responsible for most arson attacks, he doubted they would have picked on this particular boat when there were larger, more expensive ones closer to the car park and boardwalk to target. Besides, how would one of their typical juvenile arsonists from the inner city know the security code to get onto the pontoon?

'What's your feeling about this?' he asked Maidment, knowing that firefighters developed an instinct for this kind of thing, much like coppers did.

Maidment replied instantly. 'Smells bad.'

Horton agreed. It stank to high heaven and that was discounting his premonitions about this place and this incident. 'Was the security gate open when the firefighters arrived?'

'The guy from the marina office was there to let us through.'

Locked then. But he'd check that. 'Any idea who he is?'

'There was no ID on him, or if there was, it's burnt to a crisp, like the poor sod himself.'

Addressing Cantelli, Horton said, 'Get the crime scene investigators here, Barney, and call Dr Clayton. Ask if she can take a look at him and officially certify death.'

He'd rather have the pathologist here than Dr Price, the police doctor, whom he considered to be verging on incompetent because of his drink problem. Gaye Clayton might also be able to give them some information about the victim's death that could put them on the trail of this killer quickly, which was what they needed. 'I'll notify DCI Bliss.'

As Horton rang through to her direct line, he recalled that Uckfield kept his motorboat in the marina. But it was moored on a different pontoon.

Bliss answered with her customary curtness. Horton quickly apprised her of the facts, told her he had called in SOCO and Dr Clayton, and that he was about to try and discover who their victim was.

'That's not our responsibility, Inspector. You can leave it to the major crime team. I'll call them in now.'

'We don't know for certain that it is a suspicious death until Dr Clayton confirms it.' He bristled at her icy tone.

'We're grossly understaffed, Inspector, and we have enough cases of our own, such as this mugging for example. What's happening about that?'

A man's dead, probably murdered, and you're worried about the mugging of an American tourist, he thought. Serious though it was, surely this took priority? Crisply, he said, 'DC Walters is interviewing the victim at his hotel.'

'The attack occurred two hours ago. We've lost valuable time tracking down the criminals.'

For goodness' sake, who the devil did she think he was? A rookie?

Stiffly, he said, 'The uniformed response officers went in immediate search of the youths, without results. And the victim was too shocked to give an accurate description. He was taken to hospital—'

'And is that all I'll have to tell the local newspaper tomorrow? It doesn't do much for our image as a tourist destination, does it?'

Not to mention your clear-up rate, he thought. Christ, Uckfield was bad enough wanting quick results but Bliss wanted them to be instant.

'This should have been dealt with sooner.'

'If I had the manpower it would have been,' he retorted.

Five minutes into the job and she was breathing down his neck and criticizing every decision he made. It hadn't taken him long to discover that she was a control freak. If one of his officers so much as sneezed she knew the time, decibel level and direction of the sneeze before he did himself.

'I don't want excuses, Inspector Horton, I want results.' And she rang off.

'And up yours too,' he mumbled. He'd heard on the grapevine that she didn't intend staying a DCI for very long, and as far as he was concerned the sooner she moved on the better.

Cantelli came off the phone. 'Dr Clayton's on her way.'

'Good.' Despite Bliss's instructions that this was Uckfield's province, Horton said, 'I'll talk to the marina staff, Barney. You ask around on the pontoons: did anyone know our victim, when did they last see him?'

'Why don't I take the marina office, and you take the boats,' Cantelli suggested hopefully.

Horton knew that Cantelli was not one of the world's natural sailors. 'The pontoon's not going anywhere. You won't get seasick. Besides, I'll be quicker than you. I'll jog there.' He hoped he could dodge the reporters, if there were any, and the exercise would help to banish the remains of those uneasy feelings.

'I could take the car,' Cantelli said.

'And destroy the ozone layer unnecessarily for the sake of a few hundred yards! Heaven forbid.'

'Since when have you become environmentally friendly?'

'Barney, I live on a small boat with a little engine and use the wind to power it most of the time.'

'And the Harley?'

'It's less of a pollutant than the old banger you drive.'

Cantelli held up his hands in submission.

Horton broke into a jog, relieved to see that the crowd had dispersed. The Chandlery was closed, the offices surrounding it locked up for the night, and the boatyard was silent. The marina office gave on to Paulsgrove Lake, which fed into the northern end of Portsmouth Harbour.

Horton took the steps to the lock control room above the office two at a time and rapped on the door. Announcing himself with a flash of a warrant card to the swarthy-looking man in his thirties who answered the door, Horton stepped inside nodding at the slight, fair-haired woman at the controls, who introduced herself as Avril.

The run had helped to banish Horton's tensions and he scolded himself for being paranoid. God, he was glad he had said nothing to Cantelli. He asked the man, who had introduced himself as Kevin Gardner, for the victim's name.

Gardner reached for a clipboard, and after consulting papers on it, said, 'Tom Brundall. He's a visitor. Only came into the marina two days ago, on Monday afternoon.'

'From?'

'Guernsey. Is he OK?' Gardner said, concerned.

'Did he give an address?'

'No. He paid cash in advance.'

Damn. Horton might have known it wouldn't be that easy. Had Brundall lived in Guernsey or had he just motored across from visiting there? If it was the latter then Brundall could have lived anywhere. Still, Guernsey was a starting point, and Horton knew just the man to ask: his old friend, Inspector John Guilbert, of the States of Guernsey Police.

'Has he locked out of the marina whilst he's been here?' Horton addressed the young woman.

'No. Is he all right? He wasn't on his boat when . . .'

'I'm afraid so.'

'Holy shit!' exclaimed Gardner. 'Poor man.' Avril shuddered.

Horton left a short pause, which was filled by the foghorns. The sense of danger returned as the image of that charred body flashed into his mind. 'What did he look like?' he asked. *Think logically. Do what you are paid to do.*

Gardner answered. 'About your height, but in his mid-sixties, short grey hair, very thin.'

'Did he say why he'd come here?' Horton wondered if there was a Mrs Brundall who was about to hear some tragic news. If there were, he was glad he wouldn't be the one to break it to her.

'Not to me he didn't and I didn't ask. Did you speak to him, Avril?'

'No. He smiled up at me as he was going through the lock and waved. He looked a nice old man. What caused the fire?'

'We don't know yet. The fire investigation officer will make his report, but we are treating his death as suspicious.' Horton wasn't about to divulge the information he'd been given.

'The boss isn't going to like this. He's on his way over from Brighton.' Gardner was clearly agitated.

'When you reached the pontoon did you notice if the gate was open or shut?'

'Shut. I punched in the security code.' Which, thought Horton, confirmed his earlier impressions that Brundall's killer had to be either someone familiar with the marina, a boat owner or employee, or someone Brundall knew and had admitted.

'Did Mr Brundall have any visitors?'

'I wouldn't—'

'Yes, he did,' Avril interrupted.

Horton was suddenly alert. 'When?'

'Today. I was heading for the boardwalk to do a bit of Christmas shopping and I saw a man getting out of a taxi.'

'What time?'

'Just before midday.'

Disappointing, because it couldn't have been the person who threw the lighted match on board, but, if Maidment was right about this being suspicious, this visitor could have loosened the gas cooker pipe after he arrived.

'How do you know he was going to see Mr Brundall?'

'Because he asked me where pontoon G was, and said he was looking for Mr Brundall. He couldn't get on to the pontoon without the security code so I let him through and watched him until he got to Mr Brundall's boat. I saw Mr Brundall come on deck, smile and shake hands with him. Then the man climbed on board.'

So, the visitor had been expected and welcomed. That didn't eliminate him, however, from being a possible accessory to murder. 'Can you describe him?' Horton asked, hoping this might give them an early lead.

'He wore a dark suit with a white shirt and yellow tie. Quite distinguished looking, short thinning grey hair, about mid-fifties.'

Not the usual profile of a killer, thought Horton with a flicker of disappointment, but then who could tell?

'Oh, and he was carrying a briefcase,' Avril added.

So Brundall had had some business to attend to. 'Do you know what time he left?'

'No. Sorry.'

'You don't happen to know which taxi firm dropped him off,' Horton asked hopefully.

'I do actually.'

Praise the Lord for an observant woman!

'It was Acme Cars,' she continued. 'It made me think of my young brother who's got acne.'

Horton didn't recognize the name. They couldn't be local. Outside he called the CID office and got DC Walters.

'Only just returned from interviewing Mr Belmont,' Walters said before Horton could speak.

'Leave the American tourist for now; I want you to contact the States of Guernsey Police.' Horton swiftly brought Walters up to speed with events, then added, 'See if they have a record of a resident called Tom Brundall. Call me as soon as you have anything.'

He rang off to the sound of Walters grumbling and ran back to the pontoon. If Brundall had been a Guernsey resident, then why had he been killed in Portsmouth? Had he arranged to meet his killer here? Was his killer the man in the suit? Why did Brundall bring his boat here in December? It was hardly the season for it. Who *was* Tom Brundall?

Horton drew up abruptly as a thought suddenly struck him and he cursed himself for being so stupid. How did he know those charred remains were Tom Brundall's? He'd committed one of the cardinal sins for a detective in assuming it was Brundall because it was his boat, but with Avril's evidence, the dead man could easily be this man in the suit. It was impossible to recognize either of the descriptions that Kevin Gardner and Avril had given him from those charred remains, and the clothing had been singed to oblivion. Had any of the firefighters found the remains of a briefcase?

Horton reached for his mobile phone and once again called Walters. Whilst he waited for him to answer, he walked towards the pontoon, noting with surprise that Superintendent Uckfield had arrived on the scene pretty sharply. His car was parked next to the police vehicle and alongside Dr Clayton's Mini Cooper. Bliss was a quick worker but even she couldn't have got the superintendent here as fast as this. Perhaps Uckfield had had a premonition that something was happening here, Horton thought wryly, but that would be like Hannibal Lecter suddenly converting to vegetarianism. Horton supposed Uckfield must have been near to the Marina when he'd got Bliss's call.

'About time. Where have you been?' Horton snapped as Walters eventually answered.

'On the phone to Guernsey, guv.' Walters sounded peeved.

Horton ordered Walters to put out an all-ports alert for two men: the visitor with the briefcase and the man who had steered the boat into Horsea Marina on Monday afternoon. As he stepped onto the pontoon, another thought occurred to him: the victim didn't necessarily have to be either Brundall or the man in the suit; it could be someone whom Brundall

13

had lured to his boat. And furthermore how did he know that Brundall was the boat owner's real name?

He frowned with irritation. He had a feeling that this case was going to be one of those — for every step forward they'd take two back. Cantelli had told him it wouldn't be his problem, and DCI Bliss had also reminded him of that same fact. Maybe he should be grateful.

Uckfield's squat figure loomed at him from out of the fog. Maybe this one was best left to the superintendent and DI Dennings. Yet, Horton knew by the excitement he felt in his gut, and by his earlier premonition, which was still swirling around, that he didn't want that.

Never let it be said that I don't like a challenge, he thought, and felt certain that this case was going to be one.

TWO

'What's up, Steve? Worried your boat might have gone up in flames?' Horton joked with a familiarity that would have earned him a reprimand with any other senior officer, but every now and then Horton liked to remind Uckfield that they had once been close friends. He noted Uckfield's dinner jacket and bow tie underneath the camel coat. The superintendent must have been on his way to a function when he got Bliss's call.

With a flicker of annoyance Uckfield said crisply, 'What do we know about the dead man?'

Horton smiled a greeting at Dr Clayton who returned the gesture briefly before resuming her examination of the corpse. There was no sign of Dennings, and he wasn't a man to miss. His fifteen-stone muscular frame would have stood out like the Incredible Hulk.

After Horton had finished his briefing, Uckfield said, 'Great, so we think he might be this man Tom Brundall, but equally he could be any other Tom, Dick or Harry.'

'That's about the size of it so far,' Horton said, as Cantelli arrived.

'This place is like the *Mary Celeste*. I can't find a single soul on a blessed boat. Somerfield's had no joy either.'

Horton hadn't really expected anything different at this time of the year. He turned to Uckfield, and, half joking, said, 'I don't suppose you've been on your boat and seen the victim?'

Uckfield snapped, 'Of course I haven't,' and swiftly turned to Dr Clayton. 'Well?'

'He's not a very pretty sight.' Gaye glanced up. For a moment Horton thought she was referring to the superintendent.

'I can see that for myself,' Uckfield retorted. 'Was he murdered?'

'Interesting though.' She stood up, holding Uckfield's glare with composure, obviously refusing to be hurried or bullied into answering. Did Uckfield know he was addressing the daughter of one of the most eminent Home Office pathologists the country had ever seen, Samuel Ryedon? Horton doubted it or Uckfield's manner would have been sickeningly ingratiating instead of hostile. 'Could it have been an accident?' Uckfield pressed.

'Not judging by the pattern of the wound and the extent of the injury to the cranium. He was struck with a heavy object, something like a hammer.'

Horton peered once again at the body. It wasn't quite as bad the second time, though it was awful enough. But now the analytical side of his nature reasserted itself. Why had this man met with such a terrible end? Was it a case of being in the wrong place at the wrong time? Somehow Horton doubted that. It was planned, he was sure. So what kind of person could have done this and why? He knew that people were driven to murder for all sorts of reasons: greed, jealousy, revenge, hatred, love, to name but a few. But to knock a man out and then set fire to him smacked of someone cold and calculating enough to cover his tracks by wanting to destroy the evidence. Either that or someone evil enough to take pleasure in watching another human being suffer for the sheer fun of it. Maybe their killer was a bit of both. The thought sent a cold shudder through him, making him feel both sad and sickened.

Dr Clayton pulled the blanket over the corpse. 'I'll do the post-mortem as soon as I get him to the mortuary.' Turning to Horton, she added, 'I'll let you know the moment I have anything. I wouldn't want to spoil the superintendent's evening.'

Ignoring her, Uckfield addressed Horton. 'You'd better get the divers in. Not that I expect them to find anything in the marina. Our killer wouldn't be that stupid.'

'You're taking command of the case?'

'It looks like murder to me, Inspector. And that counts as a major crime in my book,' Uckfield replied, his voice heavy with sarcasm.

Horton tensed at Uckfield's sneering tone, but said casually, 'In that case we'll leave it to you and DI Dennings.' He turned and walked away.

'Not so hasty. You got a date?' Uckfield called out angrily.

No, but you have, thought Horton. Now he'd see just how important a date it was. Come on, you bastard, ask me. Either that or get your blue-eyed boy in. 'Andy.'

Horton halted and slowly turned, managing to stifle the smile of satisfaction both at being summoned and the use of his Christian name. He heard Uckfield snarl at Cantelli. 'Haven't you got anything better to do, Sergeant, than hang around on the pontoon chewing like a cow?'

Cantelli raised his eyebrows and turned to engage Dr Clayton in conversation.

Drawing level, Uckfield said in a low voice, 'Can't you follow this through, Andy? I'll clear it with DCI Bliss. Dennings is off sick with this flu bug and I've promised Alison I'd go to this dinner and dance. It's in aid of one of her charities and she's put a lot of effort into organizing it.'

Yes, and I expect her father, the chief constable, will also be there, Horton thought cynically, which was the real reason Uckfield needed to go. It was sucking-up time to the in-laws. And Horton, knowing Uckfield of old, was aware Alison could go to Outer Mongolia on her own if precious daddy wasn't anywhere on the horizon.

Uckfield continued. 'Not much will happen on this case tonight anyway, and I know I can leave a good officer like you to kick start it.'

Horton had to bite his tongue. He felt like saying if I'm that good, why didn't you appoint me your DI instead of that idiot Dennings?

'Sergeant Cantelli and I should have been off duty about two hours ago,' Horton said, holding Uckfield's stare. He wanted the man to plead yet he knew that Uckfield wouldn't. Horton had to be content with the small victory he had scored in getting the superintendent to ask for a favour in the first instance. He saw that he had made his point and before Uckfield could answer, added, 'I'll call you as soon as Dr Clayton has completed the post-mortem, Steve.' A favour didn't warrant the use of rank, not in Horton's eyes at least.

'Good.'

Horton knew Uckfield couldn't say thank you. It wasn't in his vocabulary.

Uckfield glanced at his watch. 'I'll call Sergeant Trueman on my way to the dinner and ask him to start getting the major incident suite ready. Hate these bloody things, but duty calls.'

If Uckfield had any sense of duty, Horton thought, he'd cry off. He'd always known that Uckfield was ambitious but what he hadn't realized until recently was just how ambitious.

'Was he born grumpy or has he simply perfected the art over the years?' Gaye Clayton said, nodding in the direction of Uckfield's disappearing figure.

'Must be the heavy responsibility of the job,' Horton said, recalling a very different Uckfield of their youth.

'And someone should tell him to lose some weight,' she added, picking up her case and heading down the pontoon after the superintendent. 'Not good for the heart,' she said over her shoulder.

'Not sure he's got one,' Horton heard Cantelli mutter.

'Sorry for volunteering you to continue working.'

'It's OK. I'll call Charlotte.'

The undertakers arrived the same time as the Scene of Crime Officers. Horton addressed the head of their team, who was a thin, stooping man. 'I know you'll dust the pontoon gate for fingerprints, Phil, but there's been so many of us in and out of it that it's probably useless.' He turned to the fire investigation officer who had been keeping a discreet distance from them. 'We'll need your prints and those of the firefighters.'

Maidment nodded. 'I'll organize it and I'll let you have my full report tomorrow.'

Cantelli came off the phone and they made their way back to the car. Somerfield let them through the crime-scene tape without a smile.

Seaton had probably warned her that he was in a bad mood. As the last of the fire engines trundled away, Horton saw a black Mercedes sweep into the car park. Judging by the personalized number plate he reckoned it was the marina director.

Turning to Seaton, Horton said, 'Tell him we're not yet in a position to confirm who the victim is. He's to go nowhere near the scene and if he kicks up a fuss tell him to speak to Superintendent Uckfield in the morning.' *That will serve him right for ducking out.* 'Are you on duty all night?'

'Until six, sir.'

'Then stay here with Somerfield and make sure the scene is secure. Sergeant Cantelli will organize a relief in the morning. If you or Somerfield need to take a leak then take it in turns, the same goes for eating and drinking, but no sleeping. I'll get Scrgeant Elkins of the marine unit to get the boat towed away for forensic examination as soon as Taylor says it can be moved.'

Seaton nodded, his expression serious, but Horton could tell he was pleased at being given the responsibility.

'He's not a bad lad,' Cantelli said, stretching the seat belt around him.

No, and he was a good policeman thought Horton, tilting the rear-view mirror to watch Seaton approach the casually dressed, worried-looking man climbing out of the black Mercedes. Horton wouldn't mind having Seaton in CID when the powers that be decided to allocate him extra resources, which he hoped was soon. Having lost DC Marsden to Uckfield's Major Crime Team, he was seriously undermanned.

At the station Cantelli went off to organize various tasks including carrying out Uckfield's instructions to call in the divers whilst Horton headed for the CID office where he found DC Walters pummelling a computer keyboard.

'I should have been off duty ages ago,' Walters grumbled. 'I've got a date.'

'If she loves you she'll wait for you. Has Guernsey come back with any information on Tom Brundall?'

'No.'

Maybe he could hurry them up with a call to John Guilbert. 'And the muggers?'

Walters looked up from his report. 'Late teens, early twenties, one Caucasian, one black. They were wearing those stupid hoodies. They came at the Yank suddenly from either side of him, pushed against him, roughed him up to get his wallet, which the stupid bugger kept in a kind of handbag over his shoulder, so it didn't take much, grabbed what they could and ran off. PC Jones says a witness saw them run into Curzon Howe Road but no one claims to have seen hide or hair of them.'

Which figured in that neighbourhood, thought Horton. 'Have you viewed the CCTV tapes? Queens Street, wasn't it?'

Walters looked surprised. 'The operation control officers said there was nothing on them.'

Horton sighed wearily. 'First rule of being a good detective, Walters, is never to believe anything anyone tells you. Second rule is to check it out yourself. Now, finish typing up your report, leaving out the reference to the stupid bugger, and the Yank, and get off home before you get roped into this murder investigation and miss your night of bliss.'

With surprising speed, Walters applied himself once again to the keyboard. The way he was punishing it they'd need a new one by the morning. Horton's telephone was ringing and, reaching across his desk, he picked it up, hoping it was the Guernsey Police. Instead it was DCI Bliss summoning him to her office. He'd noticed with dismay that her car was in the car park when Cantelli had driven in. She kept longer hours than him and that was saying something. Maybe she didn't have much of a home to go to either.

He entered following her abrupt order to 'come' and found her glaring at him from behind her immaculately tidy desk like an angry parent whose teenage child had stayed out too long. Where on earth did she keep all her files and paperwork? Horton wondered. In front of her there was only a single piece of paper and a rather smart-looking silver pen beside it.

She didn't ask him to sit. 'Well?'

Sod it, he sat. He could see that it irritated her. Staring at her narrow pointed face and restless eyes, Horton swiftly brought her up to date with the mugging (his version not Walters') and then with events at the marina, finishing by telling her that he and Sergeant Cantelli had volunteered for extra duty. He could tell by her scowling expression that she wasn't very pleased about that and that obviously Uckfield hadn't called her and cleared it with her as promised.

'The superintendent will pick up the overtime bill, ma'am,' he said, thinking that might cheer her up, but her frown deepened.

'I will not have overtired officers on my team. It leads to mistakes and sloppiness and I won't tolerate that.'

Where were the thanks for being dedicated to the job these days? Gone the way of *Dixon of Dock Green* it seemed, as far as Bliss was concerned. Horton had spent years juggling a caseload heavy enough to take the foundations of the Empire State Building without buckling under the strain, and he had an excellent clear-up rate. He didn't think staying on a few hours extra was going to make him fall asleep on the job tomorrow, and neither would it affect Cantelli.

He saw in her expression a determination to succeed that bordered on fanaticism. He'd seen that look before and not so long ago. It had been his own, reflected in the mirror, until Operation Extra had temporarily isolated him from the force and shown him that even when you thought you were on the inside, you weren't. It had been a hard lesson to learn, and the consequences of it were still reverberating around both his personal and professional life. But he liked to think he was beginning to come to terms with it.

Bliss continued. 'And I won't have this mugging treated lightly. It's a very serious incident, Inspector. This attack is hardly good for the city and tourism.'

Curbing his annoyance, he said, 'I'll get the community officers asking around the district and DC Walters is personally handling it.'

'Keep me informed. I'll talk to Superintendent Uckfield in the morning.'

And good luck to you, thought Horton, leaving her to scowl at the piece of paper on her desk; perhaps she was trying to intimidate it into disappearing?

'It is murder, isn't it?' Trueman said when Horton reached the incident suite. 'Because I'd hate to think I've stayed behind for the sheer bloody fun of it. I've got the number of that taxi firm by the way. They're based in Eastleigh.'

Horton's ears pricked up at that because Eastleigh was not far from Southampton airport and there were regular flights to and from Guernsey. Was the man in the suit who'd visited Brundall from the Channel Islands? It was a guess but Horton wouldn't mind betting that he was right. He glanced at his watch and was surprised to see that it was nearly ten o'clock. He reckoned Walters' girlfriend would have given him up for the night by now, unless she was truly smitten and that was hard to imagine when it came to the overweight, irritating and slovenly DC. Still, there was no accounting for taste, which made him think of his estranged wife's lover.

He reached for a telephone and dialled the taxi company's number. He let it ring for some time, drumming his fingers on the desk, before he was finally forced to accept that this particular taxi firm didn't work all night, or even late at night, leastways not from the number Trueman had given him. Still, there was little he could do now but head out there first thing tomorrow. Then he remembered that he wouldn't be on the investigation.

Cantelli threw himself down into the seat opposite Horton. 'Guernsey has called to confirm that a Tom Brundall is a resident there and that he owns a boat called *Enterprise*. He kept it in St Peter Port Marina.'

So Brundall existed, and owned the boat that had gone up in flames. It was a step forward, but it didn't necessarily mean that Brundall was their burnt offering.

'There's no previous on him,' Cantelli continued, 'but Guernsey is checking out what he did for a living. The marina manager says Brundall left St Peter Port on Monday morning but didn't tell them when he would be back. There's no answer at his home and the Guernsey police can't locate any relatives. Apparently Brundall lived in a ruddy great mansion near a place called Petit Bot Bay. Did I pronounce that right?'

'Near enough. It's on the south coast of Guernsey.' Horton recalled it well. He'd moored not far from there in nearby Portelet a couple of times, with Catherine and Emma, on Catherine's father's yacht in the days that now seemed just a distant memory.

'What about a photograph?' Horton asked. It wouldn't help with any identification but it could be used for the all-ports alert. Though he no longer thought that was necessary, as everything was pointing to the fact that their body was Tom Brundall.

'They haven't found any inside his house.'

Unusual but not necessarily suspicious. Irritating, nevertheless. More delays. It couldn't be helped, but Horton felt uneasy, as though there was an underlying urgency to this case. He pushed away the edge of his premonition as it threatened once again to rear its ugly head.

'You'd better shoot off home, Barney. There's not much point in us both hanging around. I doubt we'll get more tonight. I'll wait for Dr Clayton's initial report. Sorry you've had to work late.'

'Don't be. It saved me from late night Christmas shopping with Charlotte,' Cantelli replied, pulling a face.

That reminded Horton he needed to make some time to go shopping himself, though he had no idea what Emma wanted for Christmas. He would have to ask Charlotte; with four daughters he was sure Cantelli's wife would be able to help.

Horton loitered about the incident room occasionally glancing at the clock. He wrote the information that Cantelli had given him on to the crime board. He didn't need to stay because Dr Clayton could call him on his mobile, if she couldn't reach him at the station, but unlike Cantelli, Horton didn't have anything to go home too, and it was warmer in the police station than on his boat.

How could he take his eight-year-old daughter to a tiny, freezing-cold boat? Simple answer — he couldn't. But where could he take her? The pantomime? The zoo? The shops? He didn't fancy any of them but it was Emma's treat. And that was another thing that bugged him, he thought, gazing out of the window at the foggy night: he didn't want to be the kind of father who only gave his child treats like some benevolent uncle. He wanted to be a proper father. He'd missed out on having one himself and he was damn sure that Emma wasn't going to. He wanted to make a home for her; somewhere she could stay, and bring her friends, which ruled out his boat.

He fetched a coffee from the machine in the corner of the room and turned his mind back to the case. What had the man in the dark suit to do with the victim? Why had he visited the victim? Who was he? Why had Brundall come to Portsmouth? All questions and no answers. Not yet, but he'd get them. No, correction, DI Dennings would.

'Inspector, call for you. Dr Clayton.' At last!

'He was alive when the fire broke out,' Gaye said peremptorily. 'I found carbon monoxide in his blood and fine particles of soot in his lungs. It's my belief he was struck forcibly. His skull is fractured and there is inflammation near the injury and blistering which contains proteins.'

Horton's heart quickened. 'We're definitely looking at murder then.'

'Yes. And I can confirm by the size and shape of the wound that he was hit with something smallish and round, as I said before, possibly a hammer.' And Horton doubted they'd find that.

Gaye continued, her voice solemn. Horton heard the weariness in it. 'There is something else. He had cancer. He was riddled with it; it was in his spine and in the tissue I found in his skull. He hadn't got long to live.'

Then why come all the way across the Channel to Portsmouth? Was it a journey of nostalgia? Had he come to see someone for the last time? Did he have some unfinished business to attend to? Or had he just wanted to get away? Perhaps he had hoped to die at sea, but then that still didn't answer why he'd ended up in Horsea Marina.

'Could a woman have struck him?'

'With his being weakened by his illness it wouldn't have needed a lot of strength. Yes, a woman could have done it especially if he was crouching down or bending over when he was struck.'

'Any joy with his fingerprints?' Horton asked hopefully.

'Not enough skin left on the fingers, so you'll have to wait for DNA. I'll let you have the full report tomorrow. I'm off to bed now. I'm bushed.'

Horton didn't know how she could sleep after dissecting that corpse, but then that was her job. She had obviously perfected a technique of mentally switching off, much as he'd had to learn over the last eighteen years in the police force. Only he knew it didn't always work, and he doubted it would tonight.

He could call Uckfield to tell him about the post-mortem but then decided it would be better to discuss this with him face to face. The duty sergeant gave him the location of the superintendent's charity function and half an hour later Horton was turning into the crowded car park of the Marriott Hotel on the edge of the city.

He consulted the function board in reception and saw that Uckfield's dinner and dance was located in the main banqueting suite. He had hardly gone a few paces though when he spotted Uckfield sitting at the bar, deep in conversation with a broad-set balding man in his late forties whom Horton instantly recognized as Edward Shawford, his estranged wife's boyfriend.

Horton stiffened. If Shawford was here then Catherine must be too. Alison Uckfield and Catherine were close friends, and Horton guessed they'd come as a foursome. If it hadn't been for Operation Extra and those accusations of rape he would have been in this party instead of bloody Edward Shawford. But that was all in the past. And Jesus did it still hurt! And there was him thinking he was moving on!

So who was looking after Emma, he wondered, making his way towards the bar? His in-laws? He felt a stab of envy swiftly followed by anger that others were allowed to take care of his daughter and not her father. Uckfield looked up and caught Horton's eye. He started with surprise, then frowned and hauled himself off the bar stool. Horton watched as Shawford followed Uckfield's gaze. He caught the look of fear in the man's eyes and drew immense satisfaction from it. He should be afraid, Horton thought, recalling how he'd once come close to beating him to a pulp.

'We've had the results of the PM,' Horton said tersely. He was damned if he was going to address Uckfield by his rank, especially in front of Shawford.

'I'd better be going,' Shawford mumbled and scuttled away like a startled crab.

Horton despised him even more than he thought he possibly could.

Uckfield drew Horton away from the bar and the proximity of the banqueting suite.

'Don't I even get offered a drink, Steve?' Horton couldn't resist saying. He'd been off alcohol for three months but a soft drink might have been welcomed.

26

'You could have telephoned me,' hissed Uckfield with a glance at the banqueting suite doors, which at that moment opened and let escape a blast of music.

Horton could see Uckfield was a little tight. He relayed the information that Dr Clayton had given him and brought Uckfield up to date with Guernsey's findings, finishing with Trueman's news that he'd located the taxi company that had taken the visitor to Brundall.

'DI Dennings can talk to them in the morning.'

Uckfield said, 'I'd like you to stick with it, Andy, for tomorrow at least.'

The function room doors burst open again and this time Horton saw Alison Uckfield tumble out laughing. Beside her, in a short midnight blue dress, was Catherine. Horton caught his breath and hardened his heart. Her eyes fell on him and the smile instantly vanished from her face. Alison Uckfield glanced at her husband like a frightened child and it made Horton wonder what Uckfield had said about him, or perhaps it was Catherine who had spread evil tales. Fury surged through him, which he controlled, calling on the techniques that he'd perfected over the years spent in children's homes.

'What are you doing here?' Catherine demanded, hurrying towards him.

Uckfield answered. 'He's on duty.'

'I'm not actually, but I am on a case,' Horton corrected. He held Catherine's icy cold stare and told himself it didn't matter, but he felt a hard knot of pain inside his stomach.

Alison Uckfield's pale-skinned face puckered up with concern as she said, 'This doesn't mean you've got to leave, does it, Steve?'

Fat lot of good Uckfield would be. Horton said, 'There's not much that can be done tonight, Alison.'

She looked startled at being addressed in so familiar a manner, and dashed a look at her husband, but Horton was damned if he was going to stand on ceremony with a woman he had danced and laughed with, seen drunk, and kissed.

Taking his wife's arm and with a backward glance at Horton, Uckfield said, 'I'll clear it with Chief Superintendent Chievely tomorrow. You're on the case.'

Horton turned to Catherine. 'How's Emma?'

'Looking forward to seeing you on Christmas Eve. Don't disappoint her, Andy.'

Horton forced himself to remain calm, though he was thinking how dare she say that when he had never disappointed his daughter in her life. 'Who's looking after her tonight?' She hesitated. Her eyes flickered to the function room. He knew instantly why. 'Your mother and father are here too.'

'Yes. I've got a babysitter.'

'Who?' His stomach clenched at the thought of Emma being abandoned to a stranger.

'A girl from the village called Michelle. She's highly reliable,' Catherine replied defensively.

He had to trust her he told himself. No matter what Catherine did to him he knew she wouldn't endanger Emma, but part of him was thinking that she could have stayed with him. Yet how could she on his boat? It was totally inadequate for a child. It was inadequate for him. And then there was his job. He didn't need to be here working at midnight, but how could he have got away by seven or eight o'clock, which was probably when Catherine had wanted to leave for her function?

Admitting defeat, he said, 'Enjoy your evening,' and walked away. It wasn't until he had reached reception that he paused and turned back. Catherine had vanished, but he caught sight of another familiar face and he felt a tiny flicker of jealousy inside him. Staring up at an elegantly dressed dark-haired man in his late thirties was Frances Greywell. She didn't look as though she was going to protest either when he placed his arm across her naked shoulders.

Outside Horton breathed in the night air hoping to banish his acute sensation of isolation, but the fog was as suffocating as ever. He climbed on his Harley and rode home carefully and slowly. His route took him along the mist-shrouded seafront where the sound of the booming foghorns filled the air. There were young people milling around outside the nightclubs, and a police wagon was parked in front of the pier. Later, when club land spewed its contents on to the pavements, there would be drunken young people and scantily clad girls everywhere. He wondered if this would be Emma's fate. God, he hoped not. He wanted to play a part in her upbringing, and he knew deep in his heart that it had to be more than just a once-a-week visit.

Would the sleek, sophisticated Frances get him what he wanted? Or did she think him a loser? Had she spoken to Catherine at that dinner and dance? If so, what kind of picture had his estranged wife painted of him? With something akin to despair he climbed on board *Nutmeg* and gazed around it: two bunks, a small stove and portable toilet. It wasn't much to show for a lifetime's slog.

He lay back in the darkness, resting his hands behind his head, trying to blot out that picture at the hotel, of people laughing and drinking, of Catherine and Edward Shawford. It wasn't that he enjoyed that sort of event himself; on the contrary, he'd loathed those parties and dances. But he was expected to attend the police dinner and dance, which always took place in January and was seen as a bonding exercise by higher brass between all the units and stations across Portsmouth. Who was he going to take this year? He had thought briefly about asking Frances, but now that idea was scuppered. Once again he felt like the outsider and memories of his childhood came flooding back, the child standing alone. It churned his guts.

Mentally he pulled himself together. There was still work, and with an effort he turned his thoughts instead to that burnt body. There were many questions bothering him but one more than all the others stood out: why had someone wanted to kill a man who was already dying of cancer?

THREE

Thursday, 7.45 a.m.

The question was still troubling him the next morning when he fetched a coffee from the machine and weaved his way through the crowded incident room. One answer had sprung to mind last night and that was perhaps the murderer didn't *know* that Brundall had cancer.

Uckfield had mobilized the troops quicker than Horton had believed physically possible. But when you're wining and dining with the chief constable anything was feasible, like his secondment to the major crime team, which Bliss had told him about that morning through gritted teeth. She said that Walters had called in sick (probably suffering from a hangover or an excess of sexual activity) and that Cantelli was to run the CID office. But Bliss had added that she still expected Horton to oversee it, handle his paperwork, and make sure the mugging case was properly investigated. Some secondment, he thought cynically. Perhaps he should have eaten spinach for breakfast!

Uckfield's office blinds were shut, which meant he was either in conference or having a nap after a boozy late night, and Horton guessed it was the former.

'Brundall's GP has confirmed he had cancer,' Trueman said. 'It was at a very advanced stage. Inspector Guilbert called the doctor early this morning and rang through the information five minutes ago. Guilbert's applying for Brundall's full medical details but it looks as though he's our victim.'

Horton reckoned so. He picked up a printed photograph on Sergeant Trueman's desk. It showed a small gathering of people on board a large luxury yacht.

'That's Tom Brundall in 1996,' Trueman added over his shoulder whilst scrawling the information on the GP's confirmation of cancer on the crime board.

'Which one?'

'Him.' Trueman pointed to a slim man, in his mid-fifties with an angular face and light brown hair. He seemed surprised — or even startled — at having his picture taken. Horton got the impression he wasn't too pleased about it either. He felt a brief frisson of excitement as if there was something important in what he'd just seen. Had he recognized Brundall? He didn't think so. It must be something else, but try as he might he couldn't think what it was. It had gone.

Brundall was dressed in light-coloured trousers and an open-neck checked shirt. Beside him, reclining on the sun lounger, was a casually but well-dressed man in his mid-thirties with fair hair, sunglasses on his head and a glass of champagne in his hand, smiling into the camera. The other people in the photograph were behind them and slightly out of focus. Horton tried to banish the memory of the shrivelled blackened corpse on the pontoon and replace it with this one of Brundall. He thought Brundall looked a fairly innocuous sort of man, instantly forgettable, and the kind you might expect to meet in a bank or at an accountant's office.

Trueman continued. 'It's the only photograph that the Guernsey police can find of him. They got it from the local newspaper archives, along with this cutting.'

Horton took the piece of paper on to which the press cutting had been scanned and then emailed from Guernsey.

'Top banker claims times are good,' said the headline and they certainly looked it, if the size of that boat was anything to go by. It must have cost at least a million back in 1996.

He read the article with the practised skill of a thousand-words-a-minute man. The banker referred to wasn't Brundall, but the head of a private Guernsey bank, a man called Russell Newton who was entertaining guests aboard his yacht, including financier Tom Brundall. So that's what the dead man had done for a living. Was Newton the man on the sun lounger? Horton guessed so.

'Harrison is ageing the photograph to bring it up to date,' Trueman informed him. 'Colouring the hair grey and adding a few lines to fit the description the marina staff gave you. I should have copies in half an hour.'

'Thanks.'

'Glad someone appreciates it.' Trueman jerked his head in the direction of Superintendent Uckfield's office. 'He's like a bear with a sore arse.'

'Don't you mean head?'

'And that, judging by the amount of black coffee the super's putting away. It's DI Dennings who can't keep still.'

'I thought he was sick!' Horton said, surprised and annoyed. He didn't intend taking orders from Dennings, or playing second fiddle to the man. And neither did he intend being the DI stuck in the incident room overseeing the case; Sergeant Trueman was quite capable of that. If that was how it was going to be then he'd rather be in CID even if it did mean ploughing his way through DCI Bliss's new reporting system.

Trueman said, 'Dennings must have heard there was something going off. Doesn't want to miss his first big case.'

Bliss hadn't said anything about Dennings being back, but maybe she didn't know. He crossed to Uckfield's office, knocked once and pushed back the door. Immediately he saw that Trueman was right. Uckfield's eyes were bloodshot and his craggy face was grey.

Serves him right, Horton thought; that will teach him to go drinking with Catherine's boyfriend. Dennings didn't look too good either. His moon-like face was pale and his eyes red-rimmed and tired. Horton recalled what Cantelli had said about that film starring Paulette Goddard, and ghosts and zombies. 'Didn't expect to see you, Tony?' he said. 'You look like someone's just woken you up from a night out haunting.'

Dennings opened his mouth to reply but Uckfield got there first. 'I want you to follow up this taxi fare lead, Inspector, whilst Dennings collates things this end and liaises with Guernsey.'

Dennings' face was solemn, but Horton could tell he was fuming. Like Horton, Dennings was an action man. Perhaps Uckfield thought Dennings still under par from his flu; he certainly looked it. Horton hoped he wasn't going to infect them all with his germs. It would be about all they'd ever get from Dennings, he thought cynically. He was notoriously tight-fisted.

But it wasn't like the superintendent to be considerate and it puzzled Horton. There was no time to dwell on it or discuss the matter though, because Uckfield rose and swept out of his office, leaving them to trail in his wake. The incident room immediately fell silent as Uckfield entered it. Horton looked for Cantelli but couldn't see him. Perhaps he was in the CID office.

Uckfield didn't have much to say, mainly because there was so little information. Guernsey were picking away at Brundall's past and still trying to locate a relative. They were hoping to find some papers in Brundall's house that would tell them more about him. Horton hoped so too.

Trueman had arranged for the mobile incident unit to be set up in Horsea Marina car park in case anyone remembered seeing Brundall or his visitor. And Uckfield ordered a team to go to the marina to question the businesses there.

Half an hour later, with still no sign of Cantelli or a message from him, which wasn't like the sergeant, Horton was glad to head out of the station onto the motorway into a clear morning with no trace of fog. It had a crisp bite to it, making it feel more seasonal. He felt rather foolish and annoyed with himself when he remembered his fears last night.

Trueman had given him the address of Acme Taxis but it still took him a few minutes to locate it in a side street just off the main thoroughfare in Eastleigh.

A beanpole of a woman in her forties, with short blonde hair, and a sharp pointed face, looked up as he entered.

'Won't be a moment, luv.' She talked into a mouthpiece and tapped information into a computer. Horton heard her send a car to pick up someone from Southampton Parkway railway station. 'Now what can I do for you, dear?'

Horton showed his ID. 'One of your cars collected a fare yesterday morning at about eleven thirty a.m. and drove him to Horsea Marina. I'd like to talk to the cab driver.' Horton had calculated the time. On average, and outside rush hour, it took half an hour to travel from Eastleigh to Horsea Marina and Avril said she had spoken to the man just before midday.

The woman consulted her computer screen. 'That was Peter Kingston. He's on a run at the moment. He'll be back in about ten minutes.'

'Any idea who the fare was?'

She checked her computer as Horton stared impatiently around the cramped office with its faded and worn armchairs, coffee machine and newspapers scattered on a low table. He only had to wait ten minutes for Kingston to show, yet that already felt ten minutes too long. You've got time, he told himself, this is no race. Why then did he feel it was important to act swiftly? It wasn't just because DI Dennings had returned to work either. No, there was more to this than feelings of rivalry and professional jealousy. What though? That was the question, and one he couldn't put his finger on. It was irritating to say the least.

'The fare paid cash. I've no idea who he was.'

Damn. Horton could have traced a credit or debit card payment or a cheque. There was nothing for it but to wait until Kingston showed up. When he did, he was a small barrel of a man in his late fifties, with thinning white hair stretched across his egg-shaped head. Horton felt like a giant beside him. He didn't want to question him in front of the woman, and suggested they step outside. Kingston went one further. 'I'm off the run now. How about a coffee? There's a café three doors down on the right. I'll just sign out and meet you there. You can order me a bacon sandwich.'

It was the all-day-breakfast type with steamed-up windows, a good old-fashioned clanging bell above the door and a portly unshaven man behind a tall counter wearing an overall that looked as though it had been rescued off the rubbish tip. Health and safety would have closed this place down, if they ever got within sniffing distance, but clearly its customers loved it. It was crowded.

Horton placed the order and gazed around for a table. Two men in painter's overalls got up from the table near the window and Horton pounced on it. He sipped at his mug of black coffee, which tasted like liquorice, and wished Kingston hadn't ordered bacon because the smell of it frying brought back the picture of those charred human remains and threatened to start his stomach once again practising for the Olympic gymnastics gold medal.

The bell clanged and through a haze of cooking smoke and fried food, Kingston rolled in. Ex-navy, thought Horton, studying the gait and the slightly pompous air with which he addressed the man behind the counter. Once he had greeted the proprietor, Kingston settled himself down, and took a gulp of his coffee.

'What do you want to know?'

'Everything you can tell me about the fare you picked up yesterday morning at eleven thirty and took to Horsea Marina.'

'Is it about that boat that caught fire? I heard it on the news this morning.' Kingston had that gleam in his little grey eyes that told Horton he'd bore the pants off everyone for a month retelling the tale.

'How do you know if your fare had any connection with that?' Horton asked, watching Kingston carefully, as the man spooned another sugar into his coffee. No worries about getting diabetes there!

'Because he told me to wait for him, and I saw him go onto a pontoon. I just put two and two together. There's something dodgy about that fire, isn't there? Hey, he didn't do it, did he? He didn't look the type.'

'What was he like?'

Kingston thought for a moment. Horton curbed his impatience. He could tell this man would not be hurried or cajoled. Physically small he may be, but he was a giant in his own estimation and ego. Horton knew he would get the information he wanted. He just hoped that Kingston wouldn't embellish it in an attempt to inflate his own sense of worth.

'He hailed me outside the airport at about eleven twenty-five and got into the back of the cab. Some of them like to sit in the front, but not this guy. I asked him where he'd come from and he said Guernsey.'

Horton was encouraged. This was sounding good.

Kingston continued. 'I told him that me and the missus had got engaged there thirty years ago, and what a lovely place it was, but he just said, "How much further?" So I thought, OK, Pete, keep your mouth shut and drive. Some of the fares are like that. They want you to be invisible whilst others want to tell you their life history.'

And vice versa, thought Horton, recalling some of the cab drivers he'd met.

Kingston's bacon sandwich arrived and Horton was rather glad when Kingston spread a liberal helping of brown sauce over it. Its spicy fragrance smothered the smell of roast flesh.

Horton let him take his first bite before he asked, 'How did he seem? Worried, pleased, happy?'

'Anxious, I'd say. He kept tapping his fingers on the door, and craning his neck as if I could get there any faster.'

'How long did you wait for him at the marina?'

'About an hour. Cost him a bob or two, but he didn't seem to mind,' Kingston replied with his mouth full. 'I guess he was loaded. He told me to have a coffee. I said, "It's your money, mate." The meter was ticking all the time. I found a café that wasn't too posh amongst all those expensive shops and restaurants and when I got back to the cab he showed up five minutes later. I drove him back to the airport. He paid his bill and went off like a good boy.'

'Did he say anything on the return journey?'

'Not a word. He didn't even thank me, though he gave me a ten per cent tip.'

'Thanks enough then seeing as the fare must have been high,' Horton said, caustically.

'Not bad.' Kingston smiled and wiped his mouth with a paper napkin.

'And how did he seem when you drove him back to the airport?'

After taking the last bite of his sandwich, Kingston said, 'Annoyed, rather than worried.'

'Can you describe him?'

'Wore a dark suit. About your height, slim, mid-fifties. Biggish nose and hawk-like eyes.'

It matched the description that Avril had given him with some extra detail. 'And you've no idea of his name?' Kingston didn't have but Horton knew who would. He turned out of Eastleigh town centre and headed for the airport. At the information desk he showed his ID and asked to speak to the senior security officer. Three-quarters of an hour later he was walking back to his Harley pleased with himself.

He called Uckfield. Maybe he should have telephoned Dennings but he didn't see why Dennings should have the satisfaction of being the bearer of good news.

'Our visitor was on the ten twenty-five a.m. flight from Guernsey to Southampton yesterday,' Horton said, as Uckfield grunted down the line. 'Fortunately the flight wasn't very busy; there were only ten men on board. Three of them flew back to Guernsey from Southampton yesterday: one on the five fifteen flight, and two on the seven fifty flight. As those were the only two flights out of Southampton, and based on the taxi driver's evidence that he had dropped his fare off at the airport at half past one our man has to be the one who caught the earlier flight.' And a brief chat with the check-in girl had confirmed it.

Horton continued, 'He's called Nigel Sherbourne. His flight was booked from an address in St Peter Port, Guernsey, in the name of Sherbourne and Willings Solicitors.'

'He can't be the killer then,' said Uckfield.

'OK, so the timing's wrong for him to have thrown the lighted match onto the boat, because he was back in Guernsey, but he could have loosened the cooker pipe on his arrival. That would have allowed enough time for the gas to build up. Then his accessory comes along, knocks Brundall out and throws the match on board. That's murder in my book.'

'Why would his solicitor wish to kill him?'

'Perhaps he'll tell us if we ask nicely.'

Uckfield sniffed disbelievingly and said, 'I'll get Dennings on to Guernsey.'

On his way to Horsea Marina, Horton thought over this new information. If the solicitor was an accessory to murder then, according to Avril's evidence, Brundall had welcomed him and expected his arrival, so had Sherbourne contacted Brundall on some pretext in order to fly here and loosen the gas cooker pipe, perhaps discovering some urgent papers that needed signing? Or had Brundall summoned the lawyer to Portsmouth? Maybe Brundall had left some urgent unfinished business in Guernsey that couldn't wait until he returned. Or had something occurred here that had prompted Brundall to call his solicitor? Perhaps it was the reason why Brundall had returned to Portsmouth in the first place.

Horton hoped that visiting the scene of the crime might spark some ideas, but when he got there, his brain refused to come up with anything fresh and he saw nothing illuminating except the Christmas lights on the boardwalk. The mobile incident suite was only just being manoeuvred into place in front of the pontoon where Brundall's boat had been and Horton could see a couple of uniformed officers heading towards the shops to interview the owners.

The morning was already beginning to cloud over after such a promising start, and the water in the marina was turning a dull grey. He felt as though he was missing something important, but couldn't for the life of him think what it was. Mentally he ran through the events of the previous night, but whatever was bugging him, it refused to surface. Perhaps Cantelli would have some ideas. He made to start the bike when his phone rang. It was Cantelli.

'It's Dad. He's had a heart attack. I'm calling from the hospital.'

Horton's heart lurched. He hadn't expected this. No wonder Cantelli hadn't been at the station earlier that morning.

'When?'

'About six thirty this morning he complained about pains in his chest and arm and Mum called the ambulance. Thank God she did, because it saved his life.'

Cantelli's voice was uncharacteristically sombre and Horton thought he detected a shake in it as he spoke. He knew this would hit Barney hard as he was very close to his father. Horton felt anxious for him.

'How is he?' he asked, recalling the wiry little Italian who always had a smile on his face and a gleam in his old eyes.

'The next couple of hours are critical. I don't think I'll be able to make it into work.'

'Sod that,' Horton said crossly. 'Is there anything I can do?'

'Thanks, but no. I'm here with Mum, Isabella, Tony and Charlotte. The kids have gone to school. Marie's on her way from London.'

'Let me know how it goes. And Barney . . . all the best.' There didn't seem much else he could say.

FOUR

Horton reported Cantelli's news to Bliss as soon as he arrived back at the station, knowing that Cantelli wouldn't have told her. With Cantelli on compassionate leave, Walters off sick and DC Marsden transferred to the major crime team that left only him, and he was working on the Brundall investigation.

Bliss eyed him coldly as he pointed this out to her. She said she'd have a word with Superintendent Reine about drafting in some uniformed officers to help in CID.

Good luck to her, Horton thought. As far as he was concerned Reine was notoriously weak-willed when it came to fighting his corner with the head of the Operational Command Unit, Chief Superintendent Chievely. Still that was her problem.

He dived into the canteen, bought himself a packet of dubious looking ham and cheese sandwiches and made for the incident suite where he found Dennings frowning at the crime board as if it might suddenly reveal the answer to the mystery, provided he stared at it hard and long enough.

'What did Sherbourne have to say?' Horton asked, settling himself at an empty desk opposite Sergeant Trueman who nodded sombrely at him.

'Nothing, because Nigel bloody Sherbourne isn't in his office,' complained Dennings, spinning round and glaring at him. 'His secretary claims he's at a client's, and she'll ask him to call the Guernsey police as soon as he returns. For fuck's sake, who does she think she is? And what the hell is Guernsey playing at? I'd have hauled the bastard in, client or no client.'

Horton winced inwardly. Vice squad tactics maybe, but not exactly appropriate for CID or the major crime team. He rapidly revised his opinion of Dennings' ailments; his flushed and perspiring face was due to increased blood pressure, not fever. From his days spent with Dennings on surveillance, Horton knew he had a short fuse, as well as a coarse manner, and he didn't exactly excel in communications skills. Dennings had a lot to learn about modern and efficient policing, as DCI Bliss would have called it, and Horton wasn't convinced he was going to be a willing pupil. Still, Uckfield was Dennings' boss and maybe he didn't mind how his new DI behaved. Horton caught Trueman's glance. The sergeant's face was impassive, but Horton detected a flicker of desperation in his eyes.

He peeled back the plastic wrapper on the sandwiches and examined them. Why did they have to smother everything in mayonnaise? It was if it had just been discovered as a cure for all ills. He guessed it was used to hide the taste. Through a mouthful he said, 'Does she know why Sherbourne came to Portsmouth?'

'No. He just said he'd be out for the day. She didn't even know he'd flown here. Can you believe that? The snotty-nosed cow is covering for her boss. He's probably giving her one.'

'You've spoken to her then.'

'Too right I have. Inspector Guilbert didn't seem bothered so I thought sod it. I don't know what they feed them on in Guernsey, but they're too bloody laid back for my liking. For Christ's sake, don't they understand we're dealing with a murder investigation?'

Oh, I bet you've gone down a treat, Horton thought, wondering how John Guilbert, an officer he respected, would take that. Dennings' attitude was enough to make anyone instantly clam up. There was a time to get tough and individuals to get tough with and this was neither. 'It's a small island, with a very low crime rate. Things are done differently there.'

Dennings snorted his scepticism. 'Yeah, and Brundall was killed *here*, so they'd better get their arses in gear and do things my way.'

Horton now understood Trueman's glint of exasperation. He silenced the retort that bully-boy tactics wouldn't work. This kind of crime required using a brain, and although he'd always doubted Dennings had one, now he knew for certain that he didn't.

'What's Sherbourne's line of speciality — in law, that is?'

'Everything and anything according to Miss Snotty-Draws.'

Horton interpreted that as the secretary.

'You'd think the sun shone out of his backside,' Dennings continued. 'Mr Nigel Sherbourne can do anything except walk on water with a carrot stuck up his arse.'

Horton ignored Dennings' crudity. 'And "anything" is?' This was getting to be like extracting evidence from a reluctant witness.

'Business, property, divorce, wills, you name it, Mr wonderful Sherbourne can do it. He's been Brundall's lawyer for as long as the secretary can remember. At least for the thirteen years she's been there. She clammed up then, tight as a nun's knees — wouldn't say any more except that Brundall was a very wealthy man. Guernsey police haven't found a will but they're hoping that Sherbourne's office has a copy. I mean, *hoping*! Can you credit it! By the time they get round to checking, our killer will have spent the bloody money.'

'You think someone killed him because he changed his will?'

'Why not? He was dying of cancer.'

'If Brundall made a new will at the marina then someone would have needed to witness it, so why didn't Brundall ask the taxi driver to do it?'

'Perhaps the cab driver forgot to mention it to you.'

'I don't think so.' *Not Peter Kingston. He'd have been bursting with the news.* 'Did Sherbourne give his secretary anything to type up this morning?'

'Not from his visit to Brundall, so she says,' Dennings said disbelievingly. 'He was in a meeting when she arrived at the office this morning and then he went straight out to this client. There was no tape left on her desk or in her in-tray.'

So Sherbourne must still have whatever it was on him, or perhaps there weren't any papers, or tape, and the meeting had been simply a discussion between the two men. It was useless to speculate without the facts.

'Have we got anything more on Brundall?' Horton asked, finishing his sandwiches and tossing the packet in the bin.

'We know that he moved to Guernsey in 1980.'

'From?'

Dennings beckoned to DC Jake Marsden, who scrambled up from his desk and hurried across to them. Horton wondered how Marsden was taking to working under his new boss DI Dennings.

'Portsmouth, sir,' Marsden said.

Horton hadn't expected that, though maybe he should have done. 'He was coming back to his roots then,' he murmured thoughtfully.

Marsden nodded. 'Born 1942, the only child of Rose Almay and Eric Brundall.'

So no brothers or sisters, nieces or nephews which ruled out a whole line of possible heirs if Brundall had intended writing or changing his will and been killed because of it.

'Eric was a fisherman and Rose a machinist in Vollers,' Marsden told him, 'A lingerie factory, which has now closed down. They married in 1941. Rose died in 1956 and Eric in 1975. They lived in Cranleigh Road after the war until 1975.'

Horton knew that to be a street of narrowed terraced houses, two-up, two-down and, when first built, with a toilet in the backyard. Brundall had come far since his childhood then: living in Guernsey, being photographed with bankers and owning an expensive motorboat.

Marsden went on. 'There aren't any Brundalls or Almays listed in the telephone directory, so it doesn't look like there are any cousins either. I'm still waiting for information on Brundall's employment record.'

'And his medical records?' Horton asked.

Dennings answered. 'Inspector Guilbert's applied for a warrant to gain access to them, but of course Brundall's GP has already confirmed that he had cancer. But that's all he would say.'

Trueman said, 'DNA is being matched and the police are searching the house now for a list of his contacts.'

Horton interpreted what Trueman had left unsaid: we can't go any faster no matter how much Dennings wants to steam roller events.

Trueman added, 'The forensic team are still working on the boat but they confirm Maidment's report that the gas cooker pipe was loosened. It could have happened during the fire, but they don't think so. They can't be one hundred per cent certain though because of the damage to the boat.'

Horton said, 'And that won't look very good as evidence when we take it to court, which is exactly what our killer wanted.'

Trueman nodded his agreement. 'It's as we thought: the build-up of gas was ignited by a match or lighter. No evidence of any accelerant.'

Dennings chipped in, 'So Brundall could have lit the gas himself and caused the explosion.'

'Which is what any defence would claim. Our only evidence that it was murder comes from Dr Clayton, and that bang on Brundall's head,' Horton declared.

'And some smart-arse barrister could make that look like an accident,' Dennings added.

Horton agreed. 'Gas can slowly seep out without being detected for some days. It's possible the pipe could have been loosened in Guernsey.' Horton watched the thoughts chase themselves across Dennings' face until finally he caught the drift.

'You're saying the killer could have followed Brundall to Portsmouth?'

'Maybe our killer didn't want Brundall's death on his own doorstep.'

Dennings frowned with thought. 'Brundall might have been involved in some shady financial deal. He could have been financing drugs or arms, or even pornography.'

Horton thought it was possible, although they had no evidence to point that way. 'Maybe our killer didn't know that Brundall was already dying of cancer. Brundall could have started a business deal in Guernsey but it hadn't been concluded until after he'd left so he had to summon his solicitor.'

'Wouldn't he have stayed to see it through?' ventured Marsden.

'This is a man who didn't have time on his side. Or perhaps he wanted to see his home town one more time before he died.'

'Huh!' Dennings scoffed.

Horton said, 'On the other hand the gas cooker pipe could have been loosened soon after Brundall arrived in Horsea Marina, any time from Monday night onwards.'

Dennings glanced at his watch. 'Superintendent Uckfield is giving a statement to the press in half an hour's time. I'll brief him.'

That would bring hundreds of calls, thought Horton, the majority of which would be a waste of their time, but one might just hold some information they needed.

Would Dennings pass off Horton's comments as his own? He guessed so. Dennings needed to impress his new boss and giving credit where it was due was hardly something he remembered Dennings being famous for in the past.

'He's driving me nuts,' Trueman said with feeling after Dennings disappeared into Uckfield's office.

Horton gave a wry smile. 'It's a cross we all have to bear.' Then his expression turned serious. 'Have you heard Cantelli's news?'

'About his dad, yes.' Trueman gave a concerned frown. 'Doesn't look too good for the old boy.'

Horton returned to his office wondering how things were going for Cantelli at the hospital. There was nothing he could do to help though, so he turned his mind to the case, considering the possibility that a professional hit man could have killed Brundall because he had been involved in something illegal. As yet they had no evidence to show that, but if it seemed likely, the investigation would be handed over to the Serious Organized Crime Agency and Horton didn't think Uckfield would like that very much.

Until more information came in there seemed little Horton could do about the case: everything that could be done was being carried out by Trueman and his efficient team of officers despite, rather than because of, Dennings' annoying presence. If only they knew why Brundall had come to Portsmouth, and more importantly why Sherbourne had flown over to see him. Had Dennings asked the question of Inspector Guilbert? Horton couldn't trust him to have done so. He pulled out his mobile phone, found John Guilbert's telephone number and called him.

'Andy, good to hear from you.'

Horton smiled at the softly spoken voice, thinking how it must have wound Dennings up. But behind the slow, casual manner there was a quick, incisive brain.

'I'm working on the Brundall case with DI Dennings.'

'Rather you than me.'

'He's not renowned for his tact.'

'Or his patience. He seems to think I'm Superman and can give him answers faster than a speeding bullet.'

'Talking of which, what have you got on Brundall? And don't tell me you've already relayed it to Dennings, because I doubt he asked the right questions, or if he did then he didn't listen to the answers.'

'You know him well.'

'Unfortunately. What have you found in Brundall's house?'

'Nothing and I mean nothing. No letters, no photographs, no diary, no computer.'

'Stolen or never existed?'

'Never existed. There are no signs of a break-in and his housekeeper, Patricia Lihou, confirms he didn't have a computer. Nice lady — quiet, comfortable, well past middle age and very upset at Mr Brundall's death.'

'Mr?'

'She's worked for him for the last eighteen years and says it's always been and still is Mr.'

'Did he ever speak about his family or his past?'

'She says no, and I believe her. He was a very quiet man, and clever. He liked to do crossword puzzles, loved walking and his boat. She knew he had cancer and when he told her he was going out on the boat for a few days, she guessed it would be for the last time, but she never expected him to meet with an accident.'

'Did you tell her it wasn't accidental?' Horton asked, surprised.

'Of course, but she refuses to believe that someone could have killed such a nice man as Mr Brundall.'

Horton sniffed. 'She should have our job. What about Brundall's investments?'

'He's rolling in it, and we haven't even scratched the surface yet. When he moved here he already had millions. Mrs Lihou says Brundall never spoke about money. He was generous to her, lived well and maintained the house, but never spent much on himself except for his boat. He was a recluse, didn't mix with anyone on the island and never went on expensive holidays or business trips. I didn't know him and we've never come across him before.'

'What about Russell Newton? Brundall was photographed with him.'

'Mrs Lihou says that neither Mr Newton nor anyone else has ever visited the house. Newton's a very wealthy man and an influential one on the island. I've got to get the chief officer's authority to question him, but I will get it, Andy. It just takes time.'

'I know. Any idea who Brundall's next of kin is?'

'No. Sherbourne and Willings Solicitors tell me that Brundall has made a will, but until they speak to Nigel Sherbourne they can't let us have access to a copy, and none of the staff or Nigel's partner know what's in it anyway. Whoever Brundall has named is sitting on a small fortune, lucky sod.'

'What would you do with all that money, John?' teased Horton.

'Buy myself a bigger boat.'

'There speaks a man after my own heart. Any idea when you'll get to speak to Sherbourne?'

'He should have returned to his office an hour ago, but there's been no sign of him and no contact from him.'

Horton frowned. That was news to him, and it didn't sound too good either. Had Sherbourne absconded?

Guilbert said, 'I'm worried, Andy. His wife says he hasn't been home and there's no answer on his mobile phone. We've issued an alert for him, but he's not your killer. I know him well and you couldn't meet a more reputable lawyer or man.'

John Guilbert's word had always been good enough for Horton in the past, so why not now?

'Have you any idea of why Brundall would summon Sherbourne to England?' he asked.

'For the same reason you thought of, either to change his will or sign some business papers, and if Sherbourne's missing then it doesn't look too good, because whatever Brundall did sign, Sherbourne brought it back with him, and someone doesn't want us to find it.'

'Does Dennings know this?'

'No. I've only just found out myself. His partner in the law firm also claims he had no idea what Sherbourne's business was with Brundall. All he knows is that Brundall telephoned late Tuesday afternoon, about four fifteen. He doesn't know what the conversation was about and he didn't have any idea that Sherbourne was going to England on Wednesday. He just said he'd be out for the day. Sherbourne booked his own flight and paid with the firm's credit card. He's reliable, Andy.'

Horton thought for a moment. If Guilbert were right then either someone had followed Sherbourne from Guernsey to England and back again, or someone from here had seen Sherbourne go onboard Brundall's boat and followed him back to Guernsey. If that was so, whoever it was must have known the solicitor to have recognized him. But he was getting ahead of himself.

'Perhaps he's broken down somewhere and can't get a reception on his mobile phone,' he suggested. Or perhaps he has a lover and had switched off his mobile.

Guilbert wasn't convinced.

Horton said, 'Did Brundall have a mobile phone?'

'We can't find any record of one or any bills so I guess not.'

Which meant Brundall must have used a call box in the marina.

They spent a couple more minutes exchanging news about the family. Guilbert was sorry to hear about Horton's impending divorce and glad that the ridiculous rape charges against him had been cleared up. Then Guilbert was called away and promised to ring Horton if any fresh evidence came to light, or when they found Sherbourne.

Horton sat back deep in thought. Guilbert had said there had been no computer in Brundall's house, so how had he kept track of his investments, and how had he moved his money around?

Horton supposed he could have done it through his bank. Was that Russell Newton's bank? That wouldn't surprise Horton. Or maybe he had used a broker. And if so then Horton was sure that Guilbert would find out, but like he said it took time. However, Horton had another idea. He rang Joliffe in the forensic department and a few minutes later had the answer to his question.

'There had been the burnt-out remains of a laptop computer on Brundall's boat, but any data from it was irretrievable,' Joliffe said. He also confirmed there had been no sign of a mobile phone.

Horton relayed by phone a digest of the conversation he'd just had with Guilbert to Sergeant Trueman, asking him to pass it on to Uckfield. He felt anxious and impatient for answers, but it couldn't be hurried. Instead, he delegated as many CID tasks as he could to uniformed officers. He then made a Herculean effort to concentrate on DCI Bliss's new reporting method which seemed to be more akin to writing a revised edition of *War and Peace,* only longer. He sincerely hoped that Walters would be back tomorrow. If not then he needed Bliss to give him some manpower, as this was getting beyond a joke. Not that it was ever funny in the first place. How the hell was he supposed to deal with a serious incident if one occurred with a non-existent team? This was modern policing. Invisible.

His phone rang. He expected it to be Bliss. It was the front desk.

'There's a Reverend Anne Schofield asking for you, Inspector.'

'In reception?' he answered tetchily.

'No, on the line, sir.'

Not another attack of vandalism or theft in the church! The name wasn't familiar. He didn't have time for this but there didn't seem to be anyone left to delegate to.

'Can't you put her through to Inspector Warren?' He was Head of Territorial Operations and although Horton had already pinched some of his officers, he felt sure Warren would have a few more to spare somewhere.

'She insisted on speaking to you personally.'

'OK,' Horton said grudgingly.

'Inspector, forgive me for troubling you,' came a clear voice with a Welsh accent as soon as he announced himself, 'but are you Jennifer Horton's boy?'

Horton froze. It was the first time in years he had heard anyone speak his mother's name. The breath caught in his throat. His heart skipped a beat. Maybe he hadn't heard correctly.

'Hello,' the woman's voice came down the line to him. 'Are you there?'

'Why do you want to know?' he asked rather harshly.

'I don't mean to be rude,' she said nervously, catching his tone. 'But there is a reference to a Jennifer Horton in the late Reverend Gilmore's papers.'

Who on earth was the Reverend Gilmore? What was she talking about?

'I guess I'm not making much sense,' she continued, interpreting his silence. 'I'm Reverend Gilmore's temporary replacement at St Agnes's in Portsea. He sadly passed away yesterday evening. I've been going through the things in his study and I've found some papers that refer to you. In the margin of one there is a note in Reverend Gilmore's handwriting, which says, "Jennifer Horton's boy". I just wondered . . .'

Horton stared at the telephone with a mixture of incredulity and dismay. He didn't want to think about the woman who had abandoned him. She was the past, dead and forgotten. Or rather she had been until now. The small voice at the back of his mind was urging him to ignore this. He should leave the past alone and tell the vicar to burn the papers, but he found himself saying, 'Where are you?'

'At the vicarage in Benton Close.'

He glanced at his watch. It was already seven thirty. He was off duty and there was nothing he could do on the Brundall case. Plenty to do in CID though, whispered a little voice, and yet aloud he said, 'I'll be there in ten minutes.'

FIVE

It wasn't what he had expected. The vicarage was one of twelve council houses set around a straggly and forlorn piece of greenery that couldn't by any stretch of imagination be called grass. Horton parked the Harley outside the ugly semi-detached house typical of the 1960s and, as he gazed up at it, he wondered how the late Reverend Gilmore had known his mother. From his memory of her, he couldn't see her being friendly with a vicar. Bookmakers and gamblers maybe, he thought with bitterness. And yet what did he really know about her? She had walked out on him one November morning when he was ten. He hadn't seen or heard of her since. He didn't know if the police had investigated her disappearance, he hadn't asked, and he had never made any enquiries himself. Why should he? He'd had years, before joining the police, to fill with bitterness.

The vicarage gate squeaked as he pushed it open. He'd covered this patch as a constable and had been called to the area many times before, but he couldn't remember a Reverend Gilmore, or this house. There was a Christmas tree in the window but without its lights shining it looked like someone who had arrived at the party wearing the wrong clothes.

The garden was overgrown and neglected like the house, which badly needed a lick of paint. Perhaps the church really had lost as much money as it purported to have done over the last sixteen years. He lifted his finger to press the bell. Before he could do so, however, the door swung open and a large, square-set, rather plain, middle-aged woman with short white hair and a dog collar smiled a little warily at him. Horton guessed she hadn't expected a policeman on a motorbike dressed in black leathers.

He quickly introduced himself and showed his warrant card. Her gentle, clear-skinned face broke into a smile. It lit her pale blue eyes and made her far more attractive, but Horton could still see the concern and bafflement in her expression.

He stepped inside, surprised to find that his heart was going like the clappers. Suddenly the sense of menace that he had experienced at Horsea Marina last night was back with a vengeance. But why? There was no fog here and there was no smell of burning bodies, just a miserable looking damp house with peeling and faded wallpaper and an electric light bulb hanging from the ceiling.

'It's not very homely, is it?' she said, reading his mind. He thought her Welsh accent not nearly so strong as when he'd spoken to her over the telephone.

Why had the church allowed the Reverend Gilmore to live like this? Horton hadn't known him but he didn't think it right that a clergyman should live in such dire conditions.

Anne Schofield answered his unspoken question with an accuracy that caused him a moment's unease. 'He wouldn't let anyone help him, you know. He refused to have the place decorated. I'm afraid he was a bit eccentric and a hoarder, as you'll see.'

'How well did you know him?'

'I'd met him a couple of times. His parishioners and the Dean speak very highly of him. Coffee, Inspector?'

'No. Thanks.' He wanted this over with as quickly as possible. But he also wanted to find out more about

Gilmore and how he came to know his mother. 'How old was Reverend Gilmore when he died?'

'Fifty-five.'

Horton started with surprise. He had expected her to say at least seventy. His mind was racing. How old would his mother be now? God, it was hard to remember. He had her birth certificate, along with a photograph, in that Bluebird toffee tin under his bunk. He hadn't looked at it in years. He guessed that she must be about fifty-eight, *if* she was still alive. Could Gilmore and his mother have been lovers? Could *he* be Gilmore's son? But, no, that was ridiculous. Why? Horton had never known his father and his mother had never spoken of him. He wasn't named on his birth certificate. He'd learnt to despise the absent father for abandoning him. And he'd hardened his heart against his mother for deserting him. He didn't want to revise those opinions. It involved too much emotion. Think of practical matters, he urged himself.

'How did Reverend Gilmore die?'

'A massive stroke. He was taking the Candlelight Christmas Service last night when he collapsed.'

The church had moved quickly then to put in a replacement vicar and get her into the vicarage.

She pushed open a door on her left to reveal a forlorn-looking room with a musty smell. 'It's a bit of mess, see.'

That was a gross understatement, he thought, staring around at the chaos. He'd seen tidier rooms after they'd been ransacked by burglars.

Horton followed her as she picked her way through the books and papers that littered the floor. He couldn't help treading on most of them. Ahead, buried under an avalanche of papers, was a battered old desk and behind it a swivel leather chair.

Anne Schofield picked up a pile of yellowing newspapers which had been stacked on the floor behind the chair, and as she did so Horton glanced out of the window at the rear garden. It was tiny but seemed even smaller because of the high brick wall that gave onto the naval base. Then he caught sight of a concrete structure in the right-hand corner of the garden.

'It's an air-raid shelter left over from the war,' she explained, obviously following the direction of his glance. 'I don't know if there's anything inside it apart from rats. I haven't had the courage to look yet.'

He could see four concrete steps leading down to an entrance across which was a sheet of rusting corrugated iron.

'This is what I found.' Anne pointed at the newspaper on the Reverend Gilmore's desk.

There was a large part of him that didn't want to look, but his police training and conditioning overrode that. There, staring at him, was an article that had been written in the summer of 1995 and along with it a photograph of him holding a medal to mark the Queen's commendation for bravery. Little good it did him these days, he thought wryly. He had overpowered a thug waving a loaded gun at a postmaster on Hayling Island. He couldn't remember much about it. Instinct had taken over. He hadn't even been on duty. In the margin of the newspaper in neat rounded script were the words: "Jennifer Horton's boy?" just as Anne Schofield had told him.

It was a shock seeing his mother's name, and with it came the painful memories of hurt and shame as acute as the first time he'd experienced them. He wanted to leave, but Anne Schofield's voice pierced his thoughts. 'There's more.'

His heart sank as he flicked through the rest of the newspapers. In every single one, the Reverend Gilmore had put a circle around an article and that article was about him. Jesus! It was as if he was reading a scrapbook on his career. At any moment he expected Michael Aspel to leap out from behind the curtains with a television crew and hand him a big red book, saying, 'This is your life.'

With curiosity now overcoming his emotions he began to examine the dates. The newspapers were all later than the one where Gilmore had written his mother's name. That had been the article that had sparked this interest in him. But why this obsession?

'What can you tell me about him?' he asked, making sure to hide the emotion in his voice.

'Nothing, I'm afraid. I've come from a parish in North Hampshire. You'll need to speak to his parishioners or the Dean.'

Would he though? He wanted to move on with his life. Emma was his future. It didn't matter that she didn't have paternal grandparents. It was probably for the best that she didn't know who they were. And, he reminded himself, he didn't have time to spare. He had a murderer to catch, and if not that then a pair of yobs who had attacked an American tourist, not to mention all the other thefts, assaults and burglaries piling up on his desk!

'Thank you for showing me these,' he said politely, with, he hoped, a voice devoid of emotion. 'They're of no interest to me. Reverend Gilmore obviously knew my mother, but I didn't know him.'

He wanted to get out of here quickly. The place was depressing him. He turned to leave when his eyes caught something written on the crowded blotter. Pushing the pile of newspapers further over, he saw quite clearly standing out from the other scribblings, the words, 'Horsea Marina'. Nothing unusual in that except the words were heavily underlined and appeared to have been written recently. The lettering wasn't as faded as the rest. It was just a coincidence, but he found himself asking, 'Did the Reverend Gilmore own a boat?'

'Not that I know of,' she said, surprised. 'Why?'

'He's written the name of a marina on his blotter, or perhaps you wrote it?'

'It wasn't me.' She frowned, puzzled by his line of questioning.

Why should Reverend Gilmore choose to write those words when his parish didn't extend to the marina some seven miles to the north and west of the city? Perhaps he had a friend or relative who lived at the marina. The explanation could be perfectly simple and probably was, but Horton couldn't help thinking it an unusual coincidence. That was the policeman in him.

Anne Schofield interrupted his thoughts. 'What would you like me to do with the newspapers?'

'Burn them or throw them out for recycling,' he said quickly and firmly. The past was no use to him.

He saw her eyeing him closely. She looked troubled. 'And if I find any other reference to you or Jennifer Horton do you want me to call you?' she asked gently.

He wanted to say no, but knew he couldn't. After a moment he retrieved a card from his jacket and said, 'You can contact me on my mobile.'

It wasn't until he was on his way home that he wished he'd taken that piece of blotting paper. He told himself that lots of people lived and worked at Horsea Marina, and Gilmore could have known any of them. But that fresh blue ink bothered him as much as the discovery that Gilmore had known his mother. And it continued to nag at him when he went for a run.

He didn't have his mother down as a churchgoer, but if Gilmore had been his father then he would only have been seventeen and his mother eighteen when he'd been conceived. Had she run away from home when she had discovered she was pregnant? Perhaps she had been thrown out. In those days people weren't so tolerant towards unmarried mothers. Maybe he still had grandparents alive in Portsmouth who knew nothing about him, or rather who didn't want to know about him, which was more likely.

It was a foul night with lashing rain and gale-force winds blowing off a turbulent sea and Horton was glad to shower and get back to the boat. He called the incident room to be told there was still no sign of Sherbourne. He hadn't returned to his office or his home and calls to the hospital had drawn a blank. So where was he?

Horton shivered, not from the cold but from the conviction that something must have happened to him and it didn't bode well. If Guilbert hadn't vouched for him then Horton might have thought, like Dennings, that Sherbourne was a suspect in a murder case and had run away.

Sitting on his bunk, with the wind howling through the masts and the rain drumming on the coach roof, Horton tried not to think about his mother but it was pointless. Anne Schofield's call had resurrected so many emotions in him that he knew he couldn't put it off any longer. With a racing heart and dry throat he reached out and lifted the cushions on the opposite bunk. Stretching a hand into the space underneath, he retrieved a battered old Bluebird Toffee tin. His hand hovered over it. Then with a breath he threw open the lid and removed a photograph.

It had been years since he'd looked at it and now, with his heart beating fast, he stared at the woman with the little boy beside her. He must have been about five or six when this picture had been taken. He could recall nothing about the circumstances although he recognized the location. It had been taken at the harbour entrance where the Gosport chain ferry had once traversed across the narrow channel. His mother was holding a glass and he was clutching a packet of crisps. She was dressed in a pair of flared red trousers, a white jumper with sweetheart neckline and a wide-brimmed floppy hat over her shoulder-length blonde hair. He was in shorts and a T-shirt. It was clearly summer. How old was she? Early twenties? Who had taken the photograph? His mother's boyfriend? Could that have been the Reverend Gilmore?

Horton racked his brains, trying to recall the day, but it eluded him. Behind his mother was the sparkling blue sea of Portsmouth Harbour and to her right he could make out the dockyard as it had been before its transformation into the select waterfront complex of shops, restaurants and luxury apartments that was now Oyster Quays.

He shoved the photograph back in the tin and put it under his bunk. He tried to sleep but images and words from the day's events swirled around in his head determined to wake him every half an hour. He was rather glad when his phone rang and he reached across the bunk for it, trying to see the time.

He half expected to hear Cantelli's voice, but it was Uckfield who growled down the line. 'There's been another fire.'

'Where?' Horton was suddenly wide awake. He swung his legs over the side of the bunk and grabbed his watch. He was amazed to see it was 5.25 a.m.

'Guernsey.'

Horton's heart sank. Of course it could be Brundall's house, but Guilbert and his officers had already been inside that, so not much point in setting fire to it now. There was only one place that it could be and the thought sent a shudder through him.

He said, 'Sherbourne's office?'

'Spot on.'

Coincidence? Not bloody likely. 'How bad?'

The answer was in Uckfield's silence.

Horton caught his breath. 'Sherbourne's dead?'

'Yes.'

SIX

Friday, 6 a.m.

'It looks as though Sherbourne was already dead when the fire started at about two a.m.,' Uckfield said, as Horton unzipped his leather jacket and slinging it on a desk in the incident suite, placed his helmet on top of it. They were the only two there. So where was Dennings? Horton wanted to ask. Surely Uckfield had called him?

'Did the arsonist use Sherbourne's keys to get into the offices?' asked Horton.

'There was no forced entry if that's what you mean, although a window was broken. But the fire investigation officer says that was where the firebomb was thrown inside. The building is practically gutted and Sherbourne a mass of charred bones.'

Horton tried not to recall the picture of Brundall's remains on the pontoon, but didn't quite manage it. Peter Kingston's description of the solicitor flitted through his mind: "About your height, slim, mid-fifties. Biggish nose and hawk-like eyes." Not any more, he thought.

Uckfield said, 'Sherbourne's car has also been found flashed up. Guilbert says they'll be lucky to get its make and registration number, never mind any prints. What the hell did Brundall tell or give Sherbourne?' Uckfield cried, exasperated. 'If Sherbourne was killed because Brundall made a new will then we need to find his original heir ruddy quickly. I would say he's our prime suspect.'

'Only problem is, neither DC Marsden nor Inspector Guilbert can find a relative.'

'Must be someone else then. And all the files in that solicitor's office have gone up in smoke. Great!' Uckfield rubbed a hand across his eyes. Horton wondered what time he'd been hauled from his bed. The big man looked as though he hadn't had any sleep, and only a change of clothes told Horton he had been home. Horton doubted if John Guilbert had even had that luxury.

Uckfield said, 'I'm sending Dennings to Guernsey.'

And that will go down like a lukewarm lager on a hot summer's night. Maybe he should call Guilbert and warn him, Horton thought as Trueman walked in.

Uckfield hauled himself off the desk.

'Sergeant, get Inspector Dennings on the first available flight to Guernsey.'

Trueman looked as if he was about to say 'with pleasure' then obviously thought better of it.

Horton said, 'Where *is* Dennings?'

'On his way. I called him after I telephoned you and told him to pack a bag.'

Horton pointedly consulted his watch. 'Maybe he's lost his passport.' Uckfield scowled at him. They all knew you didn't need one for visiting Guernsey. 'Or perhaps he doesn't know what to wear.'

'He's not going to the North Pole,' snapped Uckfield.

'Ah, but does DI Dennings know that?'

Uckfield opened his mouth to reply but Horton got in first. 'Whoever killed Sherbourne knew he'd visited Brundall, but how? Either Brundall inadvertently let the cat out of the bag before he died — perhaps he called his killer or called someone who knew the killer — or someone in Sherbourne's office knew the solicitor was coming to England to see Brundall, which means they've lied to the Guernsey police, and whoever it is told the killer.'

Uckfield narrowed his eyes and sniffed noisily, as Horton crossed to the coffee machine.

'Or perhaps our killer was watching Brundall's boat and saw Sherbourne board it,' Horton continued, pressing the button for coffee, black, no sugar. 'He recognized Sherbourne and knew it could spell danger, which means the killer must be from Guernsey otherwise how else would he know Nigel Sherbourne?'

'So you think it's the same killer?'

'It seems likely.' Horton took his coffee, sipped it and pulled a face. It never seemed to get any better. 'The killer sees Sherbourne climb on board and gets worried about what Brundall's told him. He kills Brundall that night and then hotfoots it back to Guernsey to prevent Sherbourne blabbing. He knows where to locate Sherbourne, follows him, but can't get to him before he sees his client, so he waits until he comes out, abducts and kills him. He then sets fire to Sherbourne's offices to make doubly sure that whatever Brundall has told his solicitor remains a secret, which means we need to check the flights—'

'Sergeant,' Uckfield bellowed.

Trueman was less than a foot behind him.

'I want the passenger lists of all the flights from Southampton to Guernsey on Thursday morning. And you'd better check out flights from the other airports too, especially any flights that went late Wednesday evening.' The door opened. 'Inspector Dennings, what took you so long?'

'I got—'

'Never mind. Trueman, as soon as you get that passenger list relay it to Inspector Dennings; he'll be in Guernsey by then. Then I want you, Dennings, with the help of the Guernsey police, to go through it like it's that racing paper you study so keenly. Check out all the runners. I want to know if there is anyone on that list who knows or knew

Sherbourne or Brundall, and their exact movements from Sunday night until last night.'

Dennings looked puzzled and with an irritated frown Uckfield quickly relayed Horton's theory, after which Horton said, 'Of course it could be two killers and our pyromaniac here told his pyromaniac friend over there about Sherbourne's visit.'

Uckfield spun round to face Horton. 'In that case, you'd better start finding me some leads here.' To Dennings, he said, 'Get going if you're to catch the—'

'08.25 flight,' interjected Trueman, keen to push Dennings onto the earliest possible flight, so much so that he volunteered to carry his luggage for him. 'Otherwise you'll have to wait for the 11.10.'

'And that's too damn late.' Uckfield snatched a glance at his watch. 'Get a car to take you there. Blue lights all the way if necessary.'

Horton was glad to get Neanderthal Man out of the way, and Trueman, breaking with his usual habit of remaining implacable in the face of panic, bollockings and briefings, looked as if he'd received an early Christmas present.

Horton was surprised to find both Walters and Cantelli in the CID office. He could tell by Cantelli's cheerful expression that it was good news and felt overwhelmingly relieved.

'Recovered from your flu?' Horton addressed Walters.

'It wasn't flu, just an iffy stomach. Couldn't get off the toilet.'

'It's all those curries you eat.'

'I don't like curry,' protested Walters.

'Well, now that you're back, pick up where you left off on the tourist mugging. Did you get copies of the CCTV tapes?'

'No.'

'Well get them, scrutinize them and ask around the local shopkeepers in Queen Street, see if you can pick up some clue as to where our muggers are before DCI Bliss has a coronary. Cantelli, you're coming with me. How's your dad?'

63

Horton asked as they swept out of the station, thankfully making it before DCI Bliss could grab them.

'He's chatting up the nurses, so he must be feeling better,' Cantelli said brightly. 'They reckon he'll be home for Christmas.'

'I'm very glad to hear it.'

'Where are we going?'

'Horsea Marina. I'll fill you in on the way.'

By the time Cantelli pulled up in front of the pontoon where Brundall's boat had been moored Horton had brought him up to speed with the case, but not about his visit to the vicarage and the words on the Reverend Gilmore's blotter. In the chill grey morning, Horton stared across the calm surface of the marina. Opposite he could see the modern houses and apartments, to his right the boardwalk of shops, restaurants and pubs, and to his left rows of boats on blocks and the boat-moving crane. He had come here, as he had yesterday, hoping to find inspiration, but this time with those words on Gilmore's blotter imprinted on his brain. Though they couldn't have anything to do with the Brundall case, he felt that they had nudged something in his subconscious that was telling him there was something here they had all missed.

'OK,' he said, chaffing his hands in the cold morning air, 'let's go over the facts. Brundall arrives here on Monday. He takes a vacant berth. What was the weather like on Monday?'

'It started raining in the evening. I had to pick Sadie up from Guides.'

'Brundall is a sick man. He'd probably had a long day motoring across from Guernsey—'

'How long would it have taken him?' Cantelli unravelled a fresh piece of gum and offered the packet to Horton, who shook his head.

'In that boat, with its powerful engine, and the weather fair, I'd say between three to four hours.'

Cantelli looked surprised. 'That quick?'

In *Nutmeg* it would take me for ever, Horton thought, though he had done it several times with Catherine and Emma on his father-in-law's yacht.

He continued. 'Let's say Brundall came here with a purpose. He was a dying man yet he'd made a special effort. Why?'

'He wanted to see someone for the last time?'

'He's got no relatives that we can find.'

'He had unfinished business here?'

'Like what?'

Cantelli shrugged. 'Maybe he just wanted one last look at his hometown, or perhaps he came to visit his parents' grave.'

Horton spun round. That was it, of course! Why hadn't he made the connection when Marsden had mentioned the parents were dead? He said, 'If he did then how did he get around? He'd hardly have taken a bus, too awkward to get into the city from here, and he was ill and wealthy.'

'He called a taxi or maybe—'

'He hired a car,' Horton finished, excited. '*And* he would have driven that car back here.' He scanned the car park. 'It will be parked near this pontoon, and it would have been here on Wednesday when we attended the fire, which leaves . . .' Horton's eyes fell on a dark blue Ford. 'That one.' He hurried across to it and peered in at the driver's window, but there was nothing to see.

Cantelli was already calling in the registration number. Horton was annoyed; he should have thought of this earlier. They had a team of officers out here and a mobile incident suite and yet nobody had picked up on this. He didn't think the vehicle itself would yield anything but they might get some sightings of it and Brundall, between Monday and Wednesday evening.

Cantelli rang off. 'It's registered in the name of Go Far Car Hire in Buckingham Street. It hasn't been picked up for any speeding offence.'

'Call them and ask if they hired the car to Brundall, and if so get Walters over there quickly. Tell him to bring some-one from the company here right away with a set of keys. And phone Marsden and ask him to track down where Brundall's parents are buried.'

Horton walked down to the pontoon and gazed across the water to where Brundall's boat had been moored. He shuddered as the memory of that foggy night returned to haunt him. Once again he saw that charred body and felt a strong sense of foreboding. The wind stirred, rattling through the halyards for a moment, and then died down. If he had believed in ghosts he would have said that Brundall's was haunting him. But he didn't believe. And yet he felt something that he couldn't explain. A medium would call it a presence. But he wasn't any medium. He was a policeman. Facts were his stock in trade and yet . . .

Cantelli said, 'Brundall hired it all right. Walters is on his way there now.'

Horton glanced at his watch. It was almost ten thirty. Dennings would be in Guernsey talking to Inspector Guilbert.

Cantelli said, 'Is there anything wrong, Andy?'

Horton regarded him keenly. There was only concern in the sergeant's dark eyes. 'Apart from a murder, you mean?'

'You look . . . worried.'

'I'm fine,' Horton said, perhaps too sharply because Cantelli gave a slight lift of his eyebrows, but knew better than to push it. 'Have you called the hospital?' Horton asked to distract him.

'No. I'll do it now while we're waiting.'

'I'll call into the mobile incident suite.' Horton strode across the car park towards a large Portakabin facing the mul-tiplex cinema complex. He spent a few minutes talking to the officer in charge and flicking through the reports but again no one reported having seen Brundall, and he hadn't visited any of the pubs or restaurants. Neither had he eaten at the yacht club. He must have brought supplies with him.

Horton reckoned a dying man wouldn't have fancied much to eat anyway.

By the time he returned to the car, Cantelli was just coming off the phone. His dark face was puckered with concern and Horton was fearful the old man might have had a relapse.

'Marie's with Dad,' Cantelli said. 'I managed to text her and she stepped outside and called me back. He's not too bad, she says, though it seems strange to see him in bed and inactive. You know my dad — he's usually a bundle of energy. She'll have a word with the consultant when he does his rounds. Isabella and Tony are at work, the cafés don't run themselves, and Charlotte said she'd go in later this morning and take Mum. Charlotte will stay until she has to pick the twins up from school. I said I'd go up after work.'

Horton could see he was torn between wanting to be there all the time and being at work. He said, 'I'm sure they're looking after him, Barney.'

'Yeah. You just feel so helpless.'

A car swept into the car park and drew up beside them. In the passenger seat next to Walters was a slim man in his thirties with gelled hair. Walters introduced him as Darren Trenchard.

'He booked it for a week,' Trenchard said in answer to Horton's enquiry. Horton was surprised that Brundall had planned to stay that long, although there was no reason why he shouldn't do so.

'Could I have the keys, Mr Trenchard?'

Trenchard handed them across. Horton donned a pair of latex gloves, which he retrieved from his jacket pocket and zapped the car open. He walked around to the passenger side and flipped open the glove compartment. Inside was the paper work relating to the car and nothing else. The boot yielded only the spare wheel and some tools.

'Take a look at the mileage for me,' Horton said to Trenchard. 'Can you say how many miles your client has done?'

The man peered inside and then glanced at a copy of the agreement he'd brought with him. 'Forty-three.'

'And he hired it when?'

Another glance at the paperwork and Trenchard replied, 'Tuesday morning, midday.'

Forty-three miles meant Brundall must have stayed fairly local. There was no satellite navigation on the car so no record of where he had gone.

'Did Mr Brundall say anything to you when he hired the car?'

'Like what?' The man looked bewildered.

'Where he was going? What he needed a car for? Nice weather? Anything?'

'No, just that he wanted something basic and comfortable.'

'Did he collect it from your premises?'

'No. He called us and asked if we would deliver it and said he would do all the paperwork then.'

'Is that usual?'

'It happens, especially when people come here on their boats from abroad.'

He must have called from the public phone box near the cinema complex and perhaps that was where he had also summoned Sherbourne. Why hadn't anyone seen him do so then?

'Did he tell you where he had come from?' Horton asked.

'No. I checked his passport as a means of identification. It said he was British. He's that man that got killed on his boat, isn't he? Was he a drug runner?' Trenchard's eyes lit up.

'You've been watching too much television. Are your cars cleaned before they're hired out?'

'Oh yes, inside and out.'

'Good. We'll need to take it away for examination. It's all right, you'll probably get it back cleaner than when you hired it out. We'll give you a receipt.' He nodded at Walters to do the honours and drew Cantelli out of earshot. Horton hoped that the forensic team might be able to tell them something about where the car had travelled by the dust and mud in the tyre treads or under the wheel arches.

Cantelli said, 'We might get sight of Brundall on the CCTV cameras around the city.'

Horton wondered if Dennings would have thought of that if he'd been here and doubted it. Why hadn't Cantelli gone for promotion? He was far brighter than Dennings. But Horton already knew the answer to that question and he envied Cantelli. The sergeant was content with where he was and with what he had, and that, thought Horton, was a great gift.

'I'll ask Uckfield to make another statement to the press and get out a picture of this car.'

Horton left Walters to wait until the police vehicle recovery truck arrived and then drop Trenchard back to Buckingham Street. His phone rang as Cantelli turned onto the motorway heading back to the station. It was Trueman.

'There are a couple of possible sightings of Brundall that look hopeful in response to the superintendent's statement to the press yesterday. A woman who was walking her dog on Portsdown Hill on Tuesday remembers speaking to a man who fits the description. It was just after midday.'

If it was Brundall then he must have driven straight there from hiring the car: it was only a few miles away and from Portsdown Hill, Brundall would have seen the city spread out beneath him. It was a spectacular and breath-taking view and might well have been the first place a man returning to his hometown would have visited; either there or the sea front.

'And the other sighting?' he asked.

'A parishioner at St Agnes's Church, Portsea, on the same afternoon.'

Horton started in surprise. *Horsea Marina*, the words on Reverend Gilmore's blotter. Could Brundall have known Reverend Gilmore? How? Had he once been a member of St Agnes's congregation or was there more to it than that?

His spine tingled not only with excitement but also with a faint feeling of uneasiness and apprehension that he didn't much care for. Was it some kind of intuition that had told him he should have taken that piece of blotting paper when he'd left the vicarage? And wasn't it those two words that had driven him back here today to discover the hire car?

He got the details before ringing off. 'I'll talk to the parishioner,' he said to Cantelli, 'you tackle the woman with the dog.'

Cantelli pulled a face. Horton knew that Cantelli was about as good with dogs as he was on the sea.

'Why don't I take the parishioner and you take the woman with the dog?' suggested Cantelli hopefully.

But Horton couldn't let him do that.

'You might have to enter an Anglican place of worship, and I wouldn't want to offend your religion,' Horton joked uneasily. He could see Cantelli eyeing him with suspicion. Damn. But how could he tell Cantelli he'd been to the vicarage and seen those words 'Horsea Marina' on the dead vicar's blotter without revealing why he had been there? Besides, he wanted to know why Brundall had been to St Agnes's Church and on the day that both he and the Reverend Gilmore had died. It was one hell of a coincidence and he smelt trouble with a capital T and the size of the Eiffel Tower.

'St Agnes is a Catholic saint as well as an Anglican one,' Cantelli said. 'Did you know that she's the patron saint of chastity, engaged couples, rape victims and virgins, to name but a few? If I have to go inside the church I'm sure the good Lord will forgive me my sins.'

'He might but I won't. You get the dog. I get the church,' Horton said firmly.

SEVEN

The last time he'd been inside a church, when it hadn't involved investigating vandalism, had been Emma's christening seven years ago. He brought the Harley to a stop in front of a red-bricked building sandwiched between two towering council blocks. It looked more like a barracks than a place of worship, and the large Christmas tree beside the heavy wooden doors did little to make the place look more welcoming.

There were no cars outside, so thankfully no service, and none about to start. Mr Gutner's wife, the man who claimed to have seen Tom Brundall, had told him when he had called on her ten minutes ago that her husband had left for the church where he would be practising for the carol service on Sunday.

Horton pushed open the heavy wooden door and shivered despite his leathers as he stepped inside the chilly interior, trying to adjust his eyes to the gloom. Dim lights hung low from a high ceiling. A torch might have been useful, but he caught a glimmer of brightness by the altar, where a Christmas tree, this time lit, attempted to throw some light into a dull, unattractive world. Surely to God, *if* there were a God, He wouldn't have been as miserable as this? Far from uplifting, this place oozed depression. There was no sign of Kenneth Gutner. Perhaps he was in the vestry, wherever that was.

Horton's shoes made little sound on the wooden floor as he headed up the airy nave between rows of pews that looked a little worse for wear with scratches and carvings. He wasn't quite sure what God would make of 'Julie loves Darren' scratched on one of them. Perhaps He didn't mind; after all it was better than saying that Darren was a scumbag and she hated him.

This place was giving him the willies. Horton hoped that Cantelli's Roman Catholic church was brighter and more welcoming than this. He couldn't help recalling another cavernous church like this one and another aisle where Catherine had walked on their wedding day; an event where he had been forced to parade his complete lack of relatives. The only foster parents he had cared about had died by then, which was a shame because Bernard and Eileen would have delighted in his marriage. Fortunately some of his colleagues had filled up the groom's side, but it still looked totally inadequate and pathetic.

He had felt the stares of Catherine's relatives boring into his back and heard their whispers, making him feel like a leper. *'What do you mean he hasn't got anybody? Everybody has someone.'* Not him. Not then.

Uckfield had been his best man. Horton wished now it had been Cantelli, who had proved himself far more of a best man than Uckfield.

The small nativity set beside the Christmas tree reminded him of Emma. This year would be the first he wouldn't be at home. God, how he missed her! He recalled her sad little face staring out at him from her bedroom window when he'd turned up unexpectedly on the doorstep in October. It tore at his heart and the only solace he had was that he knew his daughter loved him. And this was the place to utter a silent prayer, though he couldn't quite bring himself to do so. For years his prayers had gone unanswered. *Please God bring my mum back to me.* He hadn't, so that was the end of God.

Horton brought his mind back to the job, leaning over to read the cards on the flowers that were laid out on the steps up to the altar, beside the nativity scene. Someone had cared for the Reverend Gilmore.

'We'll miss you. God Bless. Elsie and Douglas Winnacott.' 'Thanks for always being there. May you Rest in Peace. Sharon Moore.' And there were several others in the same vein.

He straightened up and stepped back, gazing around him. There was no sign of Mr Gutner. Perhaps he was in the gallery, which he could see running round the remaining three sides of the church. On his right, above him, was the organ and below this, stone pillars. In the depths of the gloom he could make out the confessional box. This church must be High Anglican if the vicar heard confessions, he thought, crossing over to it. He found some steps to its left, which he swiftly climbed. Soon he was peering down on the nave. Still no Mr Gutner. Perhaps his wife had got it wrong and he hadn't come here.

How big would the congregation be in a church like this? It had been built for hundreds, in the days when this area of Portsmouth had been a slum teaming with little houses full of poverty-stricken working-class people, many of whom would have worked in the dockyard. Now he reckoned the reverend would be hard pushed to get a handful of people here. Had Tom Brundall been one of them on Tuesday afternoon attending a special service? Why come here though? This parish church was a long way from the area where he had been raised and even further from the marina.

Horton walked towards the far end of the gallery. Now he was above the door by which he had entered. From here he couldn't see anyone entering the church.

The sound of footsteps caught his attention. He headed back to the stairs to see a man in his late seventies with white hair and a creased and crumpled leathery face rather like a walnut, settle himself at the organ. Mr Gutner, Horton presumed.

'Struth, you gave me a fright,' the old man cried, clutching his heart.

Horton apologized and decided to postpone asking questions about Brundall. He was curious to find out more about the Reverend Gilmore. Without introducing himself, he said, 'I was sorry to hear of the vicar's death.'

'So were we all. We'll miss him.'

'He was well liked?'

'Never a bad word nor a cross one. He didn't ask for much and didn't get much. Not like the kids today. Grab, grab, grab.'

'How long had you known him?'

'Since he first came here in 1995.'

Horton was surprised and shaken. He had assumed that Gilmore had been the vicar here for years. He cursed himself silently for not getting more information from Anne Schofield, and for letting his emotions overwhelm his curiosity. He should have asked more questions. Now that first article that Gilmore had put a ring round and had written his mother's name in the margin began to make more sense. Gilmore had seen it on his arrival in Portsmouth. So where was Gilmore from? And more puzzling was how would he have known his mother and Tom Brundall?

The old man continued, 'Reverend Gilmore did wonders for this place, and the community. Oh, you don't want to judge him or us by this gloomy old church; this wasn't what he was about.'

Horton didn't think he had shown any visible distaste for the church. Perhaps this man was so used to people criticizing it that he automatically went on the defensive.

'Reverend Gilmore knew what it was like to be poor. He had his fair share of tragedy too; lost his wife and daughter.' The old man's expression clouded over as he shook his head sadly.

'How?' Anne Schofield hadn't said, but then maybe she didn't know. She had told him that she was a stranger to the area. The old man lowered his voice and looked warily about him, as if he was about to divulge a secret and was afraid that Gilmore, wherever he was now, would hear. 'His little girl was killed in a boating accident, on the Reverend's yacht. She was only eight. They were out sailing when she fell overboard. She was dead by the time the Reverend could reach her.'

Horton suppressed a shudder. The church felt colder and darker than before. He tried not to imagine how he would feel if it happened to Emma whilst she was on his boat. Catherine would never forgive him, and he would never forgive himself. He wondered if he would be able to continue living.

'The Reverend's wife never got over it. She was dead within six months. Committed suicide.'

Horton felt an icy chill run through him as he imagined the poor woman's grief.

'The Reverend Gilmore had a nervous breakdown. Tried to kill himself too. He knew what despair was. He understood.' His eyes filled with tears. 'God helped him out of it, and that's when he decided to become a priest.'

'So this all happened before he was ordained.'

'Yes. After God saved him, the Reverend decided to give away all his wealth and enter the church. He went to some college up country to study and came out a priest.'

'He was once a wealthy man then?'

'Must have been to have a yacht.'

Not necessarily, thought Horton, considering his own tiny yacht; that certainly wasn't any millionaire's pad. But the old man had given him a wealth of information, much of which he would be able to check, if he wanted to, though he didn't see why he should and where it would take him except to that connection with Brundall. *If*, of course, Mr Gutner had really seen him here; his eyesight might not be a hundred per cent.

'Do you know where the Reverend Gilmore lived before he came here?' Horton asked.

The old man eyed him keenly. 'You're a copper, aren't you?'

'Does it show?' Horton smiled. He liked Gutner. Policemen can never ask questions casually, it seemed. This man was no fool.

'Can smell them a mile away, even if they're wearing leathers. You undercover?'

'No, just riding a Harley.'

'Saw it outside, nice bike. Hope it's still there when you leave.'

'So do I.' Horton returned the old man's smile. 'How come you know I'm a policeman, apart from the smell?'

'Because no one asks that many questions about someone they don't know, in a church that's off the beaten track, in a hole like this. Oh, and my wife phoned me on my mobile to say a handsome young copper in leathers was looking for me.'

Horton laughed. There didn't seem much that got past Kenneth Gutner.

'Besides I knew that sooner or later one of you lot would wake up to the fact that the Reverend's death was no accident, or a natural one.'

The laughter died in Horton's throat and the smile vanished in an instant. A chilling suspicion began to form in his mind. He tried to tell himself that the old man must be exaggerating, or that he was upset and needed someone to blame, but deep inside he knew that wasn't the case. Half afraid of where this might lead him, he said, 'What do you mean?'

'I used to be an ambulance man and I've seen a lot of deaths in my time including stroke victims, and I'm telling you that weren't no stroke the Reverend Gilmore had.'

Horton didn't like the sound of this. He eyed Gutner closely. Others might have dismissed the elderly man as being senile, but Horton wasn't that rash or stupid. His copper's antenna was radiating like it had just been struck by lightning.

'What happened, Mr Gutner?'

Gutner eyed him sharply for a couple of seconds, seemed to like what he saw and nodded. 'Reverend Gilmore had only just started to welcome the congregation to the Candlelight Christmas Service when I could see that he was having trouble getting the words out. His mouth was moving but the words sort of got stuck. And before you say that's what happens when you have a stroke, I know it does but not like this. A stroke victim doesn't have convulsions and Gilmore convulsed before he collapsed. I rushed down to help. I was playing the organ as usual that night. There was a crowd around him by the time I got to him. I pushed them aside. His breathing was all wrong. I shouted for someone to call the ambulance and spoke to Gilmore gentle like until they arrived. An hour later he was dead.' There were tears in the old man's eyes.

Horton thought he could hear the church creaking and groaning as if in sympathy with Gutner's words. One part of him said, the old man is mad; it was a natural death. And yet Horton's instincts were screaming the opposite. Why had Gilmore written Horsea Marina on his blotter? Why had Brundall come here? And why had both men died on the same night?

'What time was this?'

'The service started at six o'clock with a procession of adults and kiddies holding candles as they walked to their seats. The candles were extinguished, the congregation sat and the Reverend began the service at about six thirty. He was taken to hospital just on seven o'clock. The verger stepped in after that and we carried on with our worship, but nobody's heart was in it.'

The fire on Brundall's boat had started at seven thirty, forty-five minutes after Gilmore's collapse. *If* Gilmore's death was suspicious, and it was a big if, then it was certainly possible for the killer to have had time to get from here to Horsea Marina. Yet how could someone have killed the vicar in full view of the congregation without anyone seeing him?

'I believe you saw a man called Tom Brundall talking to the Reverend—'

'Yes, and that's another thing, why did his boat catch fire the day he visited the vicar?'

Gutner might be elderly, but there was no fooling him.

Horton said, 'It could be a coincidence.'

'Since when have the cops believed in coincidence?' Gutner scoffed.

77

He was right. With admiration for the man's intellect, which hadn't diminished with age, Horton said, 'OK, tell me what happened.'

Gutner settled back in his seat. He paused. Horton could tell it wasn't for effect but that he was marshalling his thoughts to give as accurate and concise an account as possible. He would have made a good copper.

'St Agnes's is a great big barn of a church, as you can see. The lights were on; it was a grey, miserable Tuesday, with a heavy blanket of cloud closing in on you. Even with the lights on though, there are places in this church that are still dim; it has a hundred nooks and crannies. I came up here to practise the organ and heard the door open and footsteps below—'

'The time?'

Gutner puffed out his cheeks and thought. 'About three thirty, give or take a minute. I thought it was the vicar at first but then realized it didn't sound like his tread. I looked in my mirror, here above the organ, and saw a man walk towards the nativity. It was that man whose picture was on the television, Brundall, you said his name was. Then the vicar came out of the vestry. I didn't even know he was in the church. I came in that way, and didn't see him, there's a door that leads up from there to here. He saw this stranger and looked as if he'd seen a ghost.'

'Was he pleased or afraid?' Horton asked sharply.

'Afraid,' Gutner replied instantly. 'The vicar went white and staggered back. Brundall moved forward as though to help the vicar, but he waved him away. "I'm all right," the vicar said, then, "What are you doing here? We swore never to see one another again. I've made my peace with the Lord and tried to put right what we did wrong all those years ago."'

Horton felt a thrill run down his spine. What had they done wrong? Did this have anything to do with Brundall's death? Horton wouldn't mind betting on it.

'Go on,' he encouraged, not that he really needed to; Gutner was enjoying this despite mourning his vicar.

'Brundall said, "I'm dying, cancer. I haven't got long. I want to confess and I want you to hear my confession". The vicar went even paler and he said something, but I couldn't hear what it was because he spoke so softly. Then I heard Brundall say, "Did you know that Jennifer Horton's boy's a policeman, a detective inspector here in Portsmouth?" Hey, that's you, I bet it is.'

Horton tensed. He felt the breath being sucked from his body. First Gilmore and now Brundall, and now they were both dead. Jesus! What the hell was going on? Desperately he tried to keep his face expressionless but his head was swimming with this information, and his heart was pounding as though he'd just run a marathon. He hoped he sounded neutral when he asked, 'What else did he say?'

Gutner didn't seem to notice anything untoward with him. Easily, the old man continued. 'The vicar said, "Leave it, Tom. It's over, done with". Brundall replied, "Not until I make my confession. If you won't hear it, Rowley, then I will have to find another priest", and then they moved out of earshot and sight. Brundall followed the vicar into the vestry.'

'Do you know if the vicar heard his confession?'

'No. I waited for a while before starting to play the organ. I didn't want them to think I had been eavesdropping, but they didn't come out of the vestry. Not then anyway. I started playing and didn't see the vicar until the candlelight service on Wednesday night and then he died.'

'Have you any idea what the Reverend Gilmore was referring to when he said he'd tried to put right the wrong?' Horton asked more in hope than anticipation.

'No, but it can't have been much because the vicar didn't have a bad or wicked bone in his body. And now the other man is dead too and I know for definite his death wasn't natural no matter what some smart arse doctor says.'

And Horton was inclined to agree with him. He wondered what the post-mortem on Reverend Gilmore had shown; there would have been one. If it had confirmed that the death was suspicious then he would have heard, so he assumed one hadn't been conducted yet.

Had Brundall killed Gilmore on Wednesday night? Was there time? The answer was yes. Just. After killing Gilmore, Brundall could have returned to his boat, where he was immediately accosted by his own killer who threw the match onto the gas-filled boat. But *how* had Brundall killed Gilmore in full view of a congregation? No, it didn't add up. Then a thought struck Horton. Brundall had visited Gilmore on Tuesday at three thirty and had then called Sherbourne at about four fifteen the same afternoon summoning him to Portsmouth for the next day. Had Brundall wanted to write down his confession to give to Sherbourne to read out on his death? Yes, that was possible. And someone hadn't wanted that confession heard, which meant there was a third person involved in this 'wrong' that Gilmore had spoken of and to which Brundall had wanted to confess before dying. And that third person had killed Sherbourne in Guernsey to prevent the truth from being exposed. Horton felt his heart racing with this new information. But where the blazes did his mother fit into all this? Horton certainly couldn't remember either Brundall or Gilmore.

He thanked Gutner and made to leave when the old man said eagerly, 'Don't you want me to come to the station and make a statement?'

'Later,' Horton said hastily, thinking that was the last thing he wanted. If Gutner made his statement then everyone would learn about Jennifer Horton and until Horton knew just how deeply his mother was involved in whatever had happened to Brundall and Gilmore, he wanted to keep it quiet. He could report Gutner's conversation without mentioning the bit about Jennifer Horton. He knew he shouldn't and that he was withholding vital evidence from Uckfield, but the way he saw it he had no choice. He needed more information before he was ready to expose his traumatic childhood for all and sundry at the station.

'I'll send someone round later,' he said.

Gutner seemed satisfied with this. Then he frowned. 'But you will look into the Reverend Gilmore's death, won't you?'

'I most certainly will,' Horton reassured him.

'Good.' Gutner started to pump the organ. 'It's been nice meeting you.'

And you, thought Horton, glad to escape the gloomy atmosphere of the church, and pleased to see that his Harley was still outside and in one piece. He climbed on. It was time to find out more about Reverend Gilmore and he'd start by visiting the Diocesan Offices.

EIGHT

'I was just going to lunch,' the deputy diocesan secretary grumbled, waving Horton into a seat opposite his modern desk complete with a state-of-the-art computer. Horton had been surprised to find the Diocesan Offices had been relocated to a modern office building at the entrance to the continental ferry port. He'd always assumed they were near Portsmouth Cathedral and had lost precious time trying to locate them there before someone had directed him here.

Horton didn't warm to the burly man in front of him in the dark suit and pink shirt. And he was wearing a cravat, a form of neck gear that Horton always viewed with suspicion. Yelford was in his early fifties with pockmarked skin and remarkably prominent ears. His light brown hair looked as though it was a toupee, but Horton guessed it was just the way he combed and plastered it down with lotion, which smelt of bluebells and vinegar.

'Why do you want to know about the Reverend Rowland Gilmore?'

Horton heard the defensiveness in Yelford's question. 'Just routine, sir,' he replied, drawing a sceptical look and a pursing of lips from Yelford. 'I understand the Reverend Gilmore was a very popular vicar.'

Yelford looked alarmed. 'You've been talking to his parishioners?' He ran his fingers over his cravat as if to check it was still there. 'I hope you don't think there was anything suspicious about his death.'

'There are just a couple of things we need to check, Mr Yelford.'

'Kenneth Gutner's been talking again, hasn't he? Just because he was an ambulance man he thinks he's an expert on all matters medical.'

'He's expressed his unease about the vicar's death to you then, sir?' Horton asked, injecting his tone with surprise and concern.

Yelford looked annoyed that he'd risen to the bait. 'He's an old man. He gets confused.' He gave a condescending smile that set Horton's teeth on edge. He made sure not to return the smile and was gratified to see a faint flush creep up Yelford's face.

'Mr Gutner seemed in full grasp of all his faculties when I spoke to him.'

'That was probably for only a few moments,' replied Yelford uncharitably. 'Reverend Gilmore had a stroke. No doubt it is very upsetting for Mr Gutner to lose his vicar, and the bereaved often try to find a reason for death, or someone to blame. It's a natural reaction. No one else has come forward to claim that Gilmore's death was anything but a natural one.'

No, thought Horton, noting that the Reverend had now become merely Gilmore, but that's because no one else saw Brundall visit the church and talk to the vicar. And no one else knows of the connection between the two men, except their killer. *If* Gilmore was killed.

'Of course, he will be sorely missed,' Yelford added.

To Horton's ears Yelford's remark sounded insincere, as if the man had spent years perfecting a soft quiet tone designed to make people think he cared when Horton could see that his eyes lacked any genuine sympathy.

Yelford continued as Horton remained stoically silent, 'Gilmore was a generous and devoted man and he had such a difficult parish. He could have gone far, you know. He was an extremely intelligent man, but sadly not ambitious.'

Yelford made it sound as if this was some kind of mental deficiency. Time to be firmer with this slimy toad.

'I'd like to see his file please,' Horton announced curtly.

Yelford bristled and raised his eyebrows. 'I'm not sure about that.'

Horton rose. 'Very well, I'll speak to the Bishop and return with a warrant.'

The threat worked. 'That's not necessary,' Yelford said hastily, rising. 'But I only have the briefest of details for administrative and personnel needs.'

'That will do, for now,' Horton said portentously.

Yelford frowned with irritation. 'What do you want to know?' he demanded. Horton noted the silky whisper seemed to have evaporated into thin air, and in its place was a harsh, abrupt tone.

'When was the Reverend Gilmore ordained?'

'In 1985.'

Horton made some rapid mental calculations from what Anne Schofield had previously told him. 'He would have been thirty-two then. Isn't that a little late to find his vocation?'

'It's never too late,' Yelford rejoiced, like a true sycophant. 'Gilmore didn't have a theology degree, in fact, he didn't have any qualifications, but he trained for two years before becoming ordained.'

'Where?'

Yelford glanced at the file. 'Ridley Hall in Cambridge. He did very well, excelled at everything. As I said, he was very bright.'

'I understand that his daughter drowned. Can you tell me when?'

Yelford rearranged his features to look suitably sad. 'A tragic accident. I believe it was in 1980. It's not on the file. His wife died shortly afterwards.'

'Did he come here straight from being ordained?'

Yelford consulted the file again, though Horton got the impression he didn't need to, and that it was done either for effect or to stall for time.

'No. He was based in a number of areas: Bristol, Oxford, Ross-on-Wye. He returned to Portsmouth in 1995.'

Which fitted with what Kenneth Gutner had told him and that article on Gilmore's desk. But Horton had picked up a new nugget of information. 'Returned?'

Yelford looked as though he'd been caught out committing a misdemeanour. He said stiffly, 'He was born in Portsmouth.'

Was he now? Like Brundall. And like Horton's mother. It was at least the beginnings of a connection. 'What did he do before he was ordained?'

'My file doesn't hold that kind of information, Inspector. I am sure the Dean would be only too pleased to help you, but he is a very busy man at this time of the year. I could make you an appointment to see him after Christmas; until then I hope I have given you sufficient information.'

Far from it, Horton thought, as Yelford closed the folder and stood up. Clearly he wanted Horton off the premises. 'Does the Reverend Gilmore have a next of kin?'

With a pointed sigh, Yelford opened the folder and briefly consulted it. 'There's none mentioned in the file, but I do know that he had a brother: Sebastian Gilmore. He's been in touch with the Dean over the funeral arrangements.'

Then why hadn't the Reverend Gilmore named him? 'I'd like his address.'

Yelford looked surprised and then smug as he said, 'I would have thought the police would know Mr Sebastian Gilmore.'

The name rang a bell but Horton couldn't place it: villain or hero? He wondered. Yelford rose and turned to his window. 'Gilmore's fresh fish and frozen food,' he said, looking out.

Horton crossed to the window and looked down where Yelford was pointing. Of course! That Gilmore. Below and further to the right of Horton, he could see an office block and a large warehouse emblazoned with Gilmore's name. Horton also recalled the fresh fish market at the Town Camber and the fact that Brundall's father had been a fisherman. Was it just coincidence that the Reverend Gilmore's brother operated a fishing business? Somehow he doubted it.

He left the Diocesan offices carrying with him a nasty taste that Yelford had somehow managed to leave in his mouth. Once outside he called Dr Clayton to be told that she would be free in about an hour, so he left a message to say he would like to see her then for a few minutes.

Instead of rushing back to the station, Horton found himself heading in the opposite direction towards the Town Camber. He needed time to digest what Gutner and Yelford had told him.

It was only early afternoon but it felt much later. A leaden sky was making the short winter day even darker and more oppressive than usual. In two days it would be the shortest day of the year and in six days, Christmas morning. He'd volunteered for duty. Better that than moping on the boat being haunted by the ghosts of his Christmas past. Still, before that there was Emma.

Turning right onto the Town Camber, Horton drew up on the quayside just past Gilmore's public fish market and in front of the Bridge Tavern. As he switched off the engine, he stared at the fishing boats and tugboats bobbing about in the basin. It was all so different from how he remembered it as a child. Then Lucas sailmakers would have been on his right, the old boat sheds had faced onto the Camber, one of which had still miraculously survived, and across the far side of the water there had been the ship-building engineering works instead of those new houses and apartments.

Suddenly, without warning, he was back here, as a child, sitting on the concrete quayside swinging his legs over the edge. It was summer. He was eating an ice-cream, which he now recalled his mother had bought from Cantelli's ice-cream van opposite the engineering works by the ancient harbour walls. There had always been, and still was in the summer months, a Cantelli ice-cream van there, and it was strange to think his link with the Cantellis went back so far, though he'd only met Barney through work. From that day, even though it was long ago, he could still hear the echoes of seagulls screaming overhead and smell the fish and seaweed mingling with the scent of beer.

With a racing heart he glanced behind him at the Bridge Tavern. It had hardly changed from the outside, but in his mind he saw his mother sitting on one of the wooden benches and beside her was a dark-haired man with a sharp-featured face. His mother looked upset; the man grabbed her arm, and leaned towards her, talking earnestly.

Horton snatched his head away and stared at the fishing boats with an intense feeling of anger. They were the emotions he had experienced then, as a boy of what? Eight possibly. So why had he felt like that? Why hadn't he liked the man? What had he said to Horton, or his mother? Instead of being happy eating ice-cream on a bright sunny day Horton recollected only misery and loneliness.

After a moment he turned back to look at the pub again, trying to grab some more of the memory, but it had vanished. Had that man been the Reverend Gilmore? He wished he'd asked Anne Schofield or the slimy Yelford for a photograph of him now. Horton didn't think it was Tom Brundall but then he could be wrong. His child's mind could have exaggerated the man's countenance. But it probably had nothing to do with either Brundall or Gilmore, it could just have been one of his mother's boyfriends — he seemed to recall a few of them.

Jennifer Horton's boy's a copper. Why was this so noteworthy? What was the 'wrong' Gilmore had referred to and what did Brundall want to confess? Both men had mentioned Horton's occupation and that to his mind could only mean one thing: they had committed a crime, and they hadn't been discovered. Was it worth checking the computer for unsolved crimes? He doubted it when he didn't have any idea of the timescale. Also he had the feeling that this crime had probably gone unreported.

It began to rain, so he started the Harley and headed out of Portsmouth towards the hospital on Portsdown Hill where he pulled up outside the mortuary. He found Gaye Clayton in her office and she beckoned him in with a weary smile. 'You look tired,' he said.

'It's a busy time of year for us and we've got a couple of people off sick.'

Horton sat down opposite her ancient battered desk and stretched out his long legs. 'I think I might be about to add to your burden.'

She raised her fair eyebrows. 'What is it this time — or should I say who?'

'Rowland Gilmore. He died on Wednesday evening, supposedly of a stroke.'

'I don't like the sound of this "supposedly".'

'And neither do I. I've just been talking to someone who witnessed his death, and before that the fact that Gilmore was seen talking to Tom Brundall before he was killed. I have a terrible feeling their deaths are connected and that Rowland Gilmore's might not be down to natural causes. I haven't checked the police report yet, but wondered what you could tell me. Did you do the PM?'

She was tapping into her computer before Horton had finished speaking. 'No. He's not on the system, so he must be in this pile.' She picked up a small stack of buff coloured folders and flicked through them. 'Ah, here he is. Rowland Gilmore, born the fifth of March 1953.'

That confirmed the age Anne Schofield had given him, which made him young to be his father, though not impossible.

Gaye was saying, 'He was brought in at three minutes past seven on Wednesday night. He had all the symptoms of a stroke as far as the houseman was able to ascertain and from reports given to the ambulance man, he had trouble speaking and understanding, loss of balance and paralysis.

He died at five minutes past seven.' She looked up. 'Didn't anyone come in with him?'

'I don't think so.' Gutner hadn't said.

Gaye continued. 'Because of this flu bug, and your body on the boat, his autopsy was put back. It's being done tomorrow morning. We're working overtime. I suppose you'd like me to do it.'

'Yes.'

She nodded and suppressed a yawn. 'Anything I should be looking for in particular?'

'My witness says Reverend Gilmore—'

'He was a vicar?'

'Yes. Why?'

'I'm surprised the church hasn't been on my back trying to hurry things along.'

'I rather get the impression that Gilmore wasn't one of their shining stars. His parish was in Portsea and he was a little eccentric. Apparently Gilmore was taking a service when he began to stumble over his words. He had convulsions and collapsed.'

'What time was this?'

'At six forty-five.'

She scribbled the time down. 'I'll do a thorough autopsy tomorrow.'

'Thanks. I appreciate it.'

Back at the station he looked up the incident log to see who had gone to the church, then lifted his phone and asked Sergeant Stride if PC Johns was on duty. He was. Two minutes later Johns knocked on Horton's door. He stood the other side of Horton's desk looking cocksure of himself, just as he always did.

'You were called to an incident at St Agnes's Church in Portsea on Wednesday night. The vicar was taken ill,' Horton said crisply.

'Yes, sir.'

'Tell me about it.'

'I was in the patrol car with PC Allen. By the time we got to the church the ambulance had arrived. I spoke to a couple of parishioners—'

'Their names?' Horton knew that one was Kenneth Gutner, but he wasn't going to tell Johns that.

Johns retrieved his notebook and after a moment said, 'Mr Kenneth Gutner and Miss Alice Weekes.'

'And what did they say?'

Johns looked surprised. 'Just that the vicar suddenly took ill. He started slurring his words and then collapsed.'

'Nothing else.'

'No, sir.'

'Nothing about the vicar having convulsions?'

Horton saw a sneer of contempt in PC Johns' face accompanied by a knowing smile. 'Mr Gutner did mention something about the vicar having some kind of fit.'

'But you didn't note it.'

'I thought the old man was exaggerating. He seemed to be telling the paramedics how to do their job. One of those know-it-all types.' Johns smiled.

Horton thought he'd wipe that grin from Johns' face. 'Do you know what makes a good policeman, Constable, and an even better detective? Obviously not, so let me tell you. *Never* make instant decisions about anyone based on your own prejudices. Develop an instinct or a nose about them fine, but never rely on it, and always note every little detail no matter how insignificant because it might just make the difference between catching our criminal and letting him get away. Do you understand?'

'Yes, sir.' Johns tried to look contrite but Horton could see he was livid at being reprimanded.

'It is possible that the Reverend Gilmore's death is linked to the man who was killed in the explosion on his boat.' Johns looked amazed. 'OK, you can go, and Johns . . .' Horton stopped him as he reached the door. 'Just because someone is old it doesn't mean they are senile and that their evidence should be dismissed. And neither does it mean they should be patronized. Remember that and we might make a policeman out of you, yet.'

Horton wondered if he would remember. Johns reminded him of Dennings and it wasn't just the build. Johns was the sort of copper who was good on a raid and out in the van on a Friday or Saturday night, but detection and understanding the subtleties of people would pass him by. Talking of Dennings, Horton rose and made for the incident suite. Dennings must have some information on Sherbourne's death by now, and perhaps there was something more on Brundall. Horton also thought it was about time Cantelli returned from his interview with the woman with the dog.

NINE

'Brundall told Mrs Davis that he used to live in Portsmouth years ago,' Cantelli said to Horton's enquiry. 'She claims he was much thinner than in the photograph I showed her, and which was on the television, but she can swear it was him and she described the car. This was at twelve fifteen. She walks the dog before she goes on duty. She's an agency nurse at the hospital.'

'Did she see him drive off?'

'Yes, when she came back about fifteen minutes later.'

Horton thought for a moment before saying, 'He met Reverend Gilmore at St Agnes's at three thirty, and he called Sherbourne about four fifteen. So where did he go between twelve fifteen and three thirty?'

'To his parents' grave? Marsden's discovered they're buried in Kingston Cemetery. I've contacted the CCTV control office and asked if we can check the tapes along Kingston Road. If he was heading for his parents' grave he might have driven into the city that way. And there's a camera on the corner of St Mary's Road leading to the cemetery. Seaton's picking up the tapes.'

'There's another entrance into the cemetery from New Road and no CCTV there,' Horton remarked, then, turning to Marsden, 'Take a photograph of Brundall and ask around at the cemetery. Did anyone see him there at any time, but particularly between twelve thirty and three fifteen on Tuesday afternoon? If he went there then it would have been before going to St Agnes's because it gets dark at three thirty and the cemetery closes then. Are there any flowers on his parents' grave, if so who did he buy them from? Where did he park his car? Did anyone see it? You'd better hurry because it'll be dark soon. If you get no joy today, go back tomorrow morning.'

Marsden rushed out looking relieved to escape the confines of the incident suite for a while.

Horton said, 'There are several cameras along Queens Street; we might pick up Brundall on his way to St Agnes's.'

'I'll get Walters to check.'

'Where is he, by the way?'

'Still interviewing the shopkeepers, I assume. I haven't seen him.'

'He's taking his time.'

'You know Walters, probably stopped for a three course lunch.'

'Either that or he's meeting his girlfriend to make up for lost time Wednesday night. Obviously you didn't know about her?' Horton added, seeing Cantelli's startled look.

'No, but I'd like to meet the woman who can put up with Walters. She must be quite a gal.'

'Perhaps he'll bring her to the dinner and dance.' That would be a first, thought Horton. Maybe he could ask Dr Clayton if she'd go with him. Would she accept? She probably already had a boyfriend or even a partner for all he knew.

Cantelli said, 'Talking of saints, how did you get on at the church?'

Horton told him, leaving out the bit about his mother. He might tell Cantelli, later, when he was ready, and had made some sense of it himself, but not here and not now.

Horton turned to Trueman. 'Is there anything from DI Dennings?'

'If there is the super hasn't told me. I've emailed Inspector Guilbert the passenger lists of all the flights out of England to Guernsey on Thursday morning, but it'll take some time to work through them, unless someone's name automatically jumps out.'

And Horton hoped it would but he didn't think they would be that lucky. He asked Trueman to get him all the information he could find on Sebastian Gilmore and to get an officer checking for links between Rowland Gilmore and Tom Brundall, then knocked on the superintendent's door.

Looking up from his desk, Uckfield said, 'The Guernsey pathologist has confirmed Sherbourne was strangled; there is damage to the thyroid cartilage, and the hyoid bone, just above the Adam's apple. He claims it's difficult to tell how long Sherbourne had been dead before the fire but he reckons at least four hours, which ties in with when he went missing.'

'So Sherbourne's killer is a man,' Horton said, taking the seat across the desk. 'A woman couldn't have lifted the dead weight of a tall man like Sherbourne and carried him into the building.'

'Unless she's an all-in wrestler.'

'Not many of those in Guernsey.' Horton quickly apprised Uckfield of his interview with Kenneth Gutner, again leaving out the reference to himself and his mother. Then he broke the news that Brundall's death could be linked with the Reverend Gilmore's.

Uckfield stared at him incredulously. 'You've got to be joking!'

'Do I look like I am? And before you ask, Gutner is a very reliable witness. He's not gaga. I believe him.'

'What the hell am I going to tell the press?'

'Nothing, yet. I need to talk to Gilmore's brother, Sebastian.'

Uckfield's head came up. 'You don't mean *the* Sebastian Gilmore?'

'There's more than one!' Horton asked sarcastically.

'Not of this man there ain't. Sebastian Gilmore has built up a hugely successful business. And he's an influential member of the Portsmouth Business Forum.' Uckfield frowned. 'He would have been on the phone before now if he'd thought his brother's death was suspicious. And Sebastian Gilmore doesn't mince words. He'd have told the chief constable to get his arse in gear and find out who killed his brother. Go careful with him, Andy.'

Horton eyed Uckfield, knowing he meant he could stir things up for him if he didn't.

'I'll treat him as if he was precious china.' Horton rose. 'I'll also notify the Dean that we're making inquiries into Reverend Gilmore's death.' That was if Yelford hadn't already told him.

Uckfield groaned. 'That means I'll also have the Bishop on my back. For Christ's sake, Andy, tell him to keep it to himself. I can just see the headlines if this gets out. And we'll look damn silly if we're wrong.'

You mean I will, thought Horton, noting with suspicion Uckfield's warming towards him. That's twice in one conversation he'd addressed him by his first name. Horton wondered what he was after.

'Make an appointment to talk to Sebastian Gilmore,' Uckfield said. 'He's a busy man, as well as a grieving relative. I'll make another statement to the press giving out the car registration number and description.'

Cantelli called the Dean and made an appointment for them to see him tomorrow, on a Saturday, and then went off to view the CCTV tapes for any sightings of Brundall's hire car.

Horton tried Sebastian Gilmore's office only to be told that he was out and wouldn't be in again until Monday. Horton rang off without making an appointment. As he headed back to the CID office he wondered why Anne Schofield had been going through Gilmore's things when he had a brother. Was she living in the vicarage? He didn't envy her that, if she was. Or had the church accommodated her elsewhere?

He found Walters munching a large baguette and drinking coffee. 'On holiday are you, Constable?'

'This is lunch, guv. It's taken me for ever to get round the shopkeepers in Queens Street, complete waste of time, no one saw anything. We've done better with the CCTV though. There are a couple of youths, wearing dark hoodies, lingering outside the bookies. Don't know why the control operators didn't see them, perhaps they didn't think it relevant as they don't actually show up attacking the tourist. Then they disappear into Cross Street and a few minutes later they're walking down Queens Street. I've asked for the pictures to be enhanced; we might get enough of a description to put out.'

'Check with Sergeant Cantelli, he might recognize them, and then see if they match anyone in our records. Oh, and Walters—' Horton called out on the way to his office — 'take another look at the recording and see if you can spot Brundall's car.'

'Right ho.'

Walters' reply was uncharacteristically cheerful. It was amazing what love could do, he thought with an edge of bitterness.

Horton checked his messages, cleared some of his paperwork with half a mind on it, the other half on that conversation between Brundall and Gilmore, and then reported to DCI Bliss.

Marsden returned from the cemetery, with the news that there were no flowers on the Brundalls' grave and no one had seen Tom Brundall there. He'd return tomorrow. Cantelli couldn't get a sighting of Brundall's car from the tapes either.

Another day without getting any nearer to the killer, thought Horton, heading out of the station, but at least they had gained some new and valuable information. He had reached his Harley when his mobile rang. His heart skipped a beat when he saw who the caller was: Reverend Schofield. Did she have some further information on his mother?

'I need to see you urgently,' she said without preamble.

She sounded out of breath and anxious. It was just after seven.

'Where are you?'

'In the church. Can you come now?'

He tensed and said, 'OK.'

It was wet, dark and windy and the traffic was thick with Christmas shoppers. Even though he was on the Harley, it still took him fifteen minutes to reach the church. He tried the front doors but they were locked so he hurried round to the back feeling a sense of danger so strong that his spine shivered and contracted. What had Anne discovered about his mother? Why had she sounded so upset?

It was even darker in the backyard without any street-lights, and there didn't seem to be any lights on inside the church. Perhaps she had returned to the vicarage. But surely she would have called him if she had.

As he pushed open the door his sense of menace height-ened. He felt instinctively that something was wrong. He could have switched on the light but he didn't. Was it because he had the impression that someone or something was waiting for him, or had a noise alerted him? Perhaps it was just the rain beating against the grilled windows and the wind howling round the building sounding like a hundred dead souls wailing to be let in, or should that be out, he won-dered. Whatever it was, it made his flesh crawl.

Slowly his eyes grew accustomed to the darkness. There was a sink on his right underneath the window, with a cup-board beneath it. He noted the two coffee mugs on the wooden draining board as he stepped around the table in the centre of the room towards a tall cupboard where he guessed the surplices were kept. To its left were three stone steps leading up to a door. It must open up into the church, he thought. Anne Schofield must be there.

He tried the door. It was locked, and there was no key in it. He frowned. He felt cold. *Leave. She's not here. Get out now*. He turned and something in the gloom caught his eye.

97

The cupboard door was open a fraction and wedged in it was a piece of black fabric.

With a pounding heart he twisted the handle, then cried out and leapt back as the body of Anne Schofield fell out. Revulsion and shock gave way to an upsurge of anger, but he barely had time to register this when he heard a clunk. Swiftly he turned and raced to the outside door knowing already, with a sinking heart, that the noise he had heard was someone locking it. Shit!

His senses heightened, he caught the soft shuffle of feet outside and with a flash of instinct knew what would happen next. He had to get out or he'd end up like poor Tom Brundall and Nigel Sherbourne.

Desperately he scoured the room but saw no way out. Then came a shattering of glass; he leapt as far away from the window as possible as a bottle crashed on the stone floor, and exploded with a great whoosh and a searing heat.

Horton dropped to the floor, choking and coughing. *Think of a way out of here*. There had to be one, he couldn't die here, now, like this. Gutner's words flashed into his mind as his lungs strained fit to burst and he felt as though his flesh was on fire. He'd said there was a door to the upper gallery that came up from the vestry. Yes, but where the blazes was it? Was it the one he had already tried? God, he hoped not.

He inched along the floor with his nose to the ground, spluttering and coughing. His eyes were smarting, his lungs screaming fit to burst. He could smell roasting flesh as the crackling fire devoured poor Anne Schofield. Where the devil was this other door?

The room was filled with thick black smoke, which was hard to penetrate, but to the right of the cupboard a curtain was alight. It was the only place left. It had to conceal the door. As the flames licked around his ankles he leapt up and tore at it. The burning fabric fell on his back, and he thanked the Lord he was wearing his leathers. He'd found the door. *Please God don't let it be locked*. He had to stand up to open it and fling it back before the black clawing smoke got to him. He had one chance and this was it.

He reached up, and scrabbled for the handle . . . where was it? His eyes were smarting, his lungs heaving . . . He had his fingers on it. He pushed against it and with an overwhelming sense of relief felt it open. Then he was through and slamming it behind him. He was stumbling, crawling and groping his way up a set of steps.

There wasn't any time to waste. Onwards he went until he was high enough to escape the choking black monster of smoke below. At last he came out to the right of the organ. Fumbling inside his jacket for his mobile phone, he prayed it wouldn't have melted in the heat. He punched in a number, hardly registering that his fingers were burnt, and found himself hoarsely and miraculously speaking to the emergency services.

Then he staggered on towards the far end of the gallery above the front door and collapsed onto the floor. His chest and throat were raw with pain, and his hand was stinging. When he coughed he brought up blackened phlegm and thought his ribs would be ripped apart. It seemed a lifetime until he heard the marvellous sound of the fire engines and saw the blue lights reflected in the windows. In those minutes he saw a thousand times over the burning flesh of the once kind and gentle Anne Schofield, and it sickened him.

But he was safe. He'd escaped, but for how long? He knew now that there had been no news about his mother. He had just assumed it. Anne Schofield had sounded distressed, not anxious, on the telephone because someone had forced her to make that call to him. She hadn't been the intended victim. He had. Quite clearly he had been lured here with one purpose in mind: to kill him. The killer hadn't succeeded, but he would try again. Next time Horton guessed he might not be so lucky.

TEN

Saturday, 9.30 a.m.

'Are you OK?'

'I've felt better.' Horton was touched by the worried expression clouding Cantelli's dark features. His throat felt as though he had been inhaling eighty cigarettes a day since he was fourteen, and a tight band of pain gripped his chest as if his ribs had been strapped up. His right hand was bandaged but his burns had been superficial. Apart from that, and being exhausted after a sleepless night, he was fine, and very glad to be alive.

'What happened?' asked Cantelli.

It was the same question that Uckfield had put to him last night. Horton hadn't told him the truth and he couldn't tell Cantelli. Besides, he didn't know the truth. He had suspected that someone had lured him to his death and used Anne Schofield as bait but in the cold light of day he wasn't sure about that any more.

Sitting in his office with Cantelli at the other side of his desk, Horton relayed what he'd told Uckfield and DCI Bliss: he'd called on Anne Schofield to get some background information on the relationship between Rowland Gilmore and his brother Sebastian, but had found her dead. He'd been trapped inside the building when Anne Schofield's killer had tried to destroy the evidence. Of course that didn't explain the phone call he'd received from her.

'Did the killer know you were in there?' Cantelli seemed to eye him a little suspiciously. Had he detected a lie? Had some minute gesture or inflection in his voice given him away? If anyone could read Horton then Cantelli was in with the best chance.

Horton coughed, unsure if he was stalling for time or if it was genuine, and then wished he hadn't because his chest went into a painful spasm. That would teach him to lie. He saw Cantelli frown with concern and managed to rasp, 'My Harley was parked in front of the church.'

'But why kill Anne Schofield? She's a newcomer to the area.'

Horton didn't like deceiving Cantelli, but consoled himself with the fact that the sergeant had enough on his plate at the moment with his father's illness. Croakily, Horton expounded another theory that had come to him whilst he had waited for medical attention last night at the hospital.

'Perhaps Brundall left an incriminating letter or document in the vestry when he went to see Rowland Gilmore. Or perhaps Rowland had a pang of conscience and wrote a confession which Anne Schofield discovered.'

Horton held his breath, willing Cantelli to believe that. He didn't think he was far wrong anyway, only that he guessed the incriminating letter or confession had also mentioned his mother, and Horton couldn't be allowed to discover it. But why make Anne Schofield call him? Was the killer afraid that he'd already discovered something about his mother's past life?

Cantelli looked thoughtful as Horton continued. 'I'm certain now that Gilmore's death and Brundall's are connected. Dr Clayton is doing both Gilmore's and Anne Schofield's post mortems today.'

He reached for the bottle of water on his desk and took a long draught from it. It didn't seem to help his throat very much. He could take some time and call in sick, he supposed, but how could he let an investigation that might involve his mother proceed without his involvement?

'So are we looking at the same killer for all three deaths?' Cantelli asked.

'Four if you count Rowland Gilmore.' Horton exhaled and felt the pain in his chest. 'If Gilmore *was* murdered then the MO is very different to Brundall's, Sherbourne's and Anne Schofield's deaths. I think it possible that Brundall killed Rowland Gilmore before returning to his boat. Brundall was then killed, and his killer followed Sherbourne to Guernsey, and then returned here to murder Anne Schofield. Which means our killer is no longer in Guernsey.'

Horton had expressed exactly that opinion to Uckfield earlier that morning and Uckfield had agreed. He'd called for the passenger lists of all the flights from Guernsey to England on Friday to be checked. But that wasn't the only way to travel between England and the Channel Islands, as Horton had pointed out and now explained to Cantelli.

'Our killer could be using a boat to travel back and forth.' Horton could see Cantelli following his train of thought.

'You mean if he keeps it in Horsea Marina then he'd know the security code to the pontoon and could easily have slipped onto Brundall's pontoon and killed him.'

'Yes, which means we'll have to check all the boat owners for any connection with Brundall. But it's not that straight forward.'

'That doesn't sound very simple to me,' muttered Cantelli.

'Our killer could keep his boat in Guernsey.' Horton sat forward. 'Let's say our pyromaniac follows Brundall from Guernsey but didn't moor up in Horsea Marina; I called the marina and they say no other visitor came in after Brundall either on Monday, Tuesday or Wednesday. So he must have moored nearby. He manages to get the security code for the pontoon, kills Brundall and then returns to Guernsey, by boat, but he arrives too late to stop Sherbourne from going into his office on Thursday morning. Our pyromaniac does, however, manage to catch up with Sherbourne as he leaves his office and follows him to his client's. He lies in wait for Sherbourne, abducts and kills him before dumping his body in his office and setting light to it before returning to Portsmouth by boat early Friday morning.' Horton took another swig at his water before continuing. 'Uckfield has asked Dennings to check if any boat owner left a marina in Guernsey at about the same time as Brundall and then returned late Wednesday night or early Thursday morning, plus if that same person then left Guernsey yesterday. There's only one snag though with my theory.'

'He'd have to have a pretty powerful boat.'

'That's not the problem. Anything over twenty-five feet and with a powerful engine could have done it. No, our problem is the killer might not keep his boat in a marina. He could have his own private mooring, and that will be more difficult to check. Still, Guernsey's a small place and you don't live and work on an island only thirty-one miles long and twenty-four miles square without understanding the sea and knowing who's out and about on it. Guilbert will find it, if it's there to be found, because Dennings won't have a clue where to start.'

'Does Catherine know about your dice with death?'

'No, and I made Uckfield swear not to tell her, or Alison. If Catherine finds out, she might think I'm in danger and stop me from seeing Emma on Christmas Eve.'

'We'll have the case sewn up by then.'

'That's what I like about you, Barney, your blind faith and sheer bloody optimism. Come on.' Horton rose. 'Let's go and talk to a man about his brother, after which you've got an appointment with the Dean.'

And whilst Cantelli was with the Dean, Horton was going to take a good look around the vicarage, which had been sealed off with an officer posted outside. He'd managed to forestall anyone entering the house. It hadn't been too difficult because Anne had been killed in the church. Horton wanted to be the first inside that vicarage to make sure the newspapers that mentioned him and his mother were destroyed.

Then there were the words 'Horsea Marina' on the blotting paper. Would that piece of blotting paper still be there, or had the killer taken it away after killing Anne Schofield and trying to kill him? If it had gone then Rowland Gilmore's killer couldn't have been Tom Brundall. And if it was still there . . . ? That could either mean the killer missed it or thought it unimportant, in which case he came back to the fact that Rowland Gilmore's killer wasn't Tom Brundall. He felt he was going round in circles.

'Does the Dean know about Anne Schofield's death?' Cantelli asked, breaking through his thoughts as they headed out of Portsmouth towards Sebastian Gilmore's home. Trueman had obtained the address, but Horton hadn't rung to make an appointment. Quite honestly he'd forgotten after the excitement of last night and there was no point in bothering now.

'Yes, Uckfield broke it to him last night. The Dean said he'd have both Rowland Gilmore's and Anne Schofield's files available for you.'

'What about her family?'

'There's a sister who lives in Abertillery, South Wales. The Dean notified his equivalent there last night and he and the police informed her. She's an invalid and can't get down here. There's no point in her coming anyway. We said we'd send her sister's belongings back, but I think her vicar is coming down to collect them on Monday.'

'The poor woman.'

Horton wondered if Cantelli meant Anne Schofield or her sister.

As Cantelli drove to Gilmore's home in a small village on the border between Hampshire and West Sussex, Horton mulled over the events of the previous night. He experienced that same knot of anger he'd felt last night when he had stared down at her blackened corpse. The gentle, kind woman he'd only recently met hadn't deserved such a terrible fate. She'd been an innocent victim in whatever was going on and he had vowed then, and silently reaffirmed now, that he would find the bastard who'd killed her.

When the hospital had released him at close on midnight he'd ridden home, nervously checking for anyone on his tail. But whoever it was who had tried to kill him had thought they'd finished the job; all was quiet and there was no one suspicious lurking around the marina. He was safe for one night at least. Soon, though, he guessed the killer would realize that he was still alive and would make another attempt on his life and Horton didn't intend ending up like Brundall, Sherbourne or poor Anne Schofield.

He gazed out of the window as Cantelli drove carefully through the country lanes. The rain had finally stopped and the blustery wind was tearing holes in the cloud big enough to let a glimpse of blue through; he didn't think it would last though. He wondered if he should have moved the boat this morning on the high tide, but consoled himself with the fact that the killer probably didn't know where he lived and besides it had been too windy to risk it. By the next high tide this evening it would be dark and too late to move *Nutmeg*. Perhaps tomorrow morning he might motor along Hayling Bay and up the Emsworth Channel to Northney Marina at the top of Hayling Island, and stay there for a few days, and yet he felt that was like giving in, or running away. It reminded him of his mother: had he run away from the truth of her disappearance all these years? He guessed he knew the answer to that one.

A low whistle from Cantelli made Horton look up to find they had come to a halt in front of a pair of electronically controlled gates. Beyond these Horton could see an impressive pale-pink three storey Georgian house with a kind of extension on its left that would have given Prince Charles a seizure. How the planners had allowed the glass square carbuncle to be attached to such a splendidly proportioned and listed house, Horton didn't know. Or rather he did. Hadn't Uckfield told him Sebastian Gilmore was a very influential man? What Horton hadn't reckoned on was the reach of that influence; it obviously extended out of Portsmouth into wider Hampshire. Horton couldn't help but compare this with the Reverend's ex-council house and straggling grass. Had Sebastian Gilmore ever offered to help his brother? Had that help been refused? He was very curious to learn more about their relationship.

'I didn't think there was any money in fishing,' he said as Cantelli leaned out of the car window to press the intercom. 'I remember when Gilmore had ramshackle offices on the Town Camber. They pulled them down in the late 1990s to build those posh flats. That must have made him a bob or two. My dad used to know Gilmore senior.'

'Who is it?' demanded a crackly female voice of indeterminate age.

'Inspector Horton and Sergeant Cantelli. We'd like to talk to Mr Gilmore.'

'He's not here.'

'Can you tell us where we might find him?'

'In his office; at the ferry port. What do you want him for?'

'We'll contact him there,' Cantelli quietly asserted.

There was an irritable tut before the voice said, 'I'll let him know you're coming.'

Cantelli didn't even get the chance to say thank you. Horton felt mildly irritated that Sebastian Gilmore would now be prepared for them, though why it should irk him he didn't know.

'Friendly lot, aren't they?' Cantelli said, heading back to Portsmouth. 'Seems like we've had a wasted journey.'

Not quite, thought Horton. It had been illuminating to see how the other half of the Gilmores lived.

Twenty minutes later they were pulling into Fountain Quay at the Commercial Ferry Port. After scrutinizing their identification cards, a security guard directed them to a visitor's space outside a two storey modern office block.

Horton climbed out and surveyed the area. There were a handful of cars in the car park, including a black Porsche

Cayenne. He reckoned that must be Sebastian Gilmore's because of its personalized number plate. There were a couple of fishing vessels moored up alongside the quay and the bleeping of forklift trucks behind him told him that it was business as usual on a Saturday. He watched a lorry pull up in front of a large warehouse opposite. Gilmore's security was good too, he thought, noting the cameras.

'Where do Gilmore's export?' he asked Cantelli, as they waited in reception to be announced by another uniformed security man who was telephoning to the boss. He'd emerged from a room behind the reception counter where Horton guessed he could view the security monitors. Horton noted the camera in the far corner covering reception and another over the door.

'France and Spain mainly,' Cantelli answered. 'They do a big trade in crabs, lobsters and oysters all caught locally. Tony and Isabella buy from them for the cafés and restaurants. Sebastian Gilmore's got some lucrative supermarket contracts and has worked hard to build up the business.'

And was still working hard, Horton thought, a few minutes later when a large-boned man with short greying hair and a weather-beaten, rugged face rose from behind a desk that seemed like a child's against his size. Horton felt the energy radiating from the giant like a radioactive beacon. With two strides, Sebastian was around the desk but he stalled, staring down with a puzzled frown on his broad-featured face at Horton's bandaged hands.

'Had a bit of an accident,' Horton explained lightly in a hoarse voice.

Gilmore's lips twitched but there was no smile in the gesture or in his deep brown eyes. He waved them into a seat and returned to his own, throwing himself into the chair which groaned and creaked in protest.

'What can I do for you guys?' he said, his accent betraying his Portsmouth roots. It was very similar to a Londoner's.

Horton thought how completely out of place Gilmore seemed in this room: it was too small to accommodate the man's stature and vitality. Here was someone who, despite his fifty-odd years, was very fit and active, both in mind and body.

With its cheap, rough furniture the office was also in sharp contrast to the opulence of the Georgian manor house they'd just come from, though to the left of Horton was a rather large and splendid fish tank.

'It's about your brother's death,' Horton began and saw surprise register on Sebastian Gilmore's face.

'Rowley? What about him? He had a stroke.'

There was no adjustment of Sebastian's features to show sorrow or even anger. Horton detected puzzlement and, interestingly, irritation.

Cantelli said, 'We have new evidence that suggests his death could be suspicious.'

'That's absurd!' Sebastian Gilmore focused his intense gaze on Cantelli. 'You think my brother was killed?'

Cantelli, unfazed by the contemptuous stare, stoically replied, 'It's a possibility, sir, which is why a full post-mortem is being conducted.'

'Who on earth would want to kill Rowley? He was a vicar.'

Horton could tell by Sebastian Gilmore's tone of voice that vicars weren't particularly high on his list of revered occupations. Perhaps that was what had driven the brothers apart, although he only had Anne Schofield's word that they had been estranged.

Cantelli said, 'You may have heard on the news, sir, that your brother's replacement, the Reverend Anne Schofield, died in a fire last night in St Agnes's Church, your brother's parish.'

Horton watched the expressions chase across Sebastian's face: incredulity, puzzlement, wariness.

'Are you saying that this has some connection with my brother's death?'

Placidly, Cantelli continued. 'We need to explore the possibility, sir.'

'You're not saying that Rowley knew her, are you?'

Horton remained silent and Cantelli simply looked blank. Gilmore clearly didn't like this and glared at them before shooting up from his desk and turning to stare out of the window. Horton threw Cantelli a glance, which he knew the sergeant would interpret as 'say nothing, and wait'.

After a moment Gilmore spun round. 'You're nuts. Why would anyone want to kill my brother and this other vicar?'

'When did you last see your brother, Mr Gilmore?' asked Horton.

Gilmore threw himself down in his chair, which groaned with his weight. 'Twelve years ago. He was at the Town Camber staring down at the fishing boats. My business was still there then. You can imagine my shock when I discovered he'd become a vicar.'

'Why should you be shocked?' asked Horton provocatively.

'We don't go in for religion in our family, Inspector.'

He said it as though it was something to be ashamed of. Horton heard the disgust in Gilmore's voice and felt rather sorry for Rowland Gilmore.

'Perhaps losing his wife and daughter so tragically contributed to his decision to enter the church.' Horton found himself defending the late Rowland Gilmore.

'He told me about that. But God, if there is one, which I doubt, couldn't bring them back so what's the point? What's done is done, you have to pick yourself up and move on. That's my motto anyway.'

And did you sympathize with him over his tragic loss? Like hell you did, Horton thought. He was getting the impression the brothers were like chalk and cheese.

'Was he older or younger than you, sir?'

'Younger by three years, though what that—'

'And you haven't seen him since then?'

'No.'

'Rather unusual that, for brothers,' ventured Cantelli.

'Rowley went his way and I went mine. We had nothing in common but we didn't fall out, if that's what you mean. What evidence do you have that my brother was killed?' he demanded, springing forward and glaring at Cantelli. A lesser man would have immediately pushed back his chair but Cantelli didn't budge an inch. Horton didn't even see him blink.

'We can't say, sir.'

'You mean won't say. All right, but I want to be the first to know what you find in the post-mortem,' he demanded, his tone brooking no objections.

'Of course,' Cantelli replied easily. Horton knew it wasn't strictly a lie. Sebastian Gilmore would be the first person outside of the investigation to be told the results.

After a moment's silence, Horton said, 'We believe your brother knew a man called Tom Brundall—'

'God, there's a name I haven't heard for years!'

'You know him?' Horton asked, surprised.

'Of course. We all worked together: Tom, Rowley and me. We were fishermen. Didn't you know?'

Ignoring the sneering tone, Horton recalled that DC Marsden had said Tom Brundall's father had been a fisherman so Tom must have followed in his father's footsteps, but he'd had no idea that Rowland Gilmore had also been one. Now, looking at Sebastian Gilmore, he could see that only the ocean could be big enough to encompass this giant of a man, and he wouldn't mind betting that that was where Sebastian Gilmore's heart really lay. Here was a definite connection but he didn't see how it could help him. He didn't recall his mother talking about fishing or fishermen.

He said, 'Did you know that Tom Brundall was killed in a fire on his boat in Horsea Marina on Wednesday night?'

Sebastian's eyes tightened. There was something behind them that Horton couldn't quite read. It wasn't fear and it wasn't shock. Neither was it sorrow. Before he could analyse it though the door was thrust open, and Sebastian's rugged face lit up. 'My daughter, Selina,' he introduced.

Horton swivelled round to see a slender woman in her mid-twenties. His eyes followed her as she swiftly crossed to her father's side. There was a petulant confidence in her stance and, Horton noted with interest, some hostility. She was fashionably dressed in tight jeans and a low-cut T-shirt underneath a leather jacket. She had her father's determined set of the chin, and swiftness of movement, but not his build. It was a neat little figure made taller by her high-heeled boots over her jeans.

'Selina, these are policeman. They think your Uncle Rowley was murdered.'

She looked understandably shocked, but whether it was at the abruptness of her father's announcement or the fact that Rowley had been murdered, Horton couldn't tell. A bit of both he guessed, which he found rather odd if Sebastian Gilmore was telling the truth about not seeing his brother for twelve years. How old would Selina have been then: fifteen? Sixteen? And if that was the first time Sebastian had seen Rowland since leaving Portsmouth then Selina couldn't have known her uncle very well.

Gilmore looked up at her and said, 'A man called Tom Brundall was killed in a fire on his boat and he and Rowley used to work with me years ago. I hope I'm not about to be bumped off, Inspector.'

'Is my father in danger?' she demanded with a flick of her highlighted blonde hair, and a belligerent expression.

Horton didn't know. 'When did Tom Brundall work for you, Mr Gilmore?'

'He worked for my dad first, like Rowley and me. I started on the boats in 1967. I was sixteen, but Tom had been working for Dad for some years before that. I was put with Tom on my first boat. I quickly became a skipper and then Tom used to come out with me. Rowley joined me straight from school in 1969. Dad had three boats then, sailing out of the Camber. I took over the business when he became ill in 1979, that's when Rowley decided to leave. He never really liked fishing. He left Portsmouth shortly after that.'

Horton mentally and swiftly ran through a checklist of dates: Rowland's wife and daughter died in 1980; he was ordained in 1985, and returned to Portsmouth in 1995.

Horton asked, 'When did your brother marry?'

'I can't remember. 1973 or thereabouts. Why do you want to know?' Sebastian frowned, puzzled.

Dr Clayton had told him that Rowland had been born in 1953 so he had been only twenty when he married; maybe it had been a case of having to. So how did Rowland know Jennifer Horton and when had they met? And had Sebastian Gilmore known her too? It wasn't a question he could ask yet, but Sebastian Gilmore had shown no reaction to his name.

'Did your brother have a share in your father's business?'

'I bought him out when he decided to call it quits. I gave him a fair price. He didn't complain.' Gilmore said, slightly defensively.

Interesting, thought Horton, a touchy subject as far as Sebastian Gilmore was concerned.

'Rowley took the money and that was the last time I saw him until twelve years ago.'

'And when did Tom Brundall decide that being a fisherman wasn't what he wanted?'

'1978.'

It was a year engraved on Horton's heart and mind. The year his mother left him. Horton went cold as the thoughts that had been forming in the back of his mind suddenly crystallized.

Sometimes a thing is so obvious that it has to be pushed in your face several times before you notice it and now he saw that the 'wrong' Rowland Gilmore had mentioned and which Brundall wanted to confess, could be something to do with his mother's disappearance. Had they killed her? The thought stole the breath from his body. It didn't bear contemplating. He was mad even to think it, and he had no real evidence except those newspaper articles and that overheard conversation. But that could mean anything, he told himself. Why should they kill his mother? It didn't make sense.

Gilmore said, 'We came back from fishing one day and Tom said, "That's it, I've had enough. I'm off," and I've never heard from him or seen him since.'

112

Horton was glad that Cantelli stepped in with the questioning because his throat felt like a stretched out piece of elastic, and this time the pain in his chest wasn't caused by smoke inhalation.

'And you've no idea why he did that or where he went?' Cantelli asked.

'None whatsoever, except that his old man was dead by then. His mother died when he was young, and there was no need for Tom to do as his father bid.'

'Did you know that Tom Brundall became a very wealthy man and that he lived in Guernsey?'

Horton watched Sebastian Gilmore carefully. He didn't look surprised or bothered by the fact.

'Tom was clever, and he was very good at figures. I remember he couldn't stick the smell of fish or being out in the rough weather. But back then you followed in your father's footsteps, not like now. Oh, except Selina's different.' He threw his daughter a proud and fond look.

She said, 'I'm the sales director.'

'And a damn good one,' Gilmore boasted proudly. 'We wouldn't have won that new supermarket contract without her.'

She was young for such a responsible position, thought Horton, though clearly her father's daughter by the fact that she could negotiate lucrative contracts with the supermarkets at such a tender age. A tough little cookie, and an ambitious one if Horton was any judge. Gilmore's was in secure hands. Cantelli had given him time to get his emotions under control and he needed that for his next question.

'Tom Brundall called on your brother shortly before he died. Do you know why?'

Gilmore eyed him shrewdly. 'So that's it, is it?'

'Did Brundall come to see you?'

'No.'

Truth or a lie? Sebastian Gilmore held his eye contact. Again, Horton thought he saw something which he couldn't quite fathom. 'Have you any idea why he should come to Portsmouth?'

'It was his hometown, so why shouldn't he?'

Gilmore didn't look as if he was being evasive or lying, but Horton saw in front of him a tough man well versed in the art of negotiation. Unless Horton was very much mistaken, this Gilmore could bluff, cajole, lie and bully with the best of them without blinking an eye. Rather different from his brother, Horton suspected. OK, so let's see how he reacts to the next bit of news.

'Brundall was overheard to say that he wanted to confess to your brother something that they did wrong some years ago. Do you know what he meant by that?'

Gilmore looked puzzled. 'I've no idea.'

Horton wasn't convinced. All Gilmore's reactions were right but Horton's finely tuned antennae told him that Gilmore knew a hell of a lot more than he was saying.

'Were your brother and Tom Brundall friendly outside of work?'

'I don't think so. There were eleven years between them. Tom wasn't a drinker, though Rowley liked a few.'

Horton could see that he'd get nothing further from Sebastian Gilmore. He needed the results of the post-mortem on Rowland Gilmore and he needed more background information on the two men. He rose and made to leave.

Gilmore sprang up. 'You'll let me know about Rowley? I'm sure you're wrong. I can't think why anyone would want to kill him, or Tom come to that.'

Cantelli assured him they would be in touch. As Horton reached the door he turned. 'We've had to seal off the vicarage, but you'll be able to have access to your brother's belongings as soon as we've finished, which should be within the next couple of days.'

Sebastian waved away his concerns with the sweep of an arm. 'There's nothing I want or need from there.'

Outside, Cantelli said, 'Do you think Sebastian Gilmore's in danger?'

Horton stretched the seat belt round him and considered Cantelli's question. He mulled over the interview, pushing away the thoughts of his mother, his mind connecting the strands of questioning and the undertones in Gilmore's replies.

'Brundall wanted to confess something that he and Rowland had done, and that something must have taken place when both men were here in Portsmouth and probably working together, otherwise they wouldn't have come into contact with one another. So that puts the incident between 1969 when Rowland joined the fishing boat and 1978 when Tom Brundall left.'

Cantelli pulled out of Gilmore's yard. He said, 'Even if we were to trawl through all the incidents between 1969 and 1978, it doesn't mean that whatever they did was reported, or even a criminal offence.'

Who would have connected a woman's disappearance with two fishermen? Was it connected? Who had reported Jennifer Horton missing? Horton didn't even know that. For the first time in his life his fingers itched to check.

'Would Rowland have confessed his sins before entering the church?' he asked, hopefully.

'Not sure how it works in the Anglican faith, but I guess so. You'll not get much joy there, though. The confessional is sacrosanct.'

'Pity. But we can find out about Rowland Gilmore's finances, both when he entered the church and when he died.'

'How will that help?'

'It might give us some indication of how much wealth he gave away and whether or not that compares with what his brother paid him for his share of the business. It's just a detail and probably useless, but I'd like to know. Oh, and get a photograph of Rowland Gilmore from the Dean. You can drop me off at the vicarage, and meet me back there when you've finished with him.'

And by that time, Horton thought, feeling guilty and anxious, he'd have hidden, or eliminated, anything that might mention Jennifer Horton.

ELEVEN

The vicarage was exactly how Horton had remembered it except that the gentle, welcoming and slightly puzzled Anne Schofield was missing. Damn her murderer. He stepped through the dismal hall and pushed back the door of Rowland Gilmore's study. Hurrying across to the desk he saw that the newspapers had gone. Had Anne destroyed them after his visit or had the killer taken them after setting fire to the vestry? He hoped the former.

His eyes scanned the desk for the blotter and with relief he saw that it was still there with the words 'Horsea Marina' scrawled on it. The leather chair creaked as he sat down and he pushed the other books and papers off the blotter and studied the handwriting; it was definitely the same as the other notes and jottings on the blotter, which meant that it had to be the Reverend Rowland Gilmore's. So why write those words?

Horton surveyed the desk. There was an old fashioned telephone to his right; most people when on the telephone made notes or doodled, so had Rowland Gilmore been left-handed and written 'Horsea Marina' whilst he'd been speaking on the telephone to someone? Had it been Brundall who had called Rowland and arranged to meet him in the

116

church? Perhaps Rowland had asked where he was staying and Brundall had replied, 'On my boat in Horsea Marina.' If so, then that didn't tally with Mr Gutner's evidence; he'd said that Gilmore had looked surprised and anxious when Brundall had shown up in the church. Could Gutner have been mistaken or exaggerating? It was possible. Or perhaps he had just misinterpreted Gilmore's reaction. Then again the Reverend Gilmore's surprise could have been from seeing Brundall so changed. Time plays tricks with us all and Gilmore could have been expecting the Brundall of 1978 to emerge.

There was another explanation, Horton thought, sitting back and frowning: perhaps Gilmore had returned from his encounter with Brundall and written Horsea Marina on the blotter whilst he was contemplating Brundall's desire to confess. Brundall had told him where he was staying and Gilmore had idly penned it.

Horton would get the forensic team to remove the blotting paper when they came into the house later. He knew they wouldn't be able to reveal the meaning behind the words, but they might just pick up some fingerprints in the house other than his, Anne Schofield's and the Reverend Gilmore's. If so, that might give them some lead on Anne Schofield's killer and possibly even Rowland Gilmore's. Horton just hoped that troops of parishioners hadn't been in here.

He stared around the chaotic room and shivered. It felt damp and claustrophobic and though he wasn't usually given to flights of fancy, this case was proving different. He felt a spirit of evil in this room, just as he had smelt danger at Horsea Marina on the night of Brundall's death. He considered again the thought that had struck him in Sebastian Gilmore's office: if Brundall and Rowland Gilmore *had* killed his mother then it meant she hadn't deserted him.

The thought paralysed him. For years he had hated her and now he was considering the possibility that she might not have deserved that hatred. It hadn't once crossed his mind that she could have been killed — after all, why should

117

it? No one had ever said there was anything suspicious about her disappearance. All the adults who had pushed him from pillar to post had *told* him his mother had run off with a man, so what else was he supposed to believe? Yet, the small voice inside him whispered, you could have made some attempt at an investigation when you became a policeman.

He sprang up, angry with himself and her. He was being ridiculous; the 'wrong' Brundall and Rowland Gilmore had done probably had nothing whatsoever to do with Jennifer Horton. *Then why speak of her?* Action was what he needed and he began to search through the papers on Rowland's desk, one part of his mind working like a copper but the other part, despite his best intentions, wandering back to his mother and lingering in the past.

There were stacks of sermons in the drawers, some odd scraps of notes, old shopping lists, and electric and telephone bills going back years. He picked up the books on the desk, mainly theology titles, and flicked through them. Nothing fell out. There was no mention of him or Jennifer Horton. He crossed to the bookshelves either side of a tiled fireplace. There were a number of spaces. Had these gaps been there when he'd come in here with Anne Schofield? He couldn't remember, but the fact that he was registering it made him think they hadn't been. He'd been more concerned then about finding out what Gilmore had written about his mother than worrying about what books the man had on his shelves. Was there something in one of them that might give him a clue to his mother's past? He didn't have time to go through each and every one of them and he shuddered to think that DC Walters or another junior officer would unearth something. Perhaps he could return tomorrow, on Sunday, and spend more time in this dank and miserable house trying to search for some clues to the past. But he knew he couldn't stand that. He shut the door, thinking that maybe he simply didn't want to know.

He explored the rest of the house. The living room with its brown-and-orange-patterned carpet and dull green curtains held an ancient television set, no DVD or video, and a press-button cream telephone on a chipped wooden table beside a faded light-green Dralon settee. There were two armchairs and a heavy oak sideboard, circa 1920, opposite the lurching Christmas tree that made Horton feel even more depressed.

Upstairs there were two double bedrooms, a box room and a bathroom. All looked as though they hadn't been touched since the house had been built and only Rowland Gilmore's bedroom was furnished. Here there was a single brass bed, made up with a lilac eiderdown. Beside it was a painted white bedside table on which were a few women's toilctries, a faded pink lamp with half its tassels missing and a crime novel. He picked it up and skimmed the blurb; appropriately enough it was an ecclesiastical mystery thriller. The faint smell of perfume told him that this must have been Anne Schofield's. He felt repulsed and saddened over her death. If only she hadn't come here she'd be alive today. And maybe another person finding those newspapers wouldn't even have noticed the writing in the margin and the circled articles about him, or if they had, they wouldn't have been so curious. Why had Anne Schofield taken the trouble to track him down? He should have thought of that earlier, but the shock of hearing his mother's name mentioned and seeing it written in those newspapers had overwhelmed him. Now, perhaps he'd never know.

Surveying the rest of the sad little room he saw a chest of drawers and a heavy dark wooden wardrobe, the kind that were often on sale in second-hand shops. He opened the wardrobe. Her clothes weren't inside. Had she baulked then at the thought of hanging them up alongside the dead vicar's? Where were they? He pulled open a drawer in the large chest and found her underwear and blouses neatly folded inside it. There was a suitcase underneath the chest of drawers and he drew it out. Flicking it open, he found inside a couple of pairs of trousers and a skirt. She hadn't brought much with her, hopefully anticipating a short stay and it had certainly been that!

Horton returned his attention to the wardrobe and Rowland Gilmore's clothes. Most of the jackets and trousers were worn and shabby, but then his hand froze as he felt the texture of one of the jackets. This one was different. It felt expensive.

Pulling it out, he noted the Savile Row label and gave a low whistle. It was an old-fashioned suit by today's standards, but it still screamed quality. Had this been bought on the proceeds of Gilmore's share of the fishing business? Horton was no fashion expert, and he would check, but judging by its collar and fit, and from what he already knew of Gilmore's life, he guessed it must have been purchased in the late 1970s.

Why had Rowland Gilmore kept this suit, when everything in his wardrobe looked as though it had been bought from a charity shop or jumble sale? What significance did it have for a man who had obviously cared nothing for personal belongings?

Horton's mind raced through what he'd seen here, or rather what he'd not seen. He hadn't found any photographs. So had Anne Schofield already disposed of them, or had Rowland Gilmore destroyed the ones of his wife and child, unable to bear the pain of looking at them? If so, Horton could understand that. This house was the refuge of a lonely man who had substituted the church for his family and, Horton guessed, had still found it lacking. The exhibition of poverty and deprivation Horton saw here had been to Rowland Gilmore's mind atonement for allowing his daughter and wife to die. Horton felt some empathy with him.

Gilmore had tried to kill himself before finding God and the Church and from Horton's experience suicides often killed themselves with a picture of their loved ones in front of them. This was a special suit and if that was so . . .

He reached inside the jacket pocket and his fingers curled around thick paper. Slowly, holding his breath, Horton drew it out. It was a photograph of a beautiful, dark-haired woman in a printed summer dress, pinched in at the waist with short puffed sleeves and a V-neck collar. She was laughing into the camera, or at the person behind the camera, and beside her was a little girl of about five or six with deep brown eyes, a wide smile and curly brown hair.

It was as if he was experiencing Gilmore's agony of loss. Horton sank heavily on to the bed as Gilmore's emotions assailed him: anguish, guilt, desperation . . . Was it any wonder the poor man had tried to kill himself? Horton tried to imagine the pain of losing a child. He wanted to rush out and find Emma. He wanted to hold her tight for ever, and to never let her go.

A stout knock on the front door finally jolted him out of his thoughts. He stirred himself and hurried down to let Cantelli in. Horton knew at once that there must be something different about him because Cantelli said, 'You look like you've seen a ghost.'

'Maybe I have.' And more than one, he thought. He handed Cantelli the photograph. 'Rowland's wife and daughter.'

Cantelli stared at the picture in silence. His expression softened. After a moment he said, 'What a waste.'

He made to hand it back but Horton said, 'Keep it. Find out everything you can about them and the little girl's death. And bag up the suit I found it in. I want to know when it was made, where it was sold and what it cost.'

Cantelli nodded and turned the photograph over. He read, '*Teresa and Claire. 1979. Oxwich Bay.* Where's that?'

'On the coast of Wales, not far from the Mumbles and Swansea.'

'Anne Schofield was from Wales. It's on her file. I didn't get a chance to go through it in the Dean's office but he's getting someone to copy it as well as Rowland Gilmore's. He'll send them over later. Do you think she knew him?'

Horton swiftly and mentally recalled his conversation with Anne and her expressions as they had talked. There had been nothing there to hint she had been lying but if she had known Rowland Gilmore, and he had mentioned Jennifer Horton to her, then it would explain why she had bothered to track him down after seeing those articles.

'Possibly. Did you get a photograph of Rowland Gilmore?'

'Yes.' Cantelli handed it across.

With a quickening heartbeat, Horton took it. He was staring at a slight man in his early thirties with straight brown hair thrust forward over a narrow face. It wasn't the man he had seen on the quayside. He was sure he'd never seen Rowland Gilmore in his life, and there wasn't the slightest resemblance between himself and Rowland Gilmore, so he couldn't be his father.

'That was taken on his ordination and kept in his file. The Dean said we could find a more recent photo on the Church's website.'

Horton was cross with himself for omitting to check that. 'What did the Dean tell you about Gilmore?'

They stepped inside the study, and Cantelli drew up in surprise. 'This house is awful! It makes me dislike the pompous prat I've just been talking to even more. How could the Church let him live like this?'

'I think it was Rowland's choice.'

'Some choice, eh? I've seen dogs living in better kennels.'

'The Dean?'

'He's executor of Rowland's will along with the Diocesan solicitors. Rowland didn't leave much money, which doesn't surprise me seeing this place.' Cantelli gestured at the room. 'But what he did have he left to St Agnes's, as his brother Sebastian told us. There wasn't much on his file that we don't already know. He was born in Portsmouth, was a fisherman before he was ordained. Widowed in 1980, six months after his daughter died, and that seems to be it. When he entered the Church though, he handed over the sum of just over five hundred thousand pounds.'

'That must have guaranteed his ordination.'

'You bet.' Cantelli had reached the window and was gazing into the garden. 'I . . . What the heck is—?'

'An air-raid shelter, and no, I haven't looked inside it yet.' Had Anne Schofield though? She said she hadn't.

Heading for the door, Horton said, 'Perhaps it's about time we did.' Better to have Cantelli with him than anyone else if there was something inside the shelter that referred to his mother, and better they should find it than the forensic team.

With Cantelli behind him, Horton stepped into the weed-strewn patch of garden. It was drizzling now and the day was depressingly dark and made darker by the looming dockyard wall with its barbed wire on top.

'I feel like I'm in Colditz,' Cantelli muttered. 'You got a plan for digging a tunnel or going over the wall?'

Despite his unease Horton smiled and stared at the rusting piece of corrugated iron over the entrance to the arch-shaped air-raid shelter. It looked as though it hadn't been moved in years. He stretched his fingers inside a pair of latex gloves and, taking his cue, Cantelli did the same.

'If we find a body I hope you get to it first.'

'Thanks. Give me a hand.'

Together they prised the corrugated iron sheet out of the way and leant it against the fence on their right, which gave on to a narrow alleyway before the garden of the next house. Horton noted there was a side entrance into the garden and a man's bicycle resting against the fence, the Reverend Rowland Gilmore's most probably. There were three stone steps leading down into the shelter. Inside was dark. It smelt of decay and damp and Horton could hear the soft scurrying and rustle of animals, rats most likely.

Cantelli took a pencil torch from his pocket. The thin beam pierced the dim interior. Horton could see that on either side of the small shelter was a bench. There was nothing on it except dirt.

'I wouldn't like to have been in here when the bombs were falling,' Cantelli said, with feeling.

Horton agreed. There must once have been a large house where the ex-council house vicarage now stood, which must have been bombed. Whoever had lived in it must have been mad, or very brave, to have stayed here during the war, being so close to the naval dockyard and a prime target for the Luftwaffe.

'There doesn't seem to be anything here,' Cantelli said, voicing Horton's thoughts.

He wasn't sure whether he was disappointed or not. He didn't know what he had expected to find. Cantelli's thin beam of light swept under the bench on Horton's left.

'Hang on.' Horton's heart quickened. 'Shine your torch under there again.'

Cantelli obliged. Horton entered the air-raid shelter with Cantelli close behind. Horton had to duck his head, but Cantelli could just about stand up. Horton crouched down and peered into the gloom under the bench where Cantelli shone his in adequate light.

'Old newspapers,' he said.

Horton's pulse began to race and he could feel a cold sweat prickling his spine. Surely Anne Schofield wouldn't have dumped the newspapers that had mentioned him out here? He reached under and lifted a couple of them, but the paper crumbled in his hands. No, these papers had been here a long time. 'Can you see a date on them, Barney?'

Cantelli picked up the corner of one. 'No, but they look ancient to me.'

Horton again delved under the bench and clutched another handful. The same thing happened. The paper dissolved. 'There's nothing—' His hand froze. He had felt something other than paper.

'What is it?'

'I don't know. It's right at the back. It's hard. It feels like . . . bones.'

'Animal?'

Horton heard the hopeful tone in Cantelli's voice. It could be a fox or dog perhaps. He lay on his stomach and cleared away the rest of the paper as Cantelli peered over his shoulder. Then his fingers gripped the hard narrow object and, holding it, he pulled himself up. Cantelli shone his torch but there was really no need: they both knew instantly what it was.

Horton said, 'It's a femur and it's not animal. Looks like we've found ourselves a skeleton.'

TWELVE

'The poor bugger could have keeled over in an air raid in 1940,' Uckfield said, after Horton relayed the news to him on the telephone.

'Wouldn't the builders have discovered him?'

'They probably didn't bother to look inside; you know how lazy the blighters can be.'

It was possible, but Horton had other ideas. 'It could be the "wrong" that Gilmore mentioned and Brundall wanted to confess. They could have killed this person.'

He knew it couldn't be Jennifer Horton because Rowland Gilmore had only been living in the vicarage since 1995. But he still clung to the belief that the two men had known something about his mother's disappearance, and because this skeleton couldn't be her that didn't necessarily mean that she wasn't dead, or that they hadn't had a hand in her death.

Uckfield was squawking down the line. 'Are you saying the vicar then lived with it at the bottom of his garden all these years, knowing he'd had a hand in its murder?'

Horton supposed it sounded a bit incredulous. 'Perhaps he saw it as a penance and prayed over it?'

'Huh! It's just the kind of weird thing they would do.' Uckfield scoffed, obviously of the same opinion as Sebastian

Gilmore when it came to religion. 'OK, get Taylor and his team in after they've finished in the church, and get them to bag up the bones for Dr Clayton, but it's not a priority, Inspector. We've got four deaths which are. Any results on the PMs yet?'

'No.'

'Well, hurry her up.' Uckfield rang off.

Horton had no intention of doing so. He gave instructions to the officer guarding the house to ensure that no one except Taylor and his team went in. He prayed that there would be nothing for them to find about his mother. Maybe Uckfield was right and this person had lain in the shelter for over sixty years. But Horton wasn't comfortable with that. He felt instinctively that the skeleton could be the key they needed to unlock this case.

Cantelli drove the short distance to the church. The car park had been cordoned off and a police car straddled the entrance. PC Johns hastily hid whatever it was he was reading and tried to look alert.

Apart from the occasional passer-by no one seemed to be taking any notice of the activity. Perhaps they were too busy doing their Christmas shopping, thought Horton, which reminded him of his determination to clear this case before Christmas Eve so that he personally could give his presents to Emma. Perhaps the weather was keeping everyone inside. The drizzle had turned into a relentless downpour and it had grown colder. Not cold enough for it to snow, but Horton wouldn't mind betting they'd get some sleet before the day was out.

They found Taylor and his scene of crime officers methodically ploughing through the charred remains of the vestry. Horton tensed as he stood in the doorway. The smell of burning flesh came back to him as virulently as it had been last night. It made him want to throw up. He saw himself laid out on the mortuary slab with Gaye Clayton drooling over him and Uckfield telling her to hurry up the post-mortem. Jesus, it didn't bear thinking about.

Cantelli, sensing his unease, said, 'You OK to deal with this?'

'I'm fine.' Horton pulled himself together and addressed Taylor. 'Found anything?'

He removed his mask and stepped outside the vestry under the shelter of an awning. 'There's a brass candlestick which looks as though it could be the murder weapon. We've found minute traces of blood on it.'

In a flashback, Horton saw Anne Schofield's body falling face down from the cupboard with a mass of blood in her short grey hair. He heard the sound of splintering glass, felt the rush of searing heat and relived the cold frisson of fear.

'Maidment says the fire was caused by an accelerant, which was soaked in a rag and stuffed into a glass bottle.'

Taylor's voice seemed to come to Horton from a distance. He forced himself to focus on Taylor's long thin nose and slightly prominent eyes.

'From the fragments of glass we've collected I would say that it was a beer bottle. I hear you were inside when it happened, Inspector. Rather you than me. You had a very lucky escape.'

You can say that again, thought Horton with a shiver. 'We've got another one for you, Phil,' he announced briskly. 'But this one's been dead for some time.' And he told Taylor about their find in the air-raid shelter and asked his team to make it their next job. Even Taylor's mournful face lit up at the challenge of finding some forensic evidence after so long.

Horton was glad to get out of sight of the vestry. Rounding the corner to the front of the church he saw a familiar figure leaning into the police car talking to PC Johns. The old man was getting soaked. This could be useful. Horton wondered if he'd seen Anne Schofield yesterday.

'Hello, Mr Gutner.'

Gutner straightened up and his walnut face lit up with recognition. Horton would have to take a chance on Gutner letting slip some information about his mother in front of Cantelli, but he would rather it were the sergeant than anyone else, and Horton knew he could rely on Cantelli's discretion.

'The constable says there's been a fire in the vestry and I can't go in to practise the organ,' Gutner said, puzzled.

'Not at the moment. It's a crime scene,' Horton answered.

Gutner looked surprised and then triumphant. 'I told you there was something funny about Reverend Gilmore's death, didn't I?'

'It's not—'

'What's wrong with your voice, Inspector? You got a sore throat? And what have you done to your hands?'

Horton could see the thoughts running through the old man's mind. Gutner was definitely not senile, as Yelford, the Diocese administrator, had implied.

They were getting drenched and they'd all end up with sore throats if they stood out here for much longer.

'Let's get out of this rain.'

He steered Gutner to the church door and stepped inside.

'Blimey, looks like you've got Fratton Park lights on loan.' Gutner blinked, dazzled by the unaccustomed brightness of the usually gloomy interior.

Horton smiled at the reference to the football club. Ahead, around the altar, he could see a couple of scene of crime officers. He gestured Gutner to take a pew and the elderly man removed his cap and sat down awkwardly. Horton slid in beside him whilst Cantelli slipped into the pew in front and swivelled round to face them.

Horton introduced Cantelli and then said, 'I'm afraid I've got some bad news for you, Mr Gutner. The Reverend Anne Schofield was attacked and killed last night.'

Gutner made to smile as though Horton was telling him a joke, then the truth of what Horton had said dawned on the old man. His skin paled and his eyes widened with surprise. 'You're serious?'

Horton remained silent as Gutner looked from him to Cantelli and back to Horton.

'But who . . . ? Why . . . ? My God!' breathed Gutner.

'Did you see Anne Schofield yesterday?'

'Yes. I came over in the afternoon to practise for the carol service tomorrow. We ran through the order of the service together. And now you say she's dead too. I can't believe it. What's going to happen about the carol service? Will it still be on?'

'No. I'm sorry. You'd better check the arrangements with the Dean. How did she seem? Was she worried or pre-occupied by anything?'

'No. She was fine.' Gutner ran a hand over his eyes as though wishing to blot out the thoughts that were running through his mind.

'What time was this?' Horton asked gently.

'About four o'clock. We stayed chatting until just after six when I went home for my tea. I can't believe this.'

Horton had received Anne's call at seven fifteen, and he'd arrived at the church at seven thirty-two and by then she was dead. So what had Anne Schofield done between six o'clock and seven fifteen? If she'd been praying then it hadn't done the poor woman much good. More to the point though: who had she been talking to? And he didn't mean God.

Gutner was saying, 'First the Reverend Gilmore and now her. Has someone got it in for us? I bet it has something to do with that man who came to see Reverend Gilmore, the one who mentioned—'

'Did you see or hear anyone else in the church or out-side?' Horton swiftly cut him off and avoided looking at Cantelli.

But Gutner was shaking his head. 'Not a soul.'

'Was anyone parked outside when you left?'

'No.'

Cantelli said, 'Did you see any cars that aren't normally around this area?'

'No.' Gutner eyed each of them in turn. His wrinkled face was solemn and his eyes were full of sadness. 'You think someone killed her like they killed the Reverend Gilmore, don't you?' His gaze rested on Horton and then fell to Horton's bandaged hands. 'You were here? They tried to kill you too?' he said in a flat tone.

Horton knew he was dealing with no fool. Would Gutner suddenly blurt out, 'This has something to do with Jennifer Horton'? Horton held his breath as he asked, 'Did the Reverend Gilmore ever speak to you about his past?'

Gutner eyed him keenly, then after a moment he gave a slight shake of his head. 'No, the Reverend never spoke of the past. Too painful I guess.'

Horton breathed a quiet sigh of relief. 'Have you ever been inside the vicarage?'

'Of course.' Gutner eyed Horton puzzled by so obvious a question.

'You've seen the air-raid shelter then.'

'Yes.' Despite his distress Gutner chuckled.

'What's so funny?' Horton asked, with that prickling sensation that he was about to discover something useful.

'The vicar couldn't bear to look inside it, but I told him there wasn't any bogeyman there. Me, Jimmy Tomas and his sisters used to muck about in it when we were kids. Of course, the house wasn't a vicarage then. It was an old ruin. We had a lot of fun in that old air-raid shelter.'

Horton caught Cantelli's glance and said, 'When was this?'

'You're asking something now! Let me think. It must be near on sixty years ago. The late 1940s.'

If their victim had been killed in the war, was it possible that Gutner and his young friends failed to see the human remains whilst larking around?

Horton asked, 'Have you been in it since?'

'I don't think . . . hold on a mo, yes. It wasn't long after the vicar arrived. I called on him and after we had a chat, he asked me what was in the shelter. I said nothing, but he asked me to take a look. He didn't like closed-in spaces.'

'And?'

'Same as it always was, full of dust, dirt and spiders, though it brought back some memories.' Gutner gave a grotesque wink which made Horton think of those sisters of Jimmy Tomas. 'Why do you want to know?'

Horton rose and stretched out his hand. 'You've been very helpful, Mr Gutner.'

Gutner took it, eyeing him sceptically.

'We'll run you home,' Horton said. 'It's a nasty day to be out in.'

'No. Thanks, Inspector, but I need a walk.' At the door Gutner pushed his cap down on his white hair. 'You will get whoever is doing these dreadful things, won't you?'

Horton nodded.

'Good. Go careful, Inspector, and good luck.'

'Nice old man,' Cantelli said, starting up the car and pulling away from the church. Horton flashed him a look, but saw nothing in the sergeant's expression that betrayed his curiosity about that last remark of Gutner's. The old man would have made a good police officer; he seemed bright, observant and curious to Horton. But he was also small. Too small in his day to be allowed into the police service when there had been height restrictions.

He said, 'I still think the skeleton is connected with Gilmore.'

'Those bones were well tucked away; maybe Gutner and his friends failed to spot them when they were larking around in there, and Gutner probably only stuck his head round the door when the vicar asked him to.'

Horton grunted an acknowledgement, then said, 'Gutner's sharp, though. We'll take 1995 as a starting point until SOCO or Dr Clayton tells us otherwise.'

'Can you really see Rowland Gilmore killing someone?'

Horton thought about it. 'No, I can't, though we don't really know him. Maybe Brundall killed this person and hid him in the air-raid shelter. Perhaps Rowland Gilmore didn't even know the body was there. Mr Gutner said the vicar didn't like closed-in spaces.'

'That could be a lie on Rowland Gilmore's part.'

Horton granted him that.

Cantelli continued. 'Rowland Gilmore could have got Mr Gutner to check because he suspected Brundall had killed this person and hidden him there.'

'If he did then Gutner wouldn't have failed to miss a decaying corpse or maybe smell it in 1995, which confirms my view that our victim was killed after then.'

'Maybe it was an accident.'

'But why leave the body in the air-raid shelter?'

'Because no one would think to go in there, not with the vicar on the premises.'

Yes, thought Horton, it had been a good hiding place. He glanced at his watch; it was nearly three o'clock. 'Head for the hospital, Barney, I want a word with Dr Clayton.'

Horton found her in the mortuary. He told Cantelli to check on his father and, not bothering to hide his relief or anxiety, Cantelli hurried off to the high-dependency ward.

'I thought you might have the results of the PMs,' Horton greeted her.

Gaye pulled off her green cap and ran her fingers through her short auburn hair, 'Your throat sounds bad. You've been talking too much.'

'So I've often been told.'

She smiled. 'It sounds sexy. Maybe you should cultivate a husky voice.'

'I might not have any choice if I've done permanent damage to my vocal chords.'

'Want me to take a look? I've got a nice cold slab you could lie down on.' Horton saw Tom, the mortuary assistant, grin before he started a whistling rendition of 'June is Busting Out All Over'.

Gaye crossed to the sink where she began to scrub her hands. 'Gilmore's death troubles me. I wouldn't say that to anyone but you and Sergeant Cantelli, because I like Cantelli and you both have a brain and some instinct left in you, which is more than I can say for Superintendent Uckfield and that new detective of his. Where on earth did they dig him up? He's like some prehistoric monster from the seventies.'

Horton felt inordinately pleased and tried not to show it. 'I didn't know you'd come across him that much.'

'I haven't, thank the Lord. He telephoned me from Guernsey early this morning. I was just about to begin the autopsy on Gilmore. DI Dennings insisted on speaking to me. Wouldn't take no for an answer. I don't think he's met Tom yet. I look forward to that after their brief conversation. He insisted on calling me luv, which I can handle. Not sure Tom liked being called a monkey though. He wanted to know exactly how Brundall died.'

Now why would Dennings want to know that when Horton thought he'd already seen the report? Perhaps he was comparing notes on Sherbourne's death.

'And Gilmore?'

'There are no signs of suspicious death, but equally there are no signs that he suffered a stroke or even a heart attack. He was remarkably healthy, no clogged arteries or thinning blood vessels. No tumours. In fact there was no reason why he should die. I believe he could have been poisoned, although I haven't found any trace of poison, which is what makes this case even more interesting. I've sent blood, skin and hair samples off for analysis.'

Horton was surprised. Poisoning was a bit different from being bashed on the head and being set fire to. He considered what Gaye had said. 'If Gilmore was poisoned then wouldn't he have shown signs of illness over a period of time?'

'Ah! Depends what he was poisoned with,' she replied, spinning round to face him with an eager expression. Horton felt a stirring deep in his loins, and hoped his expression didn't betray his surprise. He'd never considered her in that light before and now he found himself rather warming to the idea.

'Was there any nausea?' she asked.

'Mr Gutner, who saw him collapse, didn't mention it, and he would have done.'

133

She turned back and finished drying her hands. Horton let out a surreptitious breath.

Throwing the paper towel into the bin she continued. 'Some poisons cause paralysis of the heart muscles, others the lungs, like curare, for example, which has no effect if taken by mouth, but if injected will kill. During the death throes the victim turns blue, but no one at the hospital mentioned the victim's colour. I think even they might have noticed that despite how busy they are. Curare is almost impossible to detect after death. Then there's hemlock, which is similar to curare in that it causes paralysis of the muscles. The first symptoms can take half an hour to appear and it may take several hours for the victim to die but this victim died fairly quickly after the paralysis set in so I doubt it's curare. And it's not hyoscine, because I didn't find any trace of it in the liver. Neither is it strychnine or antimony, which is similar to arsenic, plus a few others I've ruled out. But the lab will come back with more accurate results.'

She pulled off her green gown to reveal her boyish figure in a pair of tight jeans and T-shirt. Horton wondered what she'd look like in a dress, the kind she might wear to the police dinner and dance, if he invited her. And if she accepted.

'I'm going to do some research, and I'd also like to talk to someone who saw the victim collapse.'

Horton could see nothing for it but to put her in touch with Kenneth Gutner. He would ask him not to mention the conversation he'd overheard between Brundall and Gilmore. If he told him it had to be kept quiet, as it was vital evidence, then he trusted Gutner to do so.

'And Anne Schofield?' Horton asked.

'There was no evidence of soot in the airways below the level of vocal cords, and the levels of carboxyhaemoglobin were well below ten per cent, which means that she was already dead when the fire started.'

That was a relief. He didn't like to think of her regaining consciousness to be consumed by flames.

'She was struck on the back of the head,' Gaye said, 'and, judging by the indentation in the skull, I would say you are looking for something that has an edge to it, and is five inches in length.'

Horton thought of that brass candlestick that Taylor had shown him. Its base was about the right size.

'So it's a similar pattern to Tom Brundall's death.'

'Yes. He was knocked unconscious before the fire was started but the shape of his wound is different, which means different implements were used.'

'Sherbourne was strangled before being left to burn.'

'You've let one get away from me!' she teased.

'Sherbourne was killed in Guernsey.' He wished though he could have got Gaye Clayton to examine him. It wasn't that he distrusted the Guernsey pathologist, just that he would have liked some consistency in this case.

Her face flushed red and her eyes blazed. 'So that's what prehistoric man was driving at. Did he think I'd missed something so basic like strangling?'

Gaye was going to have Dennings for breakfast when he got back. Horton hoped he'd be there to witness it. It would cheer him up no end because he was convinced that Gaye Clayton would make mincemeat of the DI.

'Sherbourne was Tom Brundall's solicitor,' he said hastily. 'He visited him on the day that Brundall died.'

'You have got your work cut out!'

'And that's not all—'

'Not another one!'

'Yes. But this one's been dead for some time. We found a skeleton in the air-raid shelter in Gilmore's garden.'

She widened her eyes at him.

'There's no indication how long it's been there, but the same man who witnessed Rowland Gilmore die says he went into the shelter in 1995 and there weren't any bones then. I'm having the bones bagged up and brought over to you. It'll probably be later today.'

'Well, never let it be said that I don't like a challenge and you're certainly giving me that with this case. Just don't let ape man anywhere near me.'

'I'll make sure all the flights from Guernsey to England are cancelled.'

She smiled. 'Are you sure he can't walk on water?'

'Not righteous enough. He's worked in the vice squad.'

'That explains it.'

'What?'

'Never mind.' She turned away and then almost instantly turned back again. 'Oh, how's Sergeant Cantelli's dad? Dave Trueman told me.'

'He's not doing too badly.'

'Good.' She held his eyes for an instant, and he found it difficult to interpret what she was thinking, only that whatever it was it made the blood once again rush to his loins.

She had reached the plastic curtained door before she called out, 'Give the sergeant my love.'

'Which one?' Horton shouted back, then wished he hadn't as his voice ended on a squeak.

'The dark romantic one.'

That had to be Cantelli, didn't it? And, surprised, Horton found himself feeling mildly jealous before she said, 'And look after that throat, Inspector.'

THIRTEEN

By the time Horton reached his office it was early evening. It had been a long day with a painful chest and a sore throat that hadn't improved as the hours had sped by. Marsden had drawn a blank at the cemetery, and Cantelli, who had been scouring the CCTV recordings for the last couple of hours for signs of Brundall's car in and around that area, had had no joy either. Walters was still trying to track down the muggers, as well as handle a spate of afternoon burglaries in Southsea where thieves had targeted Christmas presents, and DCI Bliss looked as though she was about to have a seizure unless she got some extra officers, or they managed to clear up one case, at least.

Trueman told him there had been words between her and Uckfield behind the closed door and shuttered blinds of the super's office, and he'd heard DCI Bliss had complained to Superintendent Reine. Horton wasn't sure what that would achieve; every department was stretched at this time of the year, and Reine was notoriously weak when it came to fighting his corner with Uckfield. Thankfully Bliss had left the station to attend a community meeting. Horton had half expected her to delegate the task to him, which was usual, but perhaps she'd taken pity on his throat. Either that or there was some prestige in her being there, which he suspected was nearer the truth.

He felt emotionally drained as well as physically tired as he closed his door and shut the blinds behind his desk on the wet, cold and windy December night. His prophecy had come true and it was sleeting heavily. He powered up his computer and called up the missing persons database. He'd had all day to consider this from the moment this morning when he had been interviewing Sebastian Gilmore; it had come to him that Brundall and Gilmore might have killed his mother.

He'd modified his opinion since then, but now that his curiosity was well and truly fired he wouldn't be able to rest until he found out more.

His hands were sweating and his heart was racing as he tapped her name into his computer keyboard: JENNIFER HORTON.

He felt cold even though his radiator was belting out the heat. It was the first time he had spelt her name since he was eleven when in desperation he had written a letter to her and posted it to the tower block they'd taken him from in the vain hope that she might have returned there, found him gone and was looking for him.

The thought made his heart somersault even now, as the emotions of long ago flooded back: searing optimism, excitement at the sound of the doorbell ringing in the children's home, hope at the sight of the postman. All to be followed by disappointment, hurt, bewilderment and finally, anger. That had been the first time he had run away.

He steeled himself to look at the screen. Suddenly she was there, smiling at him. The breath caught in his throat. She looked so young, barely out of her teens. If she were still alive how would she look now? Maybe he could get the technical people to produce a computer-generated picture of her. Was it possible she was still in the area and he'd actually walked past her or seen her? But, no, if she had stayed or returned to Portsmouth, surely she would have tried to find him? His guts twisted at the thought that maybe she didn't want to.

He turned his attention to the details on the screen. She was born on 25 November 1950 and had been reported missing on 30 November 1978. That meant she had disappeared on her twenty-eighth birthday. He hadn't known that, or maybe he'd forgotten it. Was it significant? Had she arranged to meet a friend or lover for a meal and a few drinks?

It took a conscious effort to keep his breathing steady as he read on. Mentally he called on his police training to consider this as a case like any other; he needed to distance himself from the emotions, but it wasn't easy. Beyond his office he could hear nothing. It was as though only he existed in the station.

She was five feet five inches tall, slim build, about nine stone, with shoulder-length, wavy blonde hair and blue eyes. She had no distinguishing features or birthmarks. There was one child, a boy. At the time of her disappearance she had been working for a year as a croupier in the casino opposite the pier. It was now a nightclub and caused the uniformed officers a great deal of trouble at kicking-out time.

On the morning of her birthday she had waved her son off to school, but hadn't shown for work in the evening. No one had bothered to find out why, they had simply assumed she'd gotten sick and later, when she still didn't show, that she had walked out on them. The last sighting of Jennifer Horton had been that morning when a neighbour had seen her leave the flat just after one o'clock. She had seemed, the neighbour said, to be in high spirits and was dressed smartly and wearing make-up. She had no family, except the boy, or so it said on the screen.

Horton sat back deep in thought. The policeman in him was asserting itself quite strongly. His mother had been meeting someone, of that he was certain, but who? Was it the sharp-featured man he recalled? Or someone else he'd forgotten about, or never met? Could it have been Rowland Gilmore, who by then was married to Teresa? Or maybe it had been Tom Brundall who she'd had a rendezvous with? At least, if Gutner was correct, it couldn't be the remains of his mother in that blessed air-raid shelter. What attempts had the police made to find her? Had they interviewed his mother's friends or work colleagues? It seemed not.

He rose, restless and angry that the organization he worked for hadn't done more. But hundreds of people went missing in a month, thousands in a year. The police were busy, he reasoned; there had been no suspicion of foul play so why should they spend time on it? But now he wanted to know more. He couldn't return to where he had been before and forget her. No matter how long it took, he had to find out what had happened to her.

He sat and began to enter an online request for the case notes, which he hoped would be with him either late Monday or early Tuesday morning. His door was suddenly and violently thrust open making him start guiltily. Uckfield stomped in with an angry expression on his craggy features. Horton quickly tapped his keyboard and his mother's face vanished from the screen as Uckfield sank heavily in the seat opposite him.

'Dennings has drawn a blank finding anyone travelling to and from Guernsey by boat,' Uckfield declared.

Horton had been expecting it. It wouldn't be that simple. This killer was clever. Horton had spoken to John Guilbert earlier about his theory that the killer could have travelled by boat and Guilbert knew as well as he did that he would be difficult to find. To someone like Dennings it would be impossible.

'It's a waste of time him staying there. He'll be back on Monday morning.'

'You'll want me off the case?'

'What did you get from the post-mortems?'

Horton noted the evasive answer and wondered at it. Perhaps Uckfield and Bliss were fighting over him. The thought pleased him. He hadn't yet spoken to Uckfield directly about Gaye Clayton's findings so he briefed him quickly and succinctly.

Uckfield listened but he appeared uneasy, shifting in his seat and letting his eye contact drift. Horton was puzzled by his manner, and why he was here in Horton's office. When he had finished, there was silence. Horton knew Steve Uckfield of old. There was something he wanted or needed to say. Horton found himself tensing. He wasn't sure he was going to like this. He had stopped trusting Steve in August when he had resumed duty after his suspension and had actually believed him capable of murder.

Finally Uckfield said, 'Sebastian Gilmore owns a boat, and he keeps it in Horsea Marina.'

Horton covered his surprise. Sebastian hadn't mentioned it, though perhaps he saw no reason to. Was that why Rowland Gilmore had written Horsea Marina on his blotter — because he'd discovered his brother kept a boat there? Perhaps Sebastian had called Rowland and it had come up in the conversation. But why would it have? Had Sebastian telephoned to Rowland to tell him Tom Brundall was moored there? Horton knew he was speculating, but he was curious and he was convinced those words on that blotter related to Brundall's death. And why hadn't Uckfield mentioned this before now? Horton would have asked him, only he saw that there was more to come.

He waited and a moment later was rewarded when Uckfield said, 'He also went out on it on Tuesday afternoon. I saw him. I was on my boat.'

So that was it. Why hadn't Uckfield said so earlier? And what had Uckfield been doing on his boat? Horton couldn't recall it being his day off.

'What kind of boat?' Horton asked.

'A Windy 52 Xanthos.'

Horton whistled softly. Sebastian Gilmore seemed to be doing very well for a humble fisherman with a boat worth over half a million pounds, a mansion house and expensive car. But, of course Sebastian Gilmore was no longer a fisherman, and neither was he humble.

Uckfield said, 'A trip on one of those, with a forty knot top speed, to Guernsey would be a doddle, but our killer can't be Sebastian Gilmore.'

'You mean you'd like it not to be him.'

'Damn sure I wouldn't.' Uckfield ran his hands through his short cropped hair.

'What time was this?'

Uckfield glared at Horton and said tautly, 'Just before two o'clock. I was checking over the boat. I thought I might take it out over Christmas if the weather improves.'

Horton knew a lie when he heard one. Since when had Uckfield taken time off from work to check out his boat?

He said, 'Did it return to the marina, or go out again?'

'I called the lock keeper. She says it didn't return until Wednesday morning at ten fifteen. I know what you're thinking, Andy.' Uckfield sprang from his seat and began to pace the small office. 'But I'm telling you, just because Sebastian Gilmore has a boat, that doesn't make him a killer. Why should he kill Brundall, Sherbourne and Anne Schofield? And I refuse to believe he poisoned his brother.'

Horton recalled to mind the giant of a man and agreed with Uckfield. Poison wouldn't be Sebastian Gilmore's cup of tea, but he could have a motive if he thought his comfortable life was being threatened in some way.

'If he was involved in whatever it was Brundall and Gilmore did wrong, which could be killing our body left in the air-raid shelter, then Sebastian Gilmore wouldn't want it revealed. He has a great deal to lose.'

Before Uckfield could reply there was a knock on the door and without waiting for an answer an immaculately made-up woman in her thirties, with dark hair and wearing a smart trouser suit, swept in. Completely ignoring Horton, her eyes alighted on Uckfield. Horton saw Uckfield start before he leapt up with an irritated frown. Suddenly all was revealed to Horton. Now he knew why Uckfield was uneasy and why he had withheld this information, choosing to bring it to Horton's door when everyone else had gone home. That look told him who Steve's latest mistress was. What was more, Horton recognized her immediately; standing before him was the woman who had been in the crowd on the night of Brundall's death. He also knew now why Uckfield had arrived so quickly on the scene; they'd been together on Uckfield's boat and it didn't take a great stretch of imagination to guess what they had been doing then and on the Tuesday Uckfield had seen Sebastian Gilmore go out on his boat.

After a quick and pointed glance at her watch she addressed Uckfield directly.

'Superintendent, are you ready? I haven't got much time.'

'I'm giving another press conference tomorrow morning,' Uckfield explained to Horton. 'This is Madeleine Dewbury, our new public relations officer. We need to go through the statement.'

'Ah.'

She held Horton's stare with a haughty contempt before spinning round and striding out.

'Do you need me there?' Horton asked, knowing full well Steve didn't.

'You just concentrate on the case.' The door slammed behind him.

Horton sat back. Did Alison Uckfield know about her husband's latest affair? Maybe she did and didn't mind. Steve was an idiot to sacrifice so much for a bit of sex, but then he never could resist women, and it made Horton cross that Uckfield got away with it, and kept his marriage intact, when his own had been destroyed on a false allegation. He had never once been unfaithful to Catherine, but he couldn't help wondering if she had been unfaithful to him. Well now he could play the field to his heart's content. He thought of Gaye Clayton and wondered . . . No, even if it was possible that she fancied him, it was too close to home for an affair, and besides he liked and respected her too much for a casual fling. A serious relationship then? He wasn't sure if he was ready for one of those yet. It meant commitment and whilst he wouldn't have said no to a bit of female company he didn't want complications, or anything that might stand in the way of gaining regular access to Emma. It shouldn't do, but the trouble was he didn't trust Catherine. If she got a sniff of anything she didn't like then she'd seize on him like a jackal and tear him to pieces. Perhaps once their divorce had come through . . .

Tomorrow he would interview Sebastian Gilmore. And he was looking forward to it. He had sensed that there was something the giant of a man was holding back, and he cursed Uckfield for not coming forward earlier. He had delayed an investigation by withholding information, but then, thought Horton, pushing a hand through his hair, so had he.

He completed the online request for his mother's case notes and then went home. His throat was sore, but he'd risk a run; it might help him pull together the many loose threads of this case which reached back into the past, including his own. When he got back from the shower he found a message on his mobile phone. It was Uckfield. Horton rang him.

'About Madeleine, she shouldn't have barged into your office like that,' Uckfield said quickly. 'There's nothing between us.'

So Madeleine had told Uckfield that she'd been in the crowd on the night of Brundall's death and that Horton must have seen her. And Uckfield was now covering his and her back-sides.

'Steve, it's up to you what you do on your boat.'

'Yes, it is. We were having a meeting on Wednesday night. It was the only time we could both make it, and I had to go on to that damn function. We were discussing the profile of the police during major crimes. OK?' Uckfield demanded angrily.

'OK.' Horton left a brief pause before adding. 'Have you told Dennings?'

'Why the hell should I? He wasn't there.'

'Sergeant Cantelli was, and he saw Madeleine.'

'Then he'd better keep his mouth shut.'

'About your meeting?' Horton sneered.

Uckfield took a deep breath. 'Look, Andy, neither Madeleine nor I saw anything, just heard a ruddy great explosion and it wasn't orgasmic. I went on deck as soon as I . . . as soon as it happened, but could see there was little point in trying to do anything. The boat was a raging inferno. I heard the fire engines, then saw a police car arrive. I told Madeleine to hang on for a while. I didn't know the silly cow would stand around gawping at the bloody fire once she left my boat.'

Horton got the impression that Madeleine Dewbury's days as Uckfield's lover and their public relations officer were numbered.

'I called in, got the details and then showed up. Good job I did too, it being a major crime.'

Horton didn't speak. Uckfield was forced to continue. 'This doesn't have to come out. We saw nothing and no one. It has no relevance to the case.'

How many times have I heard that before, thought Horton. And how many times had Steve sneered at the person saying it?

'I'll owe you one,' Uckfield added brightly.

Something in Uckfield's tone made the hairs rise on the back of Horton's neck. Suddenly the answer to many questions that had been bugging Horton for months were answered, such as how did the newly promoted DI Dennings leapfrog Horton to get into the Major Crime Team? Why had Uckfield given Dennings the job he had promised to Horton? *I'll owe you one.*

Madeleine Dewbury wasn't the first of Uckfield's extra marital conquests and she wouldn't be the last. Horton had ignored Uckfield's philandering in the past, and kept silent over it, but Dennings was a different kettle of fish. He obviously knew of Uckfield's affairs, or rather an affair, and that could only mean he had discovered it before being promoted and had threatened to tell. In return for keeping his mouth shut, Dennings had been rewarded.

Horton rang off, feeling the anger well up in him. But surely there had to be more at stake than a bit of hanky-panky to warrant Uckfield's appointing Dennings over him?

He sat down and thought back to Operation Extra, the case that had got him suspended because of a false accusation of rape. He and Dennings had been working together. Before Horton had gone undercover he'd been on surveillance watching Alpha One in Oyster Quays, an all-male health club and gym suspected of being a brothel and a cover for the importing and selling of illegal pornography. After a couple of weeks of nothing happening, Horton, on the instructions of his boss, had left the surveillance to Dennings to go under cover. Was that when Dennings had seen Uckfield with someone? It had to be. Had Dennings caught Uckfield in a compromising position with a girl, on camera, and threatened to tell? Uckfield couldn't let it come out; due before the promotion board and in with a chance for the plum job as head of the newly formed Major Crime Team, he couldn't risk any scandal. Uckfield needed Dennings' silence in return for a favour.

Uckfield was more stupid than Horton thought, and he had compounded that stupidity by getting into debt with a man whose only quality as a police officer was his physical strength. Despite feeling bitter towards Uckfield for betraying him, Horton nevertheless found himself trying to find a way to get Dennings off Uckfield's back. Why? Because he hated corruption. But was that all? If he could remove Dennings from Uckfield's team without dropping the superintendent in it would Uckfield be grateful? Would that gratitude extend to rewarding him with the position as his DI? Wasn't that just the granting of another favour and corruption too?

'Sod it.'

He checked outside the boat. There was no sign of anyone watching him. He was tired and his conversation with Uckfield had left him feeling weary and depressed. The cold and damp did little to ease the soreness in his throat. He crashed out on his bunk hoping that the pyromaniac killer wouldn't strike that night, because if he did, Horton knew he might not have the energy to resist.

FOURTEEN

Horton woke late on Sunday after a heavy, dream filled sleep, which had him running away from fire and villains brandishing axes whilst Catherine laughed at him. As a result his head felt muggy and he wasn't in the best of tempers. He cursed the gales that were still roaring through the halyards and causing the boat to rock even in the comparative calm of the marina, and when he ran down to the showers, he found that the sleet had once again become driving slashing rain.

It was too dangerous to move *Nutmeg* on the morning's high tide in this weather and the next high tide would be ten p.m., which meant he would be able to get out of the marina from seven onwards, but by then it would be dark, and *Nutmeg* was too small a boat to risk moving in both the dark and the wind. He'd have to take his chances and stay put. He could, of course, always book into a hotel if he was that worried about this pyromaniac killer coming after him. It wasn't the expense that prevented him from doing so but the fact that it felt like running away. *Nutmeg* was his home and had been since April. Cold and cramped though she was, he nevertheless loved her.

Half an hour later he was weaving his way through the Sunday Christmas traffic cursing the shoppers snaking their way into the city centre. He'd be glad when it was all over and they could get back to some semblance of normality, though in his job there was no normal.

He thought about his forthcoming interview with Sebastian Gilmore. Had he known Jennifer Horton? Both Rowland Gilmore and Tom Brundall had known his mother, so he wouldn't mind betting that Sebastian had also. But he'd given no indication of recognizing him or his name.

Horton dropped into the incident suite on the way to his office.

'Don't you ever go home?' he asked, finding Trueman hard at work.

'Like you, Andy, I just can't keep away from the place. Anyway the missus is going Christmas shopping, and I guessed this was the lesser of two evils.'

'Where's Superintendent Uckfield?'

'Said he'd be in later. His daughter's singing in a carol service at church.'

And that was about the only time you'd get Uckfield inside a church, unless a crime had been committed or the chief constable was there, which Horton guessed he would be on this occasion to listen to his granddaughter.

'Has the Dean sent over those files on Anne Schofield and Rowland Gilmore?'

Trueman shook his head. Horton was irritated. He'd had long enough. 'Chase them up, will you?'

'On a Sunday! Won't the staff be in church?'

'I don't care where they are. I want those files.'

Collecting a tired-looking Cantelli, Horton headed for Gilmore's mansion.

'Sorry to drag you out on a Sunday and your day off,' Horton said, his bad temper abating and feeling a little guilty.

'It's OK. Charlotte's taking the children to see Dad this afternoon. He was asking after them yesterday. Hospital's no place for kids but I guess he should see them just in case . . .'

Horton knew what he was thinking. 'Look, you shoot off after we've seen Sebastian Gilmore. No, I insist. I just wanted you to be with me when I interviewed him, that's all.'

148

Poor Cantelli looked too relieved to pick up on Horton's intonation, which if he had done he would have asked why Horton needed him. Why not DC Marsden or Walters? It was a sign that told Horton, Cantelli was very worried about his father's health and it made him feel even guiltier. But if anything were to emerge about his mother then Horton only wanted Cantelli to hear it.

Horton hadn't expected Gilmore to be working on a Sunday and he was proved right. After being admitted to the grounds Cantelli squeezed his Ford between Sebastian Gilmore's black Porsche Cayenne and Selina's Mercedes.

'We're the poor relations,' Cantelli said, climbing out. 'Dad should have taken up fishing when he first came to England instead of selling ice cream.'

As Horton pushed open a door that led into a small vestibule of the Georgian mansion, Selina Gilmore threw open an inner door and greeted them with a frown of irritation. She was wearing a very short, tight skirt, knee-high boots, a tight T-shirt and a good deal of make-up.

'What do you want?' she demanded curtly.

Horton repeated what Cantelli had already explained into the intercom at the gates. 'A word with your father, please.'

'Can't this wait until tomorrow?'

Horton remained silent. With a huff she swung round and obviously expected them to follow, which they did as she led them through a hall the size of a football pitch.

'This is like something out of *The Bishop's Wife*,' Cantelli said under his breath, but she heard him.

'What?' She swung round.

'The sergeant likes old movies,' Horton explained.

She glared at Cantelli as if he had a screw loose. Cantelli smiled then raised his eyebrows at Horton as soon as her back was turned.

She led them through a second door and into another hall. Horton thought the house was going to go on for ever, then she threw open a door to their left and ushered them into a gymnasium.

Curtly she said, 'I'll let my father know you're here.'

'Perhaps she thinks we need the exercise,' Cantelli said, gazing around with distaste. 'Looks like a modern torture chamber to me.'

Horton wondered why she had brought them here. In a house this size there must be other more suitable rooms for them to have waited in. OK, so the kitchen might be out of bounds if Sunday lunch was being prepared, ditto the dining room, but what about a sitting room or a study? They could even have waited in one of the two reception halls. Perhaps he was just being suspicious but he got the impression that Selina Gilmore didn't want them nosing round the house.

Horton crossed to a rowing machine as Cantelli tried an interconnecting door on the far side of the room. It was locked.

'Where do you reckon that leads to?'

'The swimming pool.' Horton jerked his head in the direction of the window to the left of the door that gave onto the carbuncle he'd seen from the gates on their first visit here.

'Very nice,' Cantelli said, gazing through it. 'Olympic size too. There's a lot of money here, Andy.'

Was it too much for one man to have made from a successful fishing business? 'Remind me to get his accounts checked out.'

Horton climbed off the rowing machine after a few easy pulls. Cantelli mooched around the room, sitting on the exercise bicycle and then standing on the running machine. He ended up on one of the benches but made no attempt to lift the weights.

'I asked Dad about the Gilmores last night. He remembers Sebastian's father, Terry Gilmore. Says he was a fierce character, everyone was scared to death of him. He was a very determined man and tough, but a worker. Dad thinks he had a stroke in the seventies which was when Sebastian must have taken over.'

As if he'd heard his name the door burst open and Sebastian stomped in. Once again Horton felt his energy fill the room, and large though the gymnasium was it suddenly felt very small. Gilmore didn't offer his hand, perhaps because he had recalled that Horton's were bandaged, though judging by the man's expression Horton guessed it was a hostile body-language gesture.

'What is it now?' Gilmore boomed in exasperation.

'You wanted to be the first to know the results of your brother's post-mortem, but if you'd rather wait . . .' Horton turned away, knowing that Gilmore would have to capitulate. He was far too impatient to be left hanging on.

'I didn't realize you'd have them so quickly.'

Horton turned back, registering Sebastian Gilmore's surprise. And was that relief he also witnessed before Gilmore scowled? The giant didn't seem quite as self-assured as he had done yesterday. Was this because they were seeing him in his home, or had he suspected them to be on some other mission?

'The post-mortem on your brother has revealed very little—'

'His death wasn't suspicious then.' Gilmore seemed to cling to the idea like a limpet to a mine.

Horton was sure there was relief in those steely eyes, but maybe he just imagined it. 'We're not yet certain—'

'I don't—'

'There appears to be no obvious reason why he died,' interrupted Horton forcefully. 'In fact he seemed remarkably healthy, which in itself makes us wonder. That, coupled with Tom Brundall's death, makes us suspicious.'

'But people do suddenly die. Sudden-death syndrome or some such thing. Perhaps it happened to Rowley.'

'That still leaves us with Tom Brundall's death.' Horton wasn't going to mention Dr Clayton's suspicions about poisoning.

Gilmore began to pace the room, frowning. Suddenly he swung round. 'A fire on board a boat can be an accident.'

'Yes, and being a boat owner you'd know that.' Horton had the satisfaction of seeing Gilmore surprised.

'You've been checking up on me.' He glared at Horton.

'As Mr Brundall's death occurred in Horsea Marina, we need to check on all the boat owners there,' Horton answered smoothly. 'Why didn't you tell us you kept a boat there?'

'You didn't ask.'

'How long have you owned it?'

'I bought it at last year's boat show. Now if there are no further—'

'Ever been across to Guernsey in it?'

'Yes, and to Jersey and France,' Gilmore snapped. 'But what has that got to do with my brother's death?'

'How long does it take you to get to Guernsey?'

'Look, what the devil is all this about?'

'Must be a couple of hours in the right conditions with those powerful engines. Where do you stay in Guernsey?'

'I don't know what the hell you're driving at, but if you must know I stay in Albert Marina, St Peter Port.'

Cantelli said, 'Did you ever see Tom Brundall there? It's where he kept his boat.'

'So that's it? I wish you'd just come out and ask the bloody questions instead of acting all ruddy Sherlock Holmes about it. I told you I haven't seen Tom from the day he walked off the fishing boat.'

Cantelli said, 'Are you married, sir?'

Gilmore glowered at Cantelli. 'What the hell has that to do with Rowley's death?' he thundered.

Horton wasn't quite sure either, but Cantelli must have had his reasons for asking the question — he always did. Perhaps he thought Sebastian had murdered his wife and put her in Rowland's air-raid shelter.

Gilmore said, stiffly, 'My wife died twenty-seven years ago. Now if you've finished—'

'How long were you married?'

Gilmore stared at Cantelli as if the village idiot had just confronted him. 'Does this have any significance?' he roared.

Cantelli shrugged and smiled as if a simpleton. Horton knew the sergeant's tricks of old. This one never failed to get

152

a reaction. He was curious to see which way Gilmore would leap; he would either humour the idiot copper in a patronizingly superior fashion or become blusteringly angry and demand explanations. Gilmore went for the former.

'If you really must know, Sergeant,' he said with some hauteur. 'We were married in 1974 and my wife died in 1981, a year after Selina was born.'

'I'm sorry to hear that, sir.' Cantelli shook his head as his pencil laboured over his notebook.

Horton saw the anger on Gilmore's face turn to puzzlement and then wariness.

He said, 'You took your boat out of Horsca Marina on Tuesday. Where did you go?'

Gilmore swung round to face Horton. Quickly recovering his composure from Cantelli's unexpected questions, he said, 'If I'd known you were going to interrogate me, I'd have called my solicitor.'

'Interrogate? I'm sorry if you got that impression, Mr Gilmore. We just need to place everyone who knew Mr Brundall before and around the time of his death. Where did you go?' Horton insisted.

Gilmore hesitated. Was he trying to think up a lie, Horton wondered, or tossing up whether to tell them to go to hell?

Finally Gilmore said, 'To Cowes on the Isle of Wight. I have an apartment there with a berth and I wanted to give the boat a run. I came back the following morning.'

That fitted with what Uckfield had told him. 'Was anyone with you, sir?'

'Look, what is this? You think I had something to do with Brundall's death? Then say so. I was on my own, satisfied?'

It would take a lot more checking to satisfy Horton. Evenly, he said, 'And where were you on Wednesday evening, sir?'

'You can't honestly believe that I had anything to do with Brundall's death? This is ridiculous. I'm going to make

153

a complaint about this. You burst in here and question me like a common criminal.'

Horton contrived to look contrite. 'I'm sorry, sir. Would you rather answer the questions at the station?'

'No, I wouldn't. If you must know, and seeing as it's obvious I am not going to get rid of you, or your ridiculous allegations, until I answer your questions, I drove to my office from my boat, OK?' Gilmore glared at Horton. Horton said nothing, forcing Gilmore to continue. 'I collected Selina and we went to a sales meeting with Tri Fare, the supermarket chain at their head office in Bristol. I didn't get back here until gone ten; there was an accident on the M4.'

'Would anyone else have access to your boat?'

'My daughter,' Gilmore sniped. 'But seeing as she was with me at Tri Fare, she didn't. Just what the fuck are you driving at?'

It was good, Horton thought, very good, but it didn't convince him. Behind those granite eyes he saw fear. He smelt wariness and concern. Gilmore knew something about Brundall's death, all right; Horton would stake his career on it.

'And your movements on Friday night between six o'clock and seven forty-five?' Now let's see what the bugger produces out of the hat for the time of Anne Schofield's death and his close encounter with eternity.

Gilmore picked up a weight. Horton could see his fist curling round it, the knuckles whitening. Here was a man desperately holding on to his temper, or was it his tongue? Did he want to explain why he had killed Anne Schofield and tried to kill him, or was Horton simply imagining it? He held Gilmore's strong intimidating stare and kept silent. He knew Gilmore was the type who hated silence and hesitation.

'I was in my office,' he said through gritted teeth.

'Alone?'

'Yes. Now if that is all . . .' Gilmore crossed to the door and threw it open.

But Horton, in true policeman fashion, said, 'There is just one more thing you can help us with.'

Gilmore tightened his grip on the weight. Horton continued, 'Did you ever visit the vicarage, your brother's house?'

'I've already told you, I saw him twelve years ago and that was it,' Sebastian Gilmore boomed with exasperation.

'Then you have no idea who the skeleton in your brother's garden is, or how it might have got there?'

'You what? You're kidding?' He looked at each of them in turn. 'You're not, are you? I haven't the faintest idea.'

Horton studied the giant of a man. His face was immobile, but his body was so tense that Horton thought you could run a truck through it and not crumple it.

'Thank you for your cooperation, Mr Gilmore. I realize how difficult a time this must be for you. We'll do all we can to find out what happened to your brother.'

Gilmore swept ahead of them and flung open the door. Horton could hear a dog barking furiously. Silent, Gilmore showed them out and firmly shut the door behind them.

It was raining but Horton took his time walking to the car and opening the door. Taking his cue, Cantelli did the same, saying, 'Gilmore's not very comfortable about something. Thought he was going to bash us over the head with that ruddy weight.'

Horton looked at the house. There were two long sash windows to the right of the main door. From one of them he could see Gilmore watching them. He climbed into the car.

'Gilmore knew that Brundall lived in Guernsey. And I reckon he met him there. Take your time starting the car, Barney, and turning it around.'

'We're being watched?'

'You bet we are.'

Cantelli obliged, making out like a learner driver. Gilmore was probably having palpitations in case he hit the Porsche.

Horton said, 'Why didn't Gilmore show more interest in the skeleton? Most people would have asked questions like, how did it get there? How long had it been there? Who is it? Even a denial like, "You don't think my brother has anything to do with that?" But nothing, it was as if everyone has a skeleton at the bottom of their garden.'

'Yeah, and he's probably got one in the closet. Is this slow enough?'

'Perfect. Any slower and you'll be going backwards. Gilmore's worried. I want his alibi for both Wednesday night and Friday night thoroughly checked.'

The gates swung open, and Cantelli stopped for a moment on the other side of them, just for effect.

Horton called Sergeant Elkins of the marine unit and relayed what Gilmore had said about being in Cowes Marina on Tuesday night. 'Find out if he's telling the truth, Elkins, and if so what time he arrived and when he left. Was he with anyone? Did he meet anyone there and if so who. Get as much information as you can. He claims he has an apartment at Cowes with a berth. Sniff around, see what you can dig up on him.'

Horton rang off, and said to Cantelli, 'What was all that stuff about a wife?'

'I just wondered if she could have been our skeleton in the garden. But the timing is wrong if Mr Gutner is correct about the bones not being there in 1995.'

'There was something else you were fishing for,' Horton said. 'I can always tell by that gleam in your watery old eyes.'

'Hey, not so much of the old.' Cantelli smiled. 'My dad also told me about Sebastian Gilmore's girlfriend.'

'What's that got to do with anything?'

'Patience. She was a real stunner by all accounts. Dad didn't say anything about her dying though.'

'Why should he? He probably doesn't remember.'

'What! My dad! He's like an elephant. He never forgets, especially when it comes to women. It was odd because when Dad was describing her she sounded a lot like Rowland Gilmore's wife.'

Horton threw Cantelli a look. 'Now that is interesting. You got that photograph of Teresa Gilmore on you?'

'Of course.'

Horton smiled. 'Then I think it's about time we paid your dad a visit.'

'I was hoping you'd say that.'

FIFTEEN

Toni Cantelli Senior was propped up in bed with suction pads and monitors attached to his narrow, grey-haired chest, and bleeping machinery surrounding him in the hot house of the high dependency unit. With his fine grey hair, lean face and very dark quick eyes he reminded Horton of a little old monkey. He seemed to perk up when they walked in. The nurse said they could have ten minutes, but no more. Horton thought that would be enough.

'Good to see you, my boy,' he greeted Horton cheerfully, and nodded at his son. 'Though I wish it wasn't in here. Still it gives me the chance to eye the pretty nurses, and where else could I have such beautiful handmaidens pandering to my whims, at my age?' He winked at a petite black-haired Philippine nurse hurrying past, flashing him a smile as she went. Her eyes swivelled to Horton, and her smile broadened. Where indeed? thought Horton.

Toni followed Horton's gaze. 'I don't blame you, Andy, especially as Barney tells me you and your wife have split up.' He leaned forward. Barney looked set to have palpitations, as the tubes moved with him and the heart monitor beeped alarmingly.

'Dad—'

'And that nurse isn't married,' Toni added in what he obviously considered to be a conspiratorially whisper, but Horton thought it loud enough to reach the hospital's main entrance, which was about a mile of corridors away. 'Neither has she got a boyfriend. What is wrong with the men today to let a pretty girl like that slip through their fingers? It wouldn't have happened in my day—'

'Dad, we're not here talk about your misspent youth.'

'No, hang on, maybe we are,' Horton interjected, turning his eye away from the nurses' station and back to the old man. He saw Barney roll his eyes and added with a smile, 'But not too far in the past, and not your youth, Mr Cantelli, but someone else's. Barney tells me you knew Terry Gilmore and his sons.'

'Ah, so that's it? Didn't think you'd come to pass the time of day with a sick old man. It's all right, son,' Toni added hastily, seeing his son's frown, 'I'm only kidding.'

'I want to know everything you can remember about them.' Horton removed his sailing jacket before he melted in the heat of the ward, and slung it over the back of the easy chair. The air was stifling and he could feel his shirt sticking to his back. 'If it won't tire you too much.'

'Son,' Toni hailed Horton affectionately, 'at my age if you ask me what I had for dinner yesterday I couldn't tell you, but ask me what happened back in 1941 and I'll give you chapter and verse. And as for tiring me, do I look tired? This is the first rest I've had in decades. At least the wife hasn't got me up a ladder cleaning windows. Talking of which she'll be in soon with Charlotte, so I'd better spill the gory bits before they get here. What do you want to know?'

'Tell me about Sebastian Gilmore and his brother Rowland.'

The old man settled back on his pillow. He closed his eyes for a brief moment, as he gathered his thoughts or maybe his reserves of energy. Then he threw open his eyes and said, 'I only know the family because I had an ice-cream van in Old Portsmouth in those days, and one on the Camber before all those fancy houses got built. Back then it was fishing and engineering and damn all else down at the harbour, except the pubs of course. There weren't the tourists like you get now, sailors maybe. Used to see them in uniform, French, American, it was a fine sight, and the girls thought so too . . . All right, son, I'm coming to it. You've got no patience.'

Horton saw Barney roll his eyes.

Cantelli senior continued. 'I wasn't in the vans myself; by then I'd started the milk parlours and cafés, but young Tony was selling ice cream. Barney put his foot down though and refused to work in the business, he only ever wanted to be a policeman and nothing else, like his granddad on his mother's side. I can remember him as a kid—'

'Dad, the Gilmores,' Barney prompted gently.

The old man smiled. 'I came across Terry Gilmore many times on the quay; we were the same age and both businessmen so we often got talking. In those days it wasn't difficult to earn a living being a fisherman, a bit different now by all accounts. They say cod's running out, and tuna. I like a nice bit of tuna with pasta and a bottle of Chianti—'

'Dad . . .'

'It's no good looking at me like that, Barney boy. I'm not one of your suspects.' But Toni Cantelli smiled lovingly at his son. 'Now where was I? Yes. Seb was the eldest. He was a restless, impatient young fellow. Tall, dark and handsome with those film star looks, a bit like Robert Mitchum and the swagger to go with it, whereas poor little Rowley wouldn't say boo to a goose. He was a quiet boy. He didn't look right in fisherman's overalls. Hardly got a word out of him. His father despaired of making him a fisherman. "Why can't he do something else?" I suggested one day. Well, you'd have thought I'd blasphemed. Gilly, as we called the old man, said, "My boys are born and bred fishermen," and there was a lot more of that rubbish. Did I give you grief, Barney, when you announced you were going to become a policeman? Or Marie when she went into teaching? No. Kids have to find their own way in the world, and you'd be best to remember that, Barney, with your five and you, Andy, with your girl.'

Horton had no idea what his daughter wanted to do when she grew up. At seven she had wanted to be a ballet dancer but then many girls went through that stage, or so Catherine said. Well, he'd be able to ask Emma soon.

'It's not for parents to foist their livelihood and desires on their kids,' Toni Cantelli said, 'but Gilly was from the old school of thought. Rowley hated fishing but he was bullied by Gilly and Seb into sticking it out, and he didn't have the guts to stand up for himself. I heard Seb bought him out in the end when old Gilly had a stroke. He was only in his mid-fifties; that must have been late 1970s. If I recall, Rowley jacked it in not long after. And I know why. Not only because he despised fishing but because of Teresa. She was stunning, a real beauty.' Toni Cantelli put his fingers to his lips and kissed the air.

Horton smiled as Barney pulled out the photograph and said, 'Is this her, Dad?'

The old man took it with thin trembling fingers. 'Yes, that's her and is this her little girl?'

'She died when she was seven, in a boating accident.'

'My God, how awful — and Teresa?'

'Suicide six months later.'

Toni Cantelli sat back on his pillow and closed his eyes. He looked a little paler. 'Perhaps we should go,' suggested Horton.

But the old man stretched out his hand and touched Horton's. 'No. I'm all right. It's just sad to think of all that beauty going to so much waste. She was so graceful, a lovely girl, came from a good family too, and she fell for Rowley in a big way. But she was Seb's girl first.'

Was she now! Horton sat up, interested and surprised. Sebastian Gilmore hadn't mentioned that his brother had taken a girlfriend from him, but then why should he? Horton hadn't asked about Rowland's wife, and Sebastian probably hadn't thought it relevant.

Then Toni Cantelli dropped his next bombshell. 'Seb and Teresa were engaged to be married. It was announced and all arranged, then two weeks before the wedding she calls it off and says she's in love with someone else who just happened to be her future brother-in-law, Rowley Gilmore.'

And what a smack in the face that must have been for a man like Sebastian! It could certainly explain why the brothers had fallen out. Horton wondered about that exchange between the brothers on the quayside at the Town Camber twelve years ago. Had Rowland told Sebastian about Teresa's death? How would Sebastian have reacted? Did he blame his brother for her death? Had Sebastian still been in love with Teresa? Did the old scars still itch? If they did he hadn't noticed Sebastian Gilmore scratching them. Could it be motive enough for Sebastian to poison his brother? But twelve years later! No. Horton was heading in the wrong direction with that thought. Sebastian Gilmore would have beaten his brother to within an inch of his life on that quayside if Teresa Gilmore had meant anything to him. He wasn't the type to harbour a grudge or brood on past disappointments. What had he said? You move on . . .

'How did Seb take it?' Horton asked.

'He put on a brave face but a man with his ego and that much pride wouldn't have liked it.'

No, and Sebastian Gilmore had married very quickly afterwards, as if to say, 'I'm not bothered, Teresa meant nothing to me.'

Cantelli said, 'Do you remember a man called Tom Brundall?'

'Course I do,' Toni Cantelli said so vehemently that Horton could see it surprised his son. 'He was a nice man, very intelligent, and quiet, like Rowley. We used to exchange the odd crossword puzzle clue. It's Tom Brundall I've got to be grateful to. He helped me to get the business going.'

Barney looked shocked. Even Horton couldn't hide his surprise. 'What do you mean?' he asked, recovering first.

Toni chuckled. 'I thought that would make you sit up. Tom was a genius when it came to money and I needed to borrow some to expand the business. I wanted to open another café at Southsea, the one Isabella runs now.' He dashed a glance at Barney. 'The lease was due on the building, just along from the pier, and there were a couple of people after it, but I wanted it. I knew it would be a good little earner and it is. I didn't like to go the bank. Tom loaned me the money.'

Cantelli's jaw dropped open in mid-chew. 'You've never said!' he declared, astounded.

'Why should I? It's never mattered before and I hope it doesn't now.' He threw Horton a worried look.

Horton hastily said, 'It's fine.'

'I paid it back within the year,' Toni Cantelli declared proudly.

Horton noticed that the old man was beginning to look very tired. Barney could see it too. Horton flashed him a look, which he knew Barney would interpret as 'nearly done'.

'Tom left fishing not long after Rowley; he was never really suited to it. He was a wizard with figures. Should have been Chancellor of the Exchequer, wouldn't be in the mess we are in now if he had been, but like poor little Rowley, Brundall's dad was a fisherman and so Tom had to become one too. As soon as he saved enough money he got out.'

The old man sank further back on his pillow and closed his eyes. Barney stood up. 'We'll be off now.' He flashed a look at Horton who rose and grabbed his coat.

'I'm not tired.' Toni's eyes snapped open. 'You just made me think back down the years, that's all, and I felt sad.'

Horton apologized. He didn't want to leave Barney's father feeling that way. 'You've been a great help, Mr Cantelli.'

Clearly with an effort the old man stirred himself, and gave a tired smile. 'You're welcome, son. Only don't you want to know about the other one?'

Horton froze. He felt a shiver of excitement run through him. 'What other one?' he asked his pulse quickening.

'I forget his name. What was it?'

'Take your time. I can come back.' Though Horton silently prayed that he wouldn't have to. This was new information and he knew that it was important. That sixth sense, or copper's intuition, call it what you may, was back with him with a vengeance. He knew Cantelli could feel it too.

Toni Cantelli said, 'There were four of them on the boat.'

Four! Horton had thought only three: Seb, Rowley and Brundall. Sebastian Gilmore had said nothing about a fourth man. Why not? Horton felt his heart racing.

'I can see him as clear as I see you, but I'm blowed if I can remember his name.'

'What did he look like?' asked Horton, his mind leaping in a direction that he could hardly take in. Could it have been the man he had seen with his mother on the quayside at the Camber? But why should it be? Why did he keep returning to that image? Had something in this case triggered that memory? It had to be.

Toni Cantelli said, 'He was good-looking, dark-haired, smart dresser, restless eyes.'

That wasn't enough to go on. The description fitted hundreds of men. Then why did Horton *feel* it must be the man with his mother? Did wishing it make it so? Shit, he was clutching at straws.

'Don't worry, it'll come to you,' Horton reassured, though he wished Mr Cantelli had remembered his name. Still, there was one man who could give him a full description and a name: Sebastian Gilmore.

Horton pressed his hand on the old man's shoulder. 'You've given us valuable information, Mr Cantelli, and I'm grateful. We can easily get his name.'

'When you do, tell me, otherwise it'll worry the devil out of me.'

Barney promised he would. Horton left Cantelli with his father and thanked the pretty dark-haired nurse. When he looked back at the entrance to the ward, he frowned. Toni Cantelli looked a lot worse than when they had entered and that hadn't been too good to begin with.

He stepped outside and switched on his mobile. There were no messages. He waited in the car watching the hospital visitors come and go thinking over the conversation with Mr Cantelli. Why had Sebastian Gilmore failed to tell them about the fourth member of his fishing crew? What was he hiding? What had happened to this fisherman? Was he the skeleton in the air-raid shelter? Damn it, he couldn't be, not in 1995, unless . . . Could he have returned and threatened to tell about the 'wrong' Rowland and Brundall had done? Had they killed him and stuffed his body in that shelter? It was possible. But what had been 'the wrong'?

Horton let his mind go into free fall. Had Brundall and Rowland Gilmore killed his mother and this man knew it or had seen, suspected or even been involved in it? Had he tracked Rowland down some years later, and Rowland had summoned Brundall to help him deal with it? But where had this fourth man been from 1978 until 1995? Abroad? In prison?

The car door opened. Horton pulled his thought back to the present.

'Is your father all right?' He could see that Barney was worried.

'I hope he's just tired, but I had a quick word with the nurse and she said she'd check him over. I'll call Charlotte and tell her Dad might not be up to much this visit.'

'Stay and tell her. No, Barney, I insist. I told you that earlier.' Suddenly Horton felt it was important that Cantelli should be there. Horton had never known his own father, and maybe that was why he felt so strongly that Cantelli should be with his. Time, Horton recognized, was precious. He wished he'd had time to talk to his mother before she had disappeared, but then he had only been a child and he'd had no idea that when he left for school that morning, it would be the last time he would see her.

'Are you sure?' Cantelli looked anxious.

'Positive.'

Cantelli's relief was palpable. Horton knew Barney wouldn't duck out of work without his agreement. Where Uckfield got the idea that Cantelli was lazy, Horton didn't know. Barney Cantelli was one of the most conscientious officers Horton had ever come across. Cantelli said, 'What are you going to do now?'

'Have another word with Sebastian Gilmore. I'd like to know why he didn't mention this fourth man.'

'Take the car.' Cantelli handed over the keys. They exchanged glances and in Cantelli's eyes Horton saw the terror of losing a loved one.

On the way back to Gilmore's house, Horton replayed in his mind the conversation with Toni Cantelli and his interviews with Sebastian Gilmore. Gilmore had had plenty of opportunity to tell him about this fourth fisherman, particularly when they'd interviewed him in his office yesterday, so why hadn't he mentioned him?

Would Dr Clayton have some further information on those bones tomorrow? He certainly hoped so, he thought, pressing the intercom and asking to speak to Sebastian Gilmore.

'What do you want now?' Selina demanded in surly tones.

Horton didn't answer. A few seconds later the gates slowly swung open and he drove up the tree lined drive. Before he had stilled the engine Gilmore was striding towards him in the rain, looking like thunder.

'I hope this is important,' he roared.

Holding Gilmore's glacial stare, Horton said, 'Who was the fourth man on your fishing boat?'

Gilmore visibly started and seemed stunned by the revelation. Was that because Horton had discovered information that Gilmore had wanted to keep a secret? Or had Gilmore genuinely forgotten this fourth man?

Recovering, Gilmore demanded, 'How do you know about him?'

'Shall we go inside, sir?'

There was a moment's hesitation before Gilmore swiftly turned and marched towards the house. Horton took this as acceptance and followed. He was intrigued by Gilmore's reaction, and excited at what he might learn. This time there was no lingering in the gymnasium; Gilmore thrust open a door beyond it on the right which led into a spacious and modern equipped study. He crossed to a cabinet on the far side of the room and poured himself a drink.

Waving the bottle at Horton he said, 'Whisky?'

Horton was surprised by the offer, but didn't show it. 'No. Thanks.'

Gilmore jerked his head at the burgundy leather sofa and as Horton sat, Gilmore settled himself in a matching leather armchair. Horton remained silent as Gilmore took a long pull at the drink. He seemed to be preparing himself for something, or was he just trying to get his story worked out? Was he about to lie?

Finally, he said, 'The other man was Warwick Hassingham.'

The name meant nothing to Horton. Had he expected it to? By the flicker of disappointment he felt inside him he guessed so. Perhaps he had been hoping to recognize it from his childhood. He must ring Barney so he could relay the name to his father.

'Why didn't you tell me about him?'

'I didn't think it important.'

But Horton could see that Gilmore was uneasy. He knew that he should have mentioned this fourth man, and the fact that he had omitted it now looked suspicious.

Horton said, 'I'd like to talk to him. Can you tell me where I can find him?'

Gilmore gave a short mirthless laugh. 'You'll need the divers. Warwick drowned in 1977.'

Horton only just hid his surprise. Toni Cantelli hadn't mentioned that. Perhaps he had forgotten the incident. It was possible. He was elderly and ill. Horton cursed silently. His surprise gave way to disappointment. This couldn't be their killer or the skeleton. And neither could it be the man his mother had run away with.

Gilmore said, 'Now you know why I didn't think it important to tell you about him.' He took another swallow of whisky. 'Warwick's been dead a long time. He can't have anything to do with Tom's death or my brother's. But it was his death that made both Rowley and Tom chuck in fishing. It was never the same once Warwick went and, as I said before, Rowley never liked fishing anyway.'

'How did he die?'

Gilmore finished his whisky and poured another. Horton wondered how many he had consumed over the lunchtime. Still, it was none of his business, and Gilmore gave no sign of being even the slightest bit intoxicated. Pity, because if he were, Horton wondered if he might get more out of him. Then he saw that Gilmore needed these drinks to be able to cope with recalling the horror of Warwick Hassingham's tragic death. Suddenly he was no longer the giant but a big teddy bear that had had all the stuffing pulled out of it.

'It was fifteenth August 1977,' Gilmore said, resuming his seat. 'When we left the harbour it was fairly calm, but there were storm warnings out for later that night. We reckoned, though, that we could get a good catch and return before the storm. But it came across quicker than anticipated.' He took a large gulp of whisky.

Horton heard a door slam somewhere in the house and a car drive away: Selina's he guessed.

Gilmore tossed back the remainder of his drink and sat forward, suddenly energized as though angry. 'The wind came up out of nowhere like a tornado and the swell was awful. We could barely keep on our feet. The sea was breaking over the vessel threatening to swamp us. Rowley was sick as a dog. Did I tell you he suffered from seasickness?'

No wonder the poor bugger hated being a fisherman. Yet he had bought himself a yacht. But Horton knew that different boats cause different movements; perhaps he wasn't seasick on his yacht, or maybe he grew out of it.

Gilmore continued. 'Then a distress call came over the radio. We weren't far from it, so we answered it to find a man alone on a motorboat. I could see immediately that his engine had gone. Bloody fool shouldn't have been out in that weather, but then some people are idiots.'

Horton knew that all too well, having had to go to the rescue of stranded sailors himself.

'We made an attempt to rescue him but a gigantic wave took hold of the vessel and before we knew it the motorboat had been swamped and there was no sign of the man. Then Warwick saw him in the water. He threw him a line.'

Gilmore rose and poured himself another drink. He was weighing his words carefully now, as though reliving a painful memory.

'Warwick always was a mad sod. He leaned over the edge of the *Frances May* — that was our fishing boat — and tried to grab the other man . . .' Gilmore paused. His eyes seemed to stretch back down the years. He took a gulp of his whisky, and said, 'A wave took him. He wasn't clipped on and he wasn't wearing a life jacket. Warwick went over just as Rowley and Tom grabbed hold of the man. They didn't know what to do. But in fact there was nothing they could do. They hauled the man aboard and Warwick went. He was found some weeks later, I forget how many. What was left of him was buried in Kingston Cemetery. I don't think Tom or Rowley ever forgave themselves for it.'

And was that the wrong that Gilmore had referred to and Brundall wanted to confess to; that they had let Warwick Hassingham die? Horton would have believed it except for two things: the skeleton and the mention of his mother.

'Why didn't you tell me this yesterday, or this morning?'

'Why should I?' Gilmore glared at Horton. 'Warwick died a long time ago.'

Gilmore was right. And they had a skeleton in Rowland Gilmore's garden that, according to Kenneth Gutner, was a lot more recent.

'What happened to the man you rescued?'

'He was taken to hospital suffering from shock, hypothermia and some pretty nasty cuts. I've no idea where he went after that. He didn't even bother coming to Warwick's memorial service, the ungrateful sod.'

'And his name?'

'Don't know. If I did know it I've forgotten it. It happened a long time ago.'

Horton eyed Gilmore closely. The man's expression was impenetrable and yet Horton sensed something — a lie? Unease? Evasiveness? Surely Sebastian Gilmore would remember the name of the man who had effectively killed Warwick? Sebastian recalled exactly what this man had suffered when rescued, so why not remember the name? Horton had a funny feeling about this. Something didn't smell right.

'You said Warwick's body was washed up some weeks after the incident; how was he identified?' After weeks in the sea, Horton knew that there wouldn't have been much left of him.

'Warwick loved his rings. He always wore a gold sovereign ring on the third finger of his right hand and a signet ring with a diamond in it on the little finger. They were on what was left of his hands, and the police matched dental records.'

'I'm surprised he was buried. Being a fisherman I would have thought the sea—'

'His mother's wishes,' Gilmore interjected, with an expression of disgust. 'Old Ma Hassingham said the sea had claimed him but she was dammed sure she wasn't going to let it swallow up what remained of him. Poor old bitch. She died eight months later.'

Horton left a short pause before asking, 'Do you have a photograph of Mr Hassingham?'

Gilmore looked surprised. 'No. What would I need that for?'

He wouldn't, but Horton wouldn't mind seeing one to check if it had been the man with his mother on the Camber. Not that it really mattered now because Hassingham had nothing whatsoever to do with his mother's disappearance.

'You bought your brother out of the business in 1978. How much did you pay him for his share?'

Sebastian looked surprised and then angry. 'That's none of your business.'

'Did you know he gave away half a million pounds to the church when he entered the ministry?'

Sebastian remained silent, glaring at Horton.

'Is that how much you paid him?' Horton persisted.

Sebastian Gilmore rose and made for the door, which he threw open. 'If you want to ask questions which have nothing whatsoever to do with my brother's death, then you can damn well do so with my solicitor present — that kind of information is personal.'

Oh no, it isn't, thought Horton, pausing before rising. 'Thank you for your co-operation, Mr Gilmore,' he said pointedly.

Gilmore showed him out in silence. As Horton ran to the car in the slanting rain and bad-tempered wind, he wondered why he was so touchy about the money. Was there something there that Sebastian Gilmore wanted to hide?

With Warwick Hassingham dead, that left Sebastian Gilmore as the only surviving member of that crew. Was he in danger? Had Brundall and Rowland's death anything to do with when they had all been fishermen together? Or did it have something to do with his mother? And now there were more questions nagging at him: who was the rescued man and what the blazes had happened to him?

SIXTEEN

They were questions he put to Uckfield an hour later. 'Has that got anything to do with this case?' Uckfield declared with exasperation, his eyes flicking impatiently beyond Horton into the busy incident suite.

Horton's idea had grown and taken shape on the drive back to the station. He didn't much care for it, however, because he wasn't sure how or if his mother fitted into it. Still, he'd have to take a chance on that.

'I think we should spend some time looking closely at Sebastian Gilmore,' he said. 'There's a lot of money around him and I'm not convinced it all comes from fishing.'

'He's built up a big business, why shouldn't he be rich?' Uckfield said, surprised.

'But *how* did he build up that business and how much did he pay his brother for his share in it? We know that Rowland gave away half a million pounds in 1979 and that's a lot of money for a humble ex-fisherman. Somehow I just can't see it all coming from running a fishing fleet in Portsmouth; remember this was before those lucrative supermarket contracts. What if Sebastian Gilmore was smuggling drugs back in the late 1970s?'

'How the hell did you arrive at that!'

172

Now Horton had Uckfield's full attention, he began to expound his theory. 'It could be the "wrong" Gilmore had tried to put right by entering the church and giving them all his money after his wife and daughter died.'

'But why drugs?'

'It pays the most and you know as well as I do that drugs are comparatively easy to smuggle in by sea, or should I say they were easy back in the 1970s. I'd like to ask the economic crime unit to find out exactly how much Sebastian paid his brother for his share of the business, and while they're at it I'd also like an investigation into Rowland Gilmore's and Tom Brundall's finances.' He could see Uckfield looking at him as if he'd gone mad. Horton sat forward. 'Tom Brundall was very wealthy and something of a recluse. He hated that photograph being taken of him; you can see that by the look on his face.' Horton stalled.

'What is it?' prompted Uckfield.

Horton didn't know. There was a flicker of an idea at the back of his mind but before he could grasp it, it had gone. Maybe it had something to do with the money. He said, 'It just doesn't add up for all three of them to have made it good. One maybe, even two of them, but all three, now I call that suspicious.'

Uckfield scratched his armpit. 'Rowland Gilmore could have taken the original pay-off from his brother and invested it, or perhaps he set up another business and made more money.'

'There's no evidence that he did either of those things. So far as we know he bought a house in Wales and a yacht and never lifted a finger again until he entered the Church. So how did he live? Even allowing for the fact that when he sold the house it had appreciated in value, you're talking about 1983 before the prices went sky high. He had sufficient funds not to work.'

Uckfield grunted and Horton took this as consent to continue.

'Then there's Tom Brundall. He jacks in fishing in 1979 and the next thing we know he appears in Guernsey with pots

173

of money. Now he, by all accounts, is a clever investor, but he would have needed a tidy sum to start with.'

'Perhaps he was prudent and a saver.'

'Perhaps,' Horton conceded, but didn't believe it. 'And Sebastian Gilmore? Large house, massive swimming pool, expensive car and boat, a property on the Isle of Wight, and I bet that's not the only one he's got. OK, so he's a good businessman but I'd still like the economic crime unit to go through his accounts.'

'Not without more evidence you don't.'

Undeterred, Horton continued. 'Let's say this man they rescued in 1977 was their supplier. They'd gone to meet him when the storm wrecked their plans and as a result Warwick Hassingham dies. That puts the dampers on Rowland Gilmore and Tom Brundall who quit not long afterwards with the money they'd already amassed. Sebastian resumes the smuggling operation with this rescued man, whose name he conveniently can't remember. Everything goes well until whoever our skeleton is shows up, he could be this rescued man aka drug supplier who wants out, or it could be someone Rowland Gilmore has spoken to when studying to be ordained.' *And was that someone Anne Schofield had also known?* 'He lets slip something about the drugs and eventually he's tracked down to Portsmouth. This person threatens to tell of Rowland's seedy past. Rowland calls either Brundall or his brother and they deal with it, or perhaps Rowland does it himself, luring him to the air-raid shelter and killing him.'

Horton interpreted Uckfield's incredulous look and added, 'Just because Rowland was a vicar it doesn't mean he wasn't capable of killing someone. Frightened men are as dangerous as angry ones.'

Uckfield grudgingly acknowledged that before saying, 'It's a bit far-fetched.'

Ignoring this, Horton said, 'Everything settles down again until Brundall shows up last Tuesday wanting to confess his sins before he dies. He wants to go to his maker with a clean sheet.'

'Cut out the poetic stuff.'

Horton smiled. 'Rowland doesn't want to hear the confession; he gets scared that Brundall will tell someone else, so he calls his brother, Sebastian, and asks his advice. Sebastian can't risk Brundall talking to anyone else, and if his alibi checks out, that means he got someone else to silence Brundall, Rowland and Sherbourne — we still need to check his alibi for Anne Schofield — and that someone could be a professional killer as we originally thought, one of his drug suppliers or our mystery man who was saved at sea.'

Uckfield exhaled. 'It's a hell of a leap between a rescued man and a drugs ring.'

Horton sat back with a frown. 'Maybe, but why didn't Sebastian Gilmore mention Warwick Hassingham and the accident unless he's got something to hide?'

'Too painful?' Uckfield suggested.

Horton recalled Gilmore's attitude that afternoon when relaying the story of Warwick Hassingham's death. Grudgingly, he admitted to himself that Uckfield could be right. Yet, he felt there was something there that didn't ring true. He wasn't going to give up on his theory yet.

'I'll contact the Marine Accident Investigation Branch first thing tomorrow and see if I can get the name of the rescued man and then we'll be able to trace him.'

'I think you're way off beam, but as we've got bugger all else to go on, you might as well go ahead.'

Horton could see that Uckfield hadn't bought his theory. He said, 'I could also talk to Customs and Revenue tomorrow; see if they've ever suspected Gilmore or his fishing fleet.'

'No, leave that for DI Dennings. Better give him something to do.'

Horton acquiesced with a secret smile knowing that Uckfield was already rueing the day he'd given in to Dennings and this was just their first case together. But if Horton knew Uckfield then he'd find a way of getting Dennings out of his hair and one which didn't risk his love affairs being exposed.

175

He said, 'It might also be worth checking Gilmore's record with the Marine and Fisheries Agency to see if any of his fishing boats or his premises have ever been inspected by their officers, and if so when? I'd also like to know if any of his boats have been inspected at sea by the Royal Navy's Fishery Protection Squad.'

'If they have, they can't have found anything otherwise we'd know about it and so would the drugs squad.'

'Would we though? Not if Gilmore was clean, and he'd been given a tip-off. Someone on the inside could be involved.'

'OK.' Uckfield held up his hands in capitulation. 'I didn't know you had such an overactive imagination.'

'There is another thing . . .'

Uckfield groaned.

Horton said, 'All fishing vessels over fifteen metres in length have to be fitted with satellite tracking devices, which are monitored from the Fisheries Monitoring Centre in London, so have there been any problems with Gilmore's tracking devices—?'

'You think they could have veered off course and picked up some merchandise?'

'Why not? But some of Gilmore's fleet is under fifteen metres, they don't have tracking devices, so maybe they make the collections. Or perhaps it's nothing to do with drugs and Gilmore is over-fishing and getting away with it.'

Uckfield sat back and stretched his hands behind his head. 'Is there money in that?'

'There's money in anything illegal. Maybe he's forging quotas.'

Uckfield sniffed loudly. 'Dennings can handle the fisheries people as well as Customs and Revenue. But let's get some hard facts first before we go barging in upsetting one of Portsmouth's most successful businessmen and risking bringing down the wrath of the media and his lawyers on us like a heap of heavy shit.'

'Just make sure you tell DI Dennings that,' Horton couldn't miss pointing out. 'I don't think he's the tread softly type.'

Uckfield shifted position. Scowling, he picked up his pen. 'Inspector Dennings knows his job.'

There was a knock on Uckfield's door. Marsden entered smiling.

'Won the lottery, Marsden, and come to give us all a hand out?' snarled Uckfield.

'No, sir.'

'Then wipe that silly grin off your face. We've got four dead people and a skeleton; there's nothing to look so cheerful about.'

'Sorry, sir.' Marsden rearranged his features as best he could but Horton could see he was brimming with some piece of news that he thought critical to the case. 'I've got a positive sighting of Brundall at the cemetery. I showed his photograph around and a woman says she saw him at a grave near her late husband's, only he wasn't at his parents' grave—'

'He was at a man's called Warwick Hassingham,' Horton interjected triumphantly, throwing a glance at Uckfield which said, didn't I tell you there's something here for us in this rescue?

Marsden looked as though someone had stolen his sweets.

Uckfield said, 'That'll teach you to be so sodding cheerful, Marsden. What time was this?'

'About two fifteen. He stayed for ten minutes and then left.'

So Brundall *had* set out on a trip down memory lane, first to Warwick Hassingham's grave, and later that afternoon to Rowland Gilmore.

Horton said, 'What's the betting he called on Sebastian Gilmore?' But there was a flaw in this, because Sebastian Gilmore said he'd returned to his office shortly after midday and had left almost immediately for his meeting at Tri

Fare. Horton could check out the CCTV tapes at the commercial port for Wednesday afternoon, but then he recalled that Gilmores also had their own CCTV. They were certainly worth a look at if he could get hold of them, although he couldn't see Gilmore giving them up without a search warrant.

Horton's phone was ringing as he reached his office and he leapt across his desk to reach for it before it stopped.

'It's Dad,' Cantelli said.

Horton went cold. He could tell immediately by Cantelli's tone that it was bad news. Please no, not that, he prayed. But it was too late for prayers, as Cantelli's next words confirmed.

'He had a massive heart attack. He died at four thirty-five p.m.'

SEVENTEEN

Horton returned to his boat that evening with a heavy heart. He recalled the little man with the twinkling eyes and the love of life and felt Cantelli's sorrow at losing so vital a human being and such a dearly loved family member. He didn't feel like eating or going for his customary run but he forced himself to do both.

The weather was so appalling that he curtailed his run at the pier and headed back to the boat with a feeling of deep dissatisfaction at the way his own life was going and the sadness of Cantelli's news. He should have rung Barney to give him the name of the fourth fisherman on Gilmore's boat before his father died. He knew it was silly and that Toni Cantelli would hardly have cared about it in the throes of a heart attack, but it bugged Horton, nevertheless. He couldn't get it out of his mind and it took him a long time to get to sleep.

He was sure he had only just drifted off when something woke him with a start and now he was staring up at the coach roof fully alert, his ears straining for the least sound. All he could hear was the rain pounding the deck, the wind whistling through the masts and the slapping of water against the sides of the boat. It was just his imagination, and yet he felt uneasy. He knew that fear heightened perceptions and the premonition he'd experienced at Horsea Marina the night of Tom Brundall's death was back with a vengeance. He hadn't forgotten that someone had once tried to kill him. He cursed himself now for not being more vigilant.

With his heart racing, he eased himself off the bunk and pulled on a sweater and tracksuit bottoms, slipping his feet into his trainers. Perhaps he had dreamt of danger and his body had involuntarily leapt into action as a result.

He listened. Nothing. And yet something was telling him that he *was* in peril. He didn't dare turn on his light in case he alerted whoever was out there. His eyes were growing accustomed to the dark. The hatchway was almost closed, with just a narrow slit open to allow air to circulate inside the cabin. He couldn't open it further without it giving an alarming screech. But he'd have to risk it because staying here wasn't an option if someone was intent on killing him.

He stiffened. Yes, he had distinctly heard the squeak of the security gate, as it swung open. It could be another boat owner, but Horton wasn't about to hang around and find out. As soon as the gate clanged shut whoever it was would be almost level with *Nutmeg*. Horton knew the timing exactly. And he didn't have minutes to lose.

With his heart racing, he eased open the storage locker underneath the bunk opposite and silently shrugged his way into a buoyancy aid.

Stealthy footsteps were getting closer, not those of any boat owner he knew. Grabbing his wallet and ripping Emma's photograph from above his bunk he took a deep breath, shoved back the hatchway and leapt into the cockpit in time to see a dark hooded figure clothed in black. Then an arm was raised. Horton didn't hesitate. As he leapt over the side of *Nutmeg* he felt a great searing heat follow him and heard the whoosh of an explosion. The sky lit up like the fourth of July and the roar of flames filled his ears. The icy sea sucked the breath from him. How long did he have before the cold swallowed him into oblivion? Ten minutes? But he was in the comparative safety of the marina; he could get to safety. He had to.

He began to swim away from the fire, the cold already numbing him, his clothes pulling him down, but the burning *Nutmeg* was guiding him across to the next pontoon. After what seemed an age but could only have been minutes he grasped the wooden decking, panting heavily, his body screaming with fatigue. He could hear shouts and cries, people running. There was no one to pull him out, the marina was almost empty, it being winter. He was slipping and going under. With numb and trembling fingers he pulled at the cord and the buoyancy aid inflated. Then someone was grabbing him by his arms and hauling him up. He found some energy and propelled himself on to the pontoon, and lay there shivering and panting.

'Are you all right, mate?'

Horton was tempted to say, 'Yes, I always go for a swim in the marina in the middle of the night in December.'

'I'll get you a blanket and call an ambulance.'

'No ambulance,' Horton managed to say, pulling himself up into a sitting position and wrenching off the buoyancy aid. 'A blanket will do for now.' He was recovering and the man seeing this climbed onto his boat and fetched a blanket, which he draped round Horton's shoulders. Pulling it across his sodden chest, Horton stared at the blazing spectacle that had been his home. He could feel the heat of the fire from here and he shuddered as he recalled how close he'd come once again to death. If he hadn't been woken by some sixth sense . . . Or was it? Now that he considered it he thought that maybe the sound of a car pulling up had alerted him. If that were so then it couldn't have been a car familiar to him. There must have been something about it that had jolted him out of his sleep, but what? And was he just imagining it?

He felt desperately sad as he watched *Nutmeg* blaze. Then anger kicked in. How dare they destroy his home? Now he had nothing except . . . With his fumbling fingers encased in soaking wet bandages he grasped the sopping photograph of Emma. He still had her, thank the Lord, but if someone was intent on killing him, then next time they might try when Emma was with him. If he didn't find this killer before Wednesday then he would have to sacrifice spending his day with his daughter, which made him furious.

'Your boat, mate?'

'Yes, or rather it was,' Horton said, recalling that the photograph of his mother had also gone up in flames. Now he had nothing to remember her by except what he carried inside him.

'What happened? Cooker explode?' his helper suggested. 'You were lucky to get out alive. There was a chap at Horsea recently who wasn't so fortunate.'

Horton remembered the blackened figure on the pontoon and shivered violently. He could hear the fire engines. Thankfully there were no boats either side of his poor *Nutmeg*. He stood up and, addressing his helper, said, 'Did you see anyone running up the pontoon?'

'No, all I heard was a great explosion, then saw you. You think someone did that deliberately?' he cried incredulously.

Oh, yes, indeed, Horton thought, but said, 'Thanks for your help, Mr . . . ?

'John Cheshire.' He reached out his hand, and Horton looked down at his own sodden wet bandaged hands.

'Better not,' he said with a wry grin.

Cheshire looked surprised and puzzled. 'You have been in the wars. Do you want to come on board? Can I get you some dry clothes?'

Horton looked at the man's stature, which was shorter and leaner than his, and said, 'Thanks, but I don't think they'll fit. I'll be all right. I'll call some mates who will help.'

Horton squelched his way up to the office where he found Eddie almost beside himself with despair; his look of relief gave Horton a warm glow. It was a nice feeling to have someone care for you. Tonight, Horton's loneliness and feelings of isolation had been so acute that he had let his guard down, and look what had happened. Still, he was alive.

Eddie rushed up to him. 'I thought you was a goner. Am I glad to see you! You all right? Do you want an ambulance? What happened?'

'What I need is a phone. Go and talk to the fire officer, Eddie, and make sure everything is OK with the other boat owners.' Eddie got his drift and hurried away leaving Horton alone in the office. He could see the firefighters running hoses down the pontoon where Eddie's colleague was already on his mobile phone to his boss. Horton suspected a fire in two of the company's marinas wasn't going to make him a happy man!

He would like to have called Cantelli but didn't want to disturb him in his bereavement. Instead he rang through to Uckfield.

'Jesus! That's twice someone's tried to kill you — why?' Uckfield exclaimed.

'If I knew that, I'd probably know who the killer is,' Horton snapped. Yet his mind was racing with the thought that this must be connected with his mother and that note in the margin of Gilmore's newspaper. And there was one person he was getting close to, whom he had interviewed that day, and who might have a lot to lose: Sebastian Gilmore.

'I'll come down and handle the investigation, myself,' Uckfield said. 'I'll send a car to collect you. Where are you going to stay?'

Horton thought he detected a hint of nervousness in Uckfield's voice. He didn't believe Uckfield would offer him a bed, so he wouldn't bother asking and suffer the humiliation of being fobbed off with excuses. He also wondered if Uckfield was worried he might ask Catherine.

'I'll sort something out.'

As Horton rang off he heard the familiar throb of the police launch and hurried outside to meet it at the waiting pontoon. He stopped for a brief moment to gaze across at *Nutmeg*; the firefighters were squirting water on her. His heart was heavy with sorrow. She had been his consolation and his refuge in the dark days following the debacle of Operation

Extra and Catherine's rejection. Watching her burn he felt as though a chapter of his life had closed. Just as his marriage to Catherine was over, so the last vestiges of that phase of his life after the accusation of rape and his subsequent suspension were completed. *Nutmeg* was being laid to rest and he should do the same with the immediate past. The past further back though was a very different matter.

His gaze took him to the car park above the marina with the fire engines and their blue lights flashing in the dark. His attacker had long gone. Did he know if he was still alive, Horton wondered. He would only have had an instant to escape the pontoon before Eddie and his colleague rushed out. Horton guessed he would have thrown the firebomb and immediately sprinted away.

'Andy, what happened? Are you OK?' Sergeant Elkins exclaimed, leaping off the launch and swiftly securing a line to the pontoon. 'I heard about the fire over the radio. I couldn't believe it when they said it was your boat.'

'I'm fine.'

'Well you don't look it, dripping all over the place and shivering like buggery.'

Horton managed a smile. 'Typical British response, sorry, force of habit. And apologizing when I don't need to.'

'Get on board. Ripley, the thermal blanket.'

Horton was glad to let Elkins take control. He settled himself in the wheelhouse as Ripley placed the silver thermal blanket around his shoulders.

Elkins opened his mouth to speak but Horton got there first.

'Don't say I should go to hospital, Dai,' Horton said, using Elkins' real name and not Dave, as he had become popularly known. 'I just need a hot shower and some clean clothes, and somewhere to stay.' The first two were easy to arrange, but he didn't know about the third. Then he had a thought. 'Let me call Superintendent Uckfield.' When connected, he said, 'Steve, I'm going back with Sergeant Elkins — yes, the police launch is here. Call an ambulance. Tell them to make it look as though they're picking me up from the water. Our pyromaniac won't be hanging around the marina, but he could be waiting somewhere down the road to see what happens. Let's make him think for a while that he's succeeded in putting me out of action. I'll call you as soon as I can to let you know where I am.' Turning to Elkins he said, 'Can you get me some dry clothes?'

'Yes. Look, I've got an idea. I need to make a call.'

As he did so, Ripley started the engine and piloted the launch into Langstone Harbour. Horton was content just to sit and think. His attacker had to be Sebastian Gilmore, and yet that couldn't be, the build was wrong. Horton couldn't mistake the giant of a man. So Gilmore must have hired someone to do his dirty work for him. If that were so, then Horton knew that his mother was the key to unlocking who was behind these killings, and that Sebastian Gilmore was afraid that Horton would turn it. Yet, it didn't quite measure up. Sebastian Gilmore had to be some kind of idiot or psychopath to think he could get away with killing a detective on the case without anyone else pointing the finger at him. And Horton didn't have Gilmore down as an idiot, which meant he must be psychotic. After all, who else would kill Anne Schofield and enjoy setting fire to people?

'It's all settled if you're happy with the arrangements,' Elkins broke through his thoughts. Horton stirred himself as Elkins continued. 'I have a friend who owns a Bavaria 44 in Gosport Marina. He's abroad working for six months. He's happy to let you live on board for as long as you like. In fact, he'd rather have someone on board, using the boat and looking after it.'

'Is he sure?' Horton felt cheered by the news. This was a stroke of luck. It sounded ideal. 'Does he know that someone's intent on setting fire to me?'

Elkins looked a little sheepish. 'Not exactly. I just told him a colleague who was a keen sailor needed a billet.'

Horton frowned, concerned. Should he insist that Elkins tell his mate the truth and risk losing the opportunity of somewhere to stay? But perhaps he could avoid anyone knowing where he was, which would be fine if he could get enough on Sebastian Gilmore to bang him up quickly.

'No one must know about it.'

Elkins nodded. 'He doesn't want any money either and says you can sail her whenever you wish.'

'He's a very generous and trusting man! What on earth does he owe you, Dai?'

Elkins flushed and bristled. 'It's not crooked if that's what you mean, Inspector.'

'I didn't think it would be.'

Elkins relaxed. 'I helped him out once, that's all—'

'Saved his life more like,' Ripley shouted over his shoulder.

'Yes, thank you, Constable. We were called to assist a rescue operation off the Isle of Wight. As we were almost on the spot we got there before the lifeboat and coastguard. I saw this man in the water and pulled him out, that's all.'

Horton suppressed a smile. He knew that wasn't just all. Through chattering teeth, he asked, 'Have you had any joy confirming whether or not Sebastian Gilmore was in Cowes Marina on Tuesday night as he claims?'

'The marina staff said to check back tomorrow when Neville's working. He was on duty last Tuesday night. Neville's a nosy bugger. If anyone knows he will.'

Within an hour, Horton had showered, changed into dry clothes — uniform trousers, shoes and a sweatshirt — and was alone on board Elkins' friend's yacht with a cup of coffee in his scarred hands. The bandages had been consigned to the rubbish bin.

'*Nutmeg*,' he said, saluting her, whilst gazing around his spacious and luxurious surroundings. His phone rang. It was Uckfield.

'There was no sign of anyone hanging around the marina, but the ambulance sped away blue lights blazing just in case.'

'And *Nutmeg*?'

'She's gone. I'm sorry, Andy.' Uckfield left a pause before adding, 'Do you want a few days off?'

'No,' Horton declared vehemently. Then he told Uckfield where he was staying and asked him to keep it quiet. 'The fewer who know the better. There's only you, Elkins and Ripley who know and I'd rather keep it that way.' Except for Cantelli, whom he would tell later and whom Horton trusted with his life. Then he relayed to Uckfield his suspicions regarding Sebastian Gilmore and added, 'When we've got more information I'd like to be the one to confront him with it. I want to know if he's surprised to see me. I take it I can go ahead and instruct the economic crime unit to look into his, Rowland Gilmore's and Brundall's backgrounds now?'

Uckfield reluctantly agreed.

Horton said, 'I don't want Dennings to know where I'm living either, or Catherine. And I'd rather you didn't say anything to Catherine or Alison about tonight.' Horton thought if Catherine knew then she would damn well stop him seeing Emma, and he had time yet to clear this up: two days, to be precise. He could sense Uckfield's hesitation and added firmly, 'As I said, Steve, let's keep this low key.'

There was a short pause before Uckfield grunted an acknowledgement.

Horton stretched out on the bunk in the aft cabin feeling strangely out of place in such comfort and luxury — he even had a shower on board — and tried to sleep. He was exhausted but he guessed that sleep would elude him for some time, as a result not only of the after effects of a massive surge of adrenalin and his unfamiliar surroundings, but also because of the thought that he knew what he had to do, and it scared him half to death because now there wasn't any doubt. He had to delve deeper into his mother's past, and he had no idea what he would find. But whatever it would be, he guessed he wasn't going to care much for it.

EIGHTEEN

Monday, 9.15 a.m.

Horton stared up at Jenson House, the tower block where he had lived with his mother on the top floor, and was surprised to find he felt neither the anger nor the pain of rejection that had plagued him for the last thirty years. Was that because he was finally taking action to solve the puzzle instead of letting it hang over his life like a black cloud? Or maybe it was the fact that the photograph and his birth certificate, the last tangible links with his mother, had been burnt in the fire? Had that had some kind of psychological effect on him, forcing him to look at this anew? Now he was getting over-analytical, he thought with a grimace, kicking down the stand on the Harley.

He didn't expect anyone still to be living here who would remember Jennifer, but that wasn't really his purpose in coming. He hoped instead to trigger a long-forgotten memory, or to release a deeply embedded clue in his sub-conscious that would tell him what had happened to her. Perhaps he'd be able to recall a boyfriend, or her mood, or something she had said.

Now he was back to behaving like Freud again. He guessed this was a pointless exercise, and he was wasting valuable police investigation time, but a slight diversion wouldn't hurt, he reasoned, heading towards the entrance. Neither Superintendent Uckfield nor DCI Bliss knew about this. As far as they were concerned he was already speeding his way to Southampton and the offices of the Marine Accident Investigations Branch.

The news of his second escape from death had spread around the station, and he was surprised and touched by the concern of many of the officers. DCI Bliss though was an exception. She made no mention of it; instead he got an ear bashing on when he was going to clear up some of his outstanding CID cases. He reminded her that Sergeant Cantelli was on bereavement leave and he was still an officer short, but she brushed both aside as being of no consequence.

He pushed open the doors of Jenson House and DCI Bliss vanished from his mind. Suddenly he was a young boy again, running across the concourse, kicking a football with the other kids, stealing hubcaps and darting up and down the stairs. He was surprised because in all the years he had been here as a PC and a detective he had never recollected the slightest thing about his short life in this tower block. He guessed he had blotted it out because of the painful memories. But now that he had opened his mind to the past, the ghosts rushed out to greet him.

They had tarted the place up since he'd last been inside, which must have been about five years ago, when he'd been seconded to the drugs squad — he'd been a sergeant then — and certainly since he'd lived here, but he felt as though nothing had changed at all. In his mind's eye he could see the small, blonde, cropped-haired little boy swinging into the vestibule whistling tunelessly, ravenously hungry, and eager to ditch his schoolbooks for football boots. He felt that same eager anticipation as the child of ten about to arrive home, but it was swiftly followed by the gut-wrenching ache of the moment he had finally realized that his mother had deserted him. He recalled the woman who had told him that she was never coming home; he could see her evil, smug face as she had imparted the news with uncharacteristic relish for a social worker. Maybe that was why he distrusted all social workers.

He pushed that memory away; there was nothing in it for him, and, while he waited for the lift, he concentrated his thoughts on Emma. He had to get this killer by Wednesday. He couldn't let Emma down, because if he did then Catherine was bound to use it as some kind of weapon to prevent him from seeing her again. Her remarks and acid tones last Wednesday night at the Marriott Hotel had made that much clear.

The lift opened with a shudder and a clunk and, pressing the button for the top floor, he thought of poor Rowland Gilmore losing his daughter and his heart missed a beat. He'd rather die himself than allow any harm to befall his daughter.

The lift slid open and he stepped out, surprised to find his heart racing. His feet propelled him forward until he was standing outside his old front door. In his mind he could see his bedroom plastered with posters of football heroes, and his schoolbooks piled on the small chest of drawers under the window. He used to lean out and watch the ships, sailing boats, and hovercraft across the Solent to the Isle of Wight beyond. Had he been unhappy? He couldn't remember, but now he recalled that the sailing boats had made him think of freedom, escape, and adventure, so maybe he had been.

Bugger. He closed his eyes and instantly saw his mother's laughing face, her blonde hair tumbling down her shoulders. He could feel the texture of her dress, smell her soft musky perfume, and hear her light laughing voice . . .

'*I'm going out, Andy. You get yourself off to bed at nine. If I come home and find you in front of that telly I'll tan your hide and there'll be no football practice for you, my boy.*'

'*Where are you going, Mum?*'

'*Where do you think? Work, of course.*'

He turned away feeling a heavy sadness within him and almost collided with an elderly woman pulling a shopping trolley. Hastily, he apologized as her lined faced looked alarmed and concerned. Strangers here meant trouble and he guessed one wearing a black leather jacket emblazoned with the Harley Davidson logo was even more suspect.

'It's OK, luv. I'm from the police.' He showed her his warrant card and she visibly relaxed.

'You can't be too sure these days. We get some funny types round here.'

'How long have you lived here, Mrs—?'

'Cobden. Thirty-two years.'

My God, she must have been his neighbour! He had been ten when he had left here; she would have been what — late forties, or early fifties? He couldn't recall her, and clearly she didn't remember him, or recognize the name on his warrant card, though he had only flashed it at her, but she might remember his mother. With a racing heart he said, 'I'm trying to trace a woman who used to live here thirty years ago. Fair, nice-looking with a little boy . . .'

'You mean Jennifer Horton.'

'Yes!' For once he was unable to hide his surprise that the elderly woman had remembered the name and there he had been telling PC Johns not to jump to conclusions about people because of their age. It felt strange to hear his mother's name, and uttered so normally. It made Jennifer come alive for him; he could almost see her here in this corridor, gossiping to the old woman, and this time he recognized that his feelings of anger and hatred towards her weren't as strong as before.

He said, 'I didn't expect you to remember her and so quickly.'

'She walked out on her little boy, the poor little mite, and he stayed in there—' she jerked her head at the door — 'waiting for his mother to come home. I had no idea. It broke my heart when the social carted the poor little blighter away.'

Horton ignored the tightening in his stomach muscles. 'Do you know what happened to her?'

'How a mother can up and leave her own child like that I don't know, but there were rumours.'

'What kind?' Horton steeled himself to hear the worst, hoping that his police training would stand him in good stead and he wouldn't betray his turmoil.

She inserted her key in the lock, and looked around as though afraid someone might overhear. Horton thought it would have been comical if it hadn't concerned him. In a low whisper she said, 'Men.'

'Any in particular?' he asked as casually as he could, though even to him his voice sounded strained. His mind went back to the Town Camber and the dark-haired man with the sharp-featured face. He wished he could recall more of him, but all he got was an impression of vitality and strength, and a sense of evil. But then that was probably his ten-year-old brain kicking in. If Rowland Gilmore had shown up wearing a dog collar he'd probably have felt the same way. He hadn't wanted anyone to steal his mother's affections from him.

The old woman peered at him warily, and for a moment Horton wondered if she had recognized him.

She said, 'Why are you interested after all these years? Is she dead?' Then her expression cleared. 'It's one of them cold cases, isn't it? Like you see on the telly. You think she's been murdered!' she cried triumphantly, with a gleam in her eyes.

'Do you think that's likely?' he asked, outwardly calm, but feeling excited and anxious inside.

She thought for a moment. 'It didn't cross my mind at the time. I just thought she didn't want to be tied down with a kid. She liked a good time. She was young. But maybe you're right. Up until she ran off, she'd been a good mother. The boy was always clean and well fed, and he seemed a happy little soul.'

Her words were like darts stabbing his heart. He had tried not to think of his childhood for so long that it was a shock to remember that there had been times when he'd been happy. The misery of his childhood after the age of ten had obliterated the good times.

'When was the last time you saw her?'

She puckered her face in thought for a moment, then said, 'It was her birthday. I bumped into her as I was coming out of the lift and she was going down. I said, "Where are you going all dressed up to the nines?" She tapped the side of her nose, smiled and said, "Ask no questions and you'll get no lies." I never saw her again.'

So who had she been going to meet? If he knew that, he'd know her killer, because now he was convinced she was dead. And he wouldn't mind betting that Sebastian Gilmore was involved in it somewhere along the line.

There was nothing more the old lady could tell him. He thanked her for her help, and left, not leaving a card with his name on it and betraying who he was. Give it a couple of days, though, and he'd return. She might have remembered something more by then, or she might know someone who had. He also hoped to have those missing-person case notes. He headed for Southampton, mulling over what the old lady had told him. She was right when she said his mother had liked men because Horton certainly remembered more than one man. But why shouldn't she have boyfriends? She had been young, pretty and single. Again he wondered who his father was; he couldn't recall his mother ever speaking of him. Had he just been a casual acquaintance, a five-minute grope in the back of a van somewhere? Or had it been a serious love affair? Horton liked to think the latter.

He pulled up in front of the Marine Accident Investigation Branch in Southampton, shelving thoughts of his mother, and turned his mind to the case of the rescued yachtsman. Although the MAIB had only come into being in 1989 it had inherited the reports from the Marine Directorate and the Maritime and Coastguard Agency. Horton knew that he would find some record of the marine tragedy that had claimed Warwick Hassingham's life.

The librarian, a slender fair woman in her late thirties with a weatherworn face and bright eyes, handed across a file.

'We haven't got all our records on to computer yet, so I'm afraid it's a case of ploughing through the paperwork. There's a summary sheet at the front. I'll leave you to it.'

Horton settled down to read.

It was Friday 15 August 1997 and the storm came up out of nowhere. Gilmore didn't have Global Satellite Positioning on the fishing boat but relied on experience and the lighthouse at St Catherine's to get his bearings. Just before midnight the Solent Coastguard received a Mayday from the motorboat, *Haven*, reporting that the engine had failed, and the helmsman was disorientated and had no idea where he was.

The rescue helicopter was scrambled and the Bembridge lifeboat alerted, but the Mayday call was also answered by the fishing vessel, *Frances May*. Skippered by Sebastian Gilmore, she was the first to reach the *Haven*, which was shipping water fast. They threw a line to the helmsman. Then, against Sebastian Gilmore's advice and instructions to wait for the rescue helicopter, Warwick Hassingham leaned over the side of the fishing boat to try and reach the man. He wasn't clipped on, a wave struck the *Frances May* and Hassingham was swept overboard. The crew of the fishing vessel threw another line to Warwick and pulled the injured man from the *Haven* on board, but Warwick Hassingham had gone. The helicopter mounted a full search and rescue operation, but there was no sign of Hassingham or the *Haven*, which was believed to have sunk. The rescued man was called Peter Croxton. He lived in Guildford.

Horton sat back. He had a name. Good. Did Croxton still live at the address in Guildford? If Horton was correct in his theory about drug smuggling and this man being the supplier, then he doubted it. There would be a coroner's report on Hassingham though and outside, Horton rang through to Sergeant Trueman and asked him to request a copy of it, and to trace Peter Croxton. On his way back to the station, he detoured to Dr Clayton to see if she had made anything of the bones they had recovered from the air-raid shelter.

'I was about to call you, Inspector,' she said, as he knocked and walked into her office. 'Come and take a look at him.'

'It's male then.' Horton followed her diminutive figure into the mortuary where the few bones Taylor had gathered up were laid out upon a slab. He nodded at Tom, who was whistling 'I'm gonna wash that man right out of my hair'.

'Yes. We were lucky to have the pelvis; it's thicker and heavier than the female pelvis. The body of the pubis is triangular in shape, whereas in a female it would be quadrangle and the sacrum is long and narrow and not short and wide, like this.' She pointed to the various bones as she spoke. 'And if that wasn't enough to confirm the sex of the skeleton then we have the skull.'

Horton stared at the bones, wondering how this poor devil had ended up in that air-raid shelter.

'He was also Caucasian. As to his height, the length of the femur puts him at five feet eleven inches.' *How tall was Peter Croxton? Could this be him?*

'With regards to the length of time he's been dead, you're certainly looking at more than five years because there are no tags of soft tissue present. I'll do some laboratory tests to give you a clearer indication of date but from what I can see, and the condition of his teeth and fillings, I'd say between five to ten years.'

Which matched what Gutner had told them — give or take a few years. If this was Croxton and Horton's theory about him being a drug supplier was correct, then maybe Croxton had decided he wanted out. Sebastian Gilmore couldn't allow that so had killed him. Sebastian knew his brother was back living in Portsmouth, he'd seen him on the quayside, and had come up with the idea of dumping his body in his brother's backyard knowing that Rowland suffered from claustrophobia and wouldn't venture inside the air-raid shelter. And if he ever did and found the body, then Rowland would keep quiet rather than risk losing his job.

'Any idea of his age?'

'From the pattern of the fusion of bone ends I would say he was about mid to late thirties when he died.'

Horton was disappointed. If he'd been killed in 1995, after Gutner had looked in the air-raid shelter, and if it were Peter Croxton, then that would make him about seventeen or eighteen at the time of the tragedy at sea. It was a bit on the young side to be involved in a complex drug smuggling operation as he had theorized, and who would have hired a motorboat to such a young man in 1977? It was still possible but it was looking more doubtful. There had been no age mentioned on the incident report. Sebastian might be able to give him some idea of the age of the rescued man, but would he tell the truth?

Gaye continued, 'I've taken pictures of the jaw and teeth and DNA survives in the bones for many years, so we'll be able to compare this with family members for closer identification.'

'If we can find any relatives. Do you know how he died?'

'Now that's where we are lucky.' Gaye turned over the skull. 'See here.' She pointed to a large indentation and handed Horton a magnifier. 'Tell me what you see.'

Horton peered closely at the cranium. 'There's a long thin crack running from the dent.' He looked up. 'Someone hit him?'

'I would say so.'

'I suppose it's impossible for you to say if he was killed then moved.'

'Sorry.'

'So we're looking for a missing person, male, mid to late thirties, five feet eleven inches tall, Caucasian, who was reported missing any time from 1998 to about 2003.'

'That's about it. *If* he was reported missing. Perhaps nobody noticed.'

Her words made him think of his mother. Someone had noticed but how hard had anyone tried to find her?

Gaye said, 'The skull can be scanned into computer and "fleshed" out to give you likely facial appearance. I'm getting on to that now, but we have no indication of his eye or hair colour. And the lip shape and size are also independent of the bony structure. It's a start, though. I'll let you have the lab results as soon as possible.'

Horton didn't like to think how many men in their mid-thirties were listed as missing between 1998 and 2003 but they'd check anyway. He told her about Cantelli's father. She shook her head sadly.

'Would you let me know when the funeral is?' she said.

'Of course.' He was surprised that she thought about going but also pleased that he would see her there.

On arriving at the station he made straight for the incident room where DC Marsden announced that Sebastian Gilmore's alibi for the night Rowland Gilmore and Tom Brundall had died had been confirmed. He had been at Tri Fare. Horton cursed. But he didn't give up all hope of pinning the murders on him. Like he had said to Uckfield, Gilmore could have hired someone to do his killing.

Horton could see Dennings in his office next to Uckfield's with his phone clamped to his ear. Uckfield wasn't around.

Horton pulled up a chair and spent some time scrutinizing the coroner's report on Teresa Gilmore's death. It confirmed what they already knew. Her clothes were found at the foot of the cliffs on the beach at Rhossili Bay on the Gower Peninsula in Wales, along with a note addressed to her husband. A walker on Rhossili Down had spotted the clothes and seen a woman in the sea. He had immediately alerted the rescue services, but by the time they reached her she was gone. What remained of her body was washed up two weeks later. The verdict was that she took her own life whilst the balance of her mind was disturbed.

He asked Marsden to take over Cantelli's task of looking into any possible connection between Rowland Gilmore and Anne Schofield, pleased to see that the files from the Dean's office had finally arrived, and was about to leave for his office when Trueman called him back.

'Andy, I might have something for you. Peters rang the coroner to ask for the report on Hassingham's death and managed to get some information over the telephone. There's a sister.'

Now, why hadn't Sebastian mentioned her? Maybe she was dead? But Trueman had said *is*. So perhaps she had emigrated, or was living in Scotland, and Sebastian hadn't thought it worthwhile bringing her up. Horton swiftly recalled the interview with Gilmore. Gilmore had interrupted him when he had expressed his surprise at Hassingham being buried at sea. 'His *mother's* wishes,' Gilmore had said, not his *family's*. And Mrs Hassingham had died eight months after the tragedy. Because of that Horton hadn't probed to find out if there was anyone else. He should have asked, though he didn't think she would be able to add anything to the case.

'Do you have an address?' he asked, not very hopeful.

'Not yet, but I know where you can find her.'

Something in Trueman's tone alerted Horton. Narrowing his eyes he peered at the sergeant. 'Where?'

'You asked me to do a company search on Gilmore before the economic crime unit took it over. A copy of his latest accounts are on their way to us, but I got a summary of them online. They all look perfectly above aboard . . .'

'And?' Horton asked impatiently, waiting for the punch line and thinking this had better be good.

'Janice Hassingham works for Sebastian Gilmore. She's his financial director.'

Is she indeed! That was twice Sebastian Gilmore had kept silent about the Hassingham connection: why? Horton was deeply interested, very curious and highly suspicious. And he guessed it was time to find out why Sebastian hadn't thought to mention her in their earlier interview.

NINETEEN

Monday, 4.45 p.m.

'Why this interest in Warwick, Inspector?'

Janice Hassingham eyed him warily, as she nodded him into the seat opposite her untidy desk piled high with files and paper. 'My brother's been dead for thirty years.'

She wasn't what Horton had expected. Instead of being slim, smart and business-like she was a short, shapeless, middle-aged woman in dull unfashionable clothes. Her straight, cropped grey hair accentuated the determined cast of her coarse-featured face and was marked with the scars of teenage acne and the lines of late middle age.

Her rather small office was crammed with box files and grey, dented filing cabinets — the kind that could be bought cheap from any ex-government surplus auction — and it overlooked the harbour. Beyond her he could see the cranes reaching over the quayside, and from the open window came the bleeping of a forklift truck below.

Sebastian Gilmore wasn't there and Horton was rather glad about that. He didn't want to explain why he had come to see Janice Hassingham, not until he had some more information. And he wanted to delay the moment when Sebastian realized he'd not been roasted alive. The security man at the reception desk had told Horton that Sebastian was at a conference in London with the Department of the Environment, Fishery and Rural Affairs. Horton had great difficulty envisaging Sebastian Gilmore stuck in an air-conditioned hotel conference room sipping mineral water and listening to officials waffle on about quotas.

Selina's Mercedes wasn't in the car park either; the security man said she was at a meeting and wasn't expected back until the afternoon. So that left him with a clear field.

Watching Janice Hassingham closely, he said, 'You may have heard about the death of a man at Horsea Marina, Tom Brundall.' He noticed a slight reaction, which she covered by shifting some papers on her desk. Was it nerves or did that gesture hide some deeper emotion, he wondered. 'And, of course, the Reverend Rowland Gilmore's death, Sebastian's brother . . .' Her eyes flashed up at him and quickly away again.

'You're interested because at one time they all worked together.'

'Yes.' For a moment he thought there was something vaguely familiar about her. He couldn't say what it was or why but he had the impression that he knew her from somewhere. 'I've read the report on your brother's accident. He was a brave man.'

'No, Inspector, he was a foolish man.'

The bitterness of her reply took him back and at the same time intrigued him. He was confident though he betrayed nothing of his feelings and was assured of this when she continued in the same crisp tone.

'The rescue helicopter would have reached the other man. Warwick should have waited, but he always was impulsive.'

She frowned and glanced at her computer screen as the tell-tale pinging of an email message popped into her inbox. She quickly fiddled with her mouse. He got the impression that she was trying to convey he was interrupting her in something far more important than her brother's death, but he saw beyond the facade. In front of him was a sad, lonely woman whose only solace he suspected was her work.

'I won't keep you long,' he said. 'I just need some background. It helps in cases like this.' He smiled reassuringly, though he needn't have bothered; Janice Hassingham had become immune to charm and perhaps even to kindness. 'Do you recall Tom Brundall and Rowland Gilmore?'

'Of course I do.' She spoke curtly yet her eyes betrayed her. So that was it! Which of them had she been in love with, Horton wondered.

'Tell me about them.' He crossed his legs and settled back in his chair as if he had all day to chat. For a moment he glimpsed irritation before sadness touched her face and he could see that the opportunity to talk about a past love was too great to let pass.

'Tom was quite a bit older than me. I was twenty when Warwick died, Tom was thirty-five. He was a quiet man and very clever.' So it was Brundall she had hankered after, but had her passion been reciprocated? Perhaps not. Or had they been lovers and Brundall had ditched her when he'd taken off? 'Rowley was the youngest of the four. He was three years younger than Sebastian and twenty-four when Warwick died.'

'You've got a good memory for figures.'

'I should have. I'm the company accountant.'

He smiled but she didn't return the gesture, not because she was hostile, he thought, but because she was cautious. It was as though she had to hold herself in for fear of saying something that might show her true feelings.

'Rowley was also quiet but in a reserved way, not like Tom, who was so knowledgeable, but never bragged about it. He had a great head for figures. I remember him once—' She stopped as though she was about to confess something important.

'Yes?'

'He was very good at forecasting the stock market.'

That wasn't what she had been about to say, but he let it go.

She added, 'I understand he made a lot of money after leaving the fishing industry. I'm not surprised.'

And maybe she glimpsed a life that she had missed out on. Did she blame her brother for that? He guessed so.

'And Warwick, what was he like?' Horton prompted, watching her carefully. A shadow crossed her face.

'Mad, is how I think most people would describe him. But Warwick was never one for doing the safe thing. Even as a child he used to worry our poor mum half to death with his antics. He was always getting into scrapes. Oh, nothing against the law, he just liked adventure — jumping off the end of the pier and risking his life, that kind of thing. But Warwick always got away with it. It was quite in character for him to try and rescue that man in the middle of a storm. It would never have crossed his mind that *he* might be swept overboard and drowned.'

She spoke with bitterness and not sadness. Oh, yes, Warwick had cocked up her life, or at least that was how she saw it. And if he was that daring, then maybe he was into smuggling drugs, with the others. What had Janice said? '*He always got away with it.*' On 15 August 1977 he hadn't.

Horton left a moment's pause before asking, 'How did the others take his death?'

She scowled at her papers, glanced fleetingly at him and away again before saying, 'They were devastated, of course. It took Sebastian days to get Rowley back on the boat, and even Tom didn't seem to have the heart for fishing anymore. He became very withdrawn. I think that was when Rowley first got religious, though the deaths of his daughter and wife were the final blow.'

'How do you know about that?'

Her head came up and she looked directly at him. 'Sebastian told me. I suppose religion gave Rowley some kind of crutch. My mother turned to spiritualism, for all the good it did her. She died within a year of Warwick's death.

Our father was already dead. It was just before my twenty-first birthday when Warwick died. Not much to celebrate, Inspector.'

He could see how much she resented her brother's death, and guessed that over the years she had come to blame it (and him) for all her misfortunes. That resentment had spawned bitterness, which had burrowed inside her and taken root, so that it had become *her* crutch.

'How long have you worked for Sebastian Gilmore?'

'Twenty-seven years. He gave me a job as soon as I qualified as an accountant and I've been here ever since.'

'You like it?'

'Sebastian has been very good to me, and with the expansion of his business I've gained promotion. Yes, I like it.'

'Do you recall the man they rescued: Peter Croxton?'

'Not really. He didn't come to the funeral.'

That more or less confirmed what Sebastian had said. So why hadn't Croxton attended the funeral of the man who had risked his life for him, and been killed as a result? There seemed only one explanation to Horton and that was he couldn't afford to be seen in public and with that fishing crew.

There seemed little more Janice could tell him about Warwick's death but there was something else that he needed to explore.

'Did your brother have any girlfriends?'

'A stream of them. They were attracted to him like flies round a dung heap.'

Interesting analogy. People usually said bees round a honey pot. Was that how she saw her brother: he was nothing but a pile of shit and the women ugly flies? Jealousy, bitterness and hatred had eaten away at this woman and looked as if they were still gnawing at her.

'Was there any particular girlfriend at the time of the tragedy?' He could feel his heart racing as he asked the question, and waited for her answer.

'Why do you want to know?' she asked sharply.

'Just routine,' he replied blandly.

She peered at him for a moment longer then, shrugging her shoulders, said, 'There was one, a blonde woman; she was just a bit older than me. I don't know what happened to her.'

He felt a quickening of his heartbeat as he asked, 'Can you remember her name?'

'No. There were so many of them.'

He tried to curb his disappointment. 'Have you got a photograph of your brother?'

'No. I destroyed them all after Mum died. His death killed her and I couldn't bear to look at them.'

Pity. There had to be a picture of Warwick Hassingham somewhere and Horton had an idea of where he might find one.

He left her to her emails and her files, and on his way out asked both the security man at reception and the one at the gate if they recalled seeing Sebastian Gilmore on Friday night. Both confirmed that Mr Gilmore had left the premises at eight thirty. So that put him in the clear for Anne Schofield's murder. When Horton suggested that seemed very late, both said it was nothing unusual for the boss to be there half the night, or all of it if he expected the fishing fleet. Interesting. Was he waiting for something special to be delivered over and above fish? Or was Horton just hoping?

He made for the library, where he asked to examine the microfiche records of the local newspaper. He felt certain they would have covered the tragedy at sea. He had just settled down to scroll through them when his mobile phone rang. He was tempted to ignore the call but recognized the number as that of his solicitor. His chest went tight as he answered it.

'Can you talk?' Frances Greywell began. Horton heard the uncustomary hesitation in her voice and knew this was bad news. He steeled himself for what he was about to hear.

'What is it?'

'I've had a call from Catherine's solicitor.'

The tension inside him hardened into a ball of pain.

'He says that Catherine is refusing you access to Emma on Wednesday on account of it being too dangerous for her to be with you at the moment. I understand that you're on a case where someone has tried to kill you by setting fire to your boat. Is it true?'

She sounded concerned, but his disappointment and anger were so overwhelming that he ignored it. 'Hello, are you there?'

He must have grunted because she continued. 'I insisted that this had all been agreed and that Catherine couldn't go back on her word, but I'm afraid she can if she has a legitimate reason to think your daughter's life might be in danger.'

Slowly Horton counted to ten, hoping to quell the anger inside him. It didn't help. The anger was still there, only now he shifted the focus of it. Who the hell had told Catherine? If it was Uckfield, he'd have him by the balls, superintendent or not.

Finally he found his voice and said, 'Emma will be safe with me.'

'I said that of course, and told him that whatever case you were working on, it could be over by Wednesday, but, Andy . . .'

It was the first time she had used his Christian name. There was worse to come.

'Emma's gone away for Christmas with Catherine and her parents. They flew out from Gatwick to Cyprus at midday today. I've just got back into the office and found a message from her solicitor. I rang him straightaway. I'm really sorry.'

The bitch! Horton wouldn't mind betting she had planned this all along. Their flights had probably been booked ages ago. Catherine had had no intention of letting him see his daughter over Christmas. Christ, how it hurt.

'I'll get onto things the moment they get back from holiday,' Frances Greywell continued, 'and make sure you see Emma as soon as possible in the New Year. I know how disappointed you must be and how much this meant to you but we'll get something arranged.'

'You can arrange something now,' he said, tight-lipped. 'I can't—'

'I want to speak to my daughter on Christmas Day. You can manage that, can't you?'

He didn't mean to sound so curt; his anger wasn't directed at her.

After a moment she said, 'Leave it with me,' and rang off.

He thought about calling Catherine on her mobile and sounding off at her, but that would achieve nothing except make him more frustrated. If Frances couldn't get him permission to call and speak to his daughter on Christmas Day then he'd damn well do it anyway, all day and every ten minutes until someone answered the phone. He couldn't bear the thought that Emma might think he had forgotten her.

He found it difficult to turn his mind to the case, but now he was even more determined to resolve it by Christmas Eve and prove that Emma would have been safe with him. He toyed with the idea of trying to get a flight out to Cyprus. He knew where Catherine's parents' villa was. Yes, he could do that, and he could also find out who had told Catherine about the fire. The two thoughts kept him going while he trawled through the microfiche until he found what he had been looking for. Then he shelved his personal problems and concentrated on the articles in front of him.

The rescued man was mentioned by name, but unfortunately there was no photograph of him and neither was there one of Warwick Hassingham. Horton was disappointed. Instead the newspaper had used photographs of the *Frances May*, which they had obviously taken whilst she'd been moored up in the Town Camber.

Horton scrolled on to the coverage of the funeral. There was a photograph of the funeral procession with the hearse being pulled by two black horses. Walking behind the hearse was a hunched older woman, her hatless head lowered. Horton assumed her to be Warwick Hassingham's mother. Beside her, head held high, was a young Janice Hassingham with shoulder-length hair and wearing a black trouser suit.

Behind them Horton saw a burly figure of an older man, and either side of him two young men: one clearly Sebastian and the other Rowland. The older man must be Terry Gilmore, their father. Rowland was smaller and thinner than his elder brother, not bad looking in a slightly feminine way with those neat features and long hair, which, of course, was fashionable then. Following them was a man and a woman, before the bulk of the mourners whom, unfortunately, Horton couldn't make out.

The man he guessed was Tom Brundall and the woman possibly Teresa, Rowland Gilmore's wife. He made a note of the date the article appeared. There was no more information on Peter Croxton.

He found the obituary on Terry Gilmore. He'd died on 15 November 1978, ten days after Jennifer had disappeared and fifteen months after the tragedy that had taken Warwick Hassingham. Gilmore Senior was described as a driven man who had loved the sea; he'd seen a niche in the market for fishing in Portsmouth and established the thriving business in the Town Camber, which Sebastian had made even more successful. There was nothing there that Horton didn't already know.

He sat back, deep in thought. He wouldn't mind reading all the articles that had been written over the years on the Gilmores. Not only might it give him valuable background information on their business, but it might spark some ideas of the 'wrong' that Brundall had mentioned to Gilmore, other than it being drug running or that skeleton. And there might be an article that carried a photograph of the fishermen, including Warwick Hassingham. Before he checked that though there was something he had to do.

He returned to the station, and sought out Uckfield. Without knocking he burst into his office. 'Catherine's taken Emma to Cyprus for Christmas. You told her about the fire.'

'I didn't—'

'Don't lie to me, Steve,' Horton snapped, scrutinizing him carefully. 'You told Alison and she went squealing to

Catherine. Don't you know how much it meant to me to see Emma, and you've ruined it?'

Uckfield rose and closed his office door. Turning back to face Horton he said, 'I didn't say a word to either of them. Alison's father read the report and mentioned it to Alison. I tried to stop her telling Catherine but I was too late.'

'And you expect me to believe that!' Horton cried contemptuously.

'You can believe what you damn well like, it's the truth,' Uckfield snapped. Then more quietly he added, 'Perhaps if you'd told her yourself, you could have stopped her taking Emma away.'

'When I want your advice on my personal life I'll ask for it.' And Horton swept out, fury and disappointment eating into him.

He was glad no one stopped him on his way to his office and that DCI Bliss wasn't around. He closed his office door and sat for some time staring at nothing. Did he believe Steve Uckfield? He didn't know. Had Catherine planned all the time to take Emma away? He knew it was pointless rushing out to Cyprus; Catherine would call it harassment and use it to further prevent him seeing his daughter. Cantelli's theory was that Catherine was jealous of Emma's love for him. Horton couldn't believe that, but why was Catherine so against him seeing Emma? He needed to find a way of getting to the truth of that. For now, though, he had other mysteries to solve and they might help distract him from his personal anger and frustration.

He powered up his computer and logged on to the press cuttings service that the constabulary used and entered a request for all the articles that had been published on Gilmores over the last twenty years to be sent to him by email. He might only get the ones scanned to computer but it was a start.

He searched amongst the steadily rising pile of papers on his desk for the file on Jennifer Horton, but it wasn't there. He was disappointed. He had hoped to take it home that night. His phone rang and he was surprised to hear Cantelli's voice.

'How's the investigation going?'

Horton was tempted to tell him about the incident on his boat last night and Catherine's betrayal over Emma, but he didn't want to speak over the phone, and he guessed that Cantelli had enough on his plate.

He said. 'I'll bring you up to date later.'

'Yeah, OK.' Cantelli hesitated.

'You've got enough to do, Barney.'

'Isabella and Tony have got it all pretty much sussed. If you don't mind, I'd like to come in tomorrow.'

Reading between the lines Horton thought Cantelli wasn't so much peeved that his older brother and sister had elbowed him out of making funeral arrangements, but that he was desperately looking for something to stop him brooding over his loss.

'I'll be glad to see you.' He rang off feeling that it wasn't right for Cantelli to work, but he knew that he couldn't prevent him from coming in. Cantelli's voice had sounded terse, and Horton recognized all too well the emotions behind it. The sergeant was in denial. He didn't want to believe or even think that his father had died, and he couldn't face talking about it or making funeral arrangements. Horton's heart went out to him and it helped to ease his own pain over Emma.

He made for the canteen where he found Dennings tucking into a Christmas dinner. Horton didn't really want to sit with him, but he didn't have much choice, as there wasn't anywhere else free.

'What did you get from Customs and Revenue and the Fishery Agency?' he asked, putting a plate of curry down in front of him.

'Gilmore is squeaky clean.'

'No one's that,' Horton replied.

'Well, the bugger's clever enough not to have got caught. I hear you had an accident last night on your boat.'

'Yeah.' Horton began to tackle the curry. It wasn't hot enough for his taste.

'And you think that it was Sebastian Gilmore?'

Uckfield had obviously been talking. Horton just hoped he hadn't told Dennings, or anyone else, where he was now living.

'No. Wrong build. I wouldn't be surprised though if he hired someone, just like he could have done to kill the others.'

Before Dennings could comment Horton's mobile rang. He listened for a while then rang off. 'That was Sergeant Elkins. The marina manager has confirmed that Gilmore's boat was moored up in Cowes Marina on Tuesday night and he left Cowes Wednesday morning about ten thirty. Someone in the apartment block also saw Gilmore Wednesday morning just after nine thirty. He was alone.'

'What did he go there for?'

'I'll ask him when I see him.'

'Which you won't. It's my case, remember.'

'How could I forget?' Horton sipped his Coke and ate his curry.

Through a mouthful of turkey, Dennings said, 'I told the super that it was about time we hauled Sebastian bloody Gilmore in and formally questioned him.'

'I don't think Uckfield wants to do that without more evidence, knowing how influential Gilmore is.'

'Well, that's where you're wrong.' Dennings scraped back his chair. 'Because we're bringing him in tomorrow morning.'

'On what grounds?'

'That he might be our killer.'

Might wasn't good enough as far as Horton was concerned. Not with forceful characters like Sebastian Gilmore. You needed firm evidence or at least the appearance of it, and Horton knew they didn't have this. A solicitor would tear holes through their vague suspicions in seconds. He was surprised at Uckfield.

He said, 'Gilmore has an alibi for Brundall's death and Anne Schofield's.'

Dennings paused. Horton saw the triumphant, half cocky gleam in his eye. 'Alibis can be falsified.'

Had Dennings broken Sebastian Gilmore's alibi, he wondered as he watched him strut out of the canteen. If he had then Horton was annoyed he hadn't been told, and peeved he hadn't discovered it himself.

He tossed back his Coke, mentally running through the facts of the case. No, he was sure Dennings was bluffing. But he had a point. Could Sebastian Gilmore have lied about his whereabouts when Brundall was killed? If he had, then his daughter had also lied as had the sales director at Tri Fare. It wasn't beyond the realms of fantasy. And maybe it was worth putting some pressure on that sales director.

He rose and took his tray of used crockery back to the trolley next to the kitchen, earning himself a smile from the young catering assistant. He was confident that Dennings would get very little out of Sebastian Gilmore. Uckfield had probably agreed to it out of desperation that he was getting nowhere fast with the case.

Back in his office, Horton called Inspector Guilbert in Guernsey and updated him on the case, assuming that Dennings wouldn't have done so, and he was right.

'I'm interviewing Russell Newton tomorrow,' John Guilbert said. 'Anything in particular you want me to ask him?'

'Find out all you can about that party on board his boat. Who was there? Who did Brundall talk to? How well did Newton know him? You know the kind of thing. Oh, and there is one more thing you can ask . . .' Horton hesitated; he was going to ask Guilbert to find out from Newton if Brundall had ever mentioned Jennifer. But Horton couldn't quite bring himself to say it. 'Did Brundall ever talk about his past as a fisherman, or mention a man called Warwick Hassingham?'

That night Horton carefully checked outside the boat at Gosport Marina. There was no sign of anyone loitering and with the marine unit keeping a close eye, Horton was able to relax a little. Reaching his hands behind his head he lay on the bunk and deliberately forced his thoughts away from Catherine and Emma and onto the case.

Had Sebastian Gilmore killed Jennifer Horton because her boyfriend, Warwick, had told her about the drugs? Had his mother been a junkie and Warwick her supplier? He didn't remember her as such, but he didn't know the difference between his true memory and what other people, and his boyhood pain of rejection, had put there in its place. Then another thought occurred to him. Had Warwick Hassingham's death really been an accident? Had Warwick been about to betray the others, or had he already betrayed them to Jennifer? Did the three other fishermen push Warwick over the side of that fishing boat? Did this Peter Croxton know that? He was threatening to tell, perhaps blackmailing Brundall and Sebastian Gilmore who from 1995 onwards had been very wealthy men. So he had been silenced and dumped in the air-raid shelter. It made sense except for the age of the skeleton. Could Gaye Clayton be mistaken?

Sebastian could have given Warwick's sister the job of accountant because of a guilt complex for killing her brother. But the secret that Brundall had wanted to confess to Rowland hadn't been killing Warwick; it had been murdering Peter Croxton and, once Rowland had heard that, he couldn't let it rest. He must have called his brother to tell him he was going to the police, and hence he'd been silenced. Like Dennings had said, alibis can be false. Anne Schofield was killed because she had found a confession that Rowland must have written and in it there had been something about Jennifer and how she had been involved back in 1977, which was why she had called Horton.

Horton rose and began to pace the boat, testing out his theory. After Warwick's 'accidental' death had Sebastian comforted Jennifer Horton as a means of finding out what she knew? Had Jennifer become a liability, so had to be killed? If so, which of them had done it? Sebastian or Brundall? Horton just couldn't see Rowland in that role. Well, Brundall was dead. But if Sebastian Gilmore had consigned him to those years of children's homes whilst he'd lived in comfort and security, then by God Horton would make him suffer. Who said revenge was a dish best served cold? Too right it was and he would serve it right in Gilmore's face.

TWENTY

Tuesday, 8 a.m.

Horton rose early and managed to clear a mountain of paper-work before Cantelli knocked and entered. Swiftly, Horton brought the sergeant up to date with events.

'So when are you going to tell me about almost being fried alive?' Cantelli declared.

Horton cursed silently. The station grapevine was work-ing well. He could see that Cantelli was concerned and the last thing he wanted was him worrying. Light-heartedly he said, 'I was saving the best bit until last.'

'You should have called me.' Cantelli looked peeved.

'Barney, you've got enough to cope with at the moment—'

'That's no reason to neglect my friends.'

Horton was warmed by Cantelli's words. It was typical of him to consider others even in the depths of his own sor-row, and Horton knew how deep that was. He could see by the haunted look in his dark eyes, sunk like caverns in his lean face, that Cantelli had had little sleep and was grieving inside. He should be with his family; this wasn't the place for him but Horton could hardly order him home.

Cantelli said, 'I hear the boat's a write-off. So, where are you staying?'

Horton had to tell him. He trusted Cantelli more than anyone else. He glanced at his door; it was open but there was no one immediately outside. Nevertheless, he lowered his voice as he said, 'Elkins got me a billet on this boat in Gosport Marina. It's like living in Buckingham Palace after slumming it on poor little *Nutmeg*. No one knows except Elkins, PC Ripley, Uckfield and you. I'd rather it stay that way until I know who's after me.'

'But why, Andy? Why you? And don't give me all that stuff about being in the wrong place at the wrong time. I know it's tosh.'

Horton sat back and frowned. He should have guessed that Cantelli would see through him, and that he would get to the nub of the matter before either Uckfield or Dennings. Yet, it was difficult for Horton to speak of his mother. He felt this was a defining moment. Should he tell Barney, or whitewash it? But Cantelli deserved more than waffle. This was the man who had stood by him no matter what had been said about his morals, behaviour and professional conduct. Cantelli deserved the truth. After a moment he said, 'Close the door, Barney.'

Cantelli did as he was told. When he was seated, Horton told him about the newspapers in Gilmore's study, the conversation that Gutner had overheard and his worries about his mother's involvement. He didn't find it easy. He tried to speak dispassionately, as though he was giving a report, and yet he couldn't ignore the tension inside him. Maybe it showed in his voice? If it did then Cantelli gave no sign he saw it. Cantelli was the first and only person inside the force he had ever spoken to about Jennifer.

The sergeant listened in silence, looking at first puzzled and then deeply concerned, but not pityingly. Horton was glad; he couldn't have stomached that, but then he wouldn't have expected pity from Cantelli. Even though Cantelli had never known the kind of rejection that Horton had experienced, having been raised in a loving family, Horton knew from working with him over the years that he felt it and understood. He could see it in his expression, too. Cantelli was one of only a handful of people who already knew that he'd been raised in children's homes and with foster parents, though they rarely spoke of it. Why should they? Horton had consigned it to history until now.

Cantelli said, 'So we need to tackle Sebastian Gilmore and find out what he knows. No more pussy-footing round gymnasiums and swimming pools.'

Horton was heartened by Cantelli's fervour and yet reined in by it. Maybe that was what Cantelli had wanted to achieve. A kind of reverse psychology. Now he was beginning to think like a shrink.

'Dennings is bringing him in this morning. If he'll come,' Horton added.

Knowing Sebastian, Horton reckoned it would only be in the company of his solicitor. Sebastian Gilmore was smart; they'd get nothing out of him. But before Horton could comment further his phone rang and he was surprised to hear Selina Gilmore's voice.

'My father's not come home. I'm worried.'

She should be telephoning Dennings, but she had asked for him, probably because he was the only detective she had met on the case.

'I didn't realize he hadn't come home until our housekeeper told me. She said that Dad had not been down for breakfast and he always is by six thirty sharp. I called his office and I've tried his mobile, but there's no answer.'

Horton didn't like the sound of this. Could Sebastian Gilmore have done a runner, believing the police to be on his tail? Had Dennings or someone else in the station warned him he was about to be brought in for questioning? But would a man like Gilmore run away? Horton doubted it. Would he leave his house, business and daughter? Perhaps he had wealth stashed away in some offshore account and

Selina was in on this too? Should he tell Dennings? Like hell he would.

'We'll meet you at the office in ten minutes.' Replacing his phone he addressed Cantelli. 'That was Selina Gilmore. Her father's gone missing.'

On the way to Gilmore's offices Horton was tempted to tell Cantelli about Catherine taking Emma away but decided against it. He knew Cantelli would be upset and angry on his account and Horton didn't want to burden him with more of his problems. Instead, Horton wondered aloud if his interview with Janice Hassingham had spooked Gilmore.

Cantelli said, 'Maybe he's with a woman his daughter knows nothing about.'

It was possible, Horton thought, as Cantelli drew up outside the office. It was raining heavily, but the yard was humming with activity.

'Gilmore's car is here,' Horton said. It was parked next to Selina's Mercedes. 'Perhaps he's shown up.'

But Selina greeted them in her office, along the corridor from her father's, with a worried frown. 'Dad returned from his conference in London late yesterday afternoon. I left him here at seven o'clock,' she said, looking understandably concerned. 'He said he had some things to attend to. I went home, had a shower, changed and then went out with some friends for a meal. I didn't get back until midnight; I thought Dad had gone to bed. When I got up he wasn't in the house and his car had gone from the garage so I assumed he'd come to work. But he's not here. I've checked everywhere and asked around. No one's seen him.'

Horton saw the panic in her eyes and heard the concern in her voice. If her father had run out, and she was party to it, then she was a damn good actress.

'Was your father's car in the garage at home last night?'

'I don't know. I didn't look. I caught a taxi home. I'd been drinking.'

'Is there anywhere he could have gone?'

'I've tried all his friends and contacts. The manager at Cowes Marina said Dad's not there and his boat is still at Horsea Marina. Our housekeeper at our place in Portugal hasn't seen or heard from him. Do you think something could have happened to him? If it has then I blame you; you should have given him protection.' Her voice was getting louder and angrier.

Horton said evenly, 'How did he seem yesterday?'

'His usual self.'

'He didn't seem worried or preoccupied about anything?'

'Only business matters, but that was normal.' Her phone rang. She snatched it up.

Horton crossed to the window and looked down into the yard. Across the car park he could see one of Gilmore's two warehouses. There was a forklift truck whizzing in and out with a flashing light and a bleeping sound. The rain swept in off the sea in a blanket of grey. He heard Selina say, 'Can't Bill deal with it?' Then Horton's attention was caught by a man rushing out of the warehouse. He was calling something out to a colleague who immediately dropped what he was holding and the two men ran back inside the warehouse. Horton spun round.

'Stay here,' he commanded. 'Sergeant.'

'What is it? What's happening?' Selina cried out after them, slamming down the phone.

Horton was aware that she was hurrying behind them as they raced down the stairs into reception. Whatever had caused the commotion Horton caught the tension of it here before sprinting across the yard.

He pushed back the heavy plastic curtain and stepped into the chilly warehouse with its huge tanks and its smell of fish. The radio was belting out rubbishy Christmas songs. There was no one to stop him. Even the forklift truck had been abandoned. He heard Selina's heavy breathing as she caught up with them. There were voices coming from a room further down and on their right.

'Cantelli, stay with Selina.'

But Selina pushed Cantelli away and Horton nodded at Cantelli to let her go.

He strode forward purposefully, in front of them, his heart hammering against his chest, praying that what he thought might be happening actually wasn't.

'Police,' he said forcefully. The crowd parted before him to reveal a door opening into a freezer. Horton stared down at the frozen giant on the floor, huddled in the foetal position, with icicles hanging off his hair and his eyelashes, his fists clenched around his chest, his eyes wide open, covered in frost.

'Dad!'

Selina screamed and tried to push past him but Cantelli now took hold of her firmly. It was only a few seconds before the fight went out of her. Cantelli rapidly scanned the crowd, found a sympathetic and homely face on a woman and handed Selina into her care.

Horton said, 'Stop that music someone.' It didn't escape him that it was belting out the strains of 'Frosty the Snowman'. He doubted anyone else, except Cantelli, would notice the irony of the song though. That was policemen for you.

Cantelli began to clear the warehouse and Horton tentatively stepped into the freezer, not wanting to destroy any evidence. He didn't think there would be much to see, apart from signs of the desperate struggle of a man not wanting to freeze to death.

The music stopped. Thank God for that! Now all Horton could hear was the humming of the freezer and the water bubbling and running in the giant fish tanks. He pulled out a pair of latex gloves and stretched his fingers inside them. Then he crouched down on his haunches and gently closed Gilmore's eyes. That was better. He studied the body closely without touching it, shivering from the cold, despite the warmth of his sailing jacket. He could see no physical signs of attack. It would take a lot to assault a man the size and strength of Sebastian Gilmore and if he had put up a fight his assailant would have known it.

It didn't look as though there was anything in Gilmore's clenched fists, but he'd leave that for Dr Clayton to examine either here in situ or on the mortuary slab.

He felt annoyed with himself for not preventing this killing, but he was angrier still with Sebastian Gilmore. If the fool had only told him the truth then he might be alive today, and Horton might also have got closer to the truth about his mother. Now, he wondered if the facts behind her disappearance would go to the grave with Sebastian Gilmore.

He pushed such thoughts away and concentrated on the frozen corpse. It looked to him as though Gilmore had stepped inside the freezer and then someone had slammed the door on him. There would have been no way out, and no one would have heard his cries. Horton shuddered at the thought of such a slow and terrifying death.

Carefully, he patted the frozen pockets of Gilmore's trousers and loose-fitting casual jacket, and extracted a set of keys. There was no mobile phone. Not that it would have done the poor man much good if he'd had one; he probably wouldn't have been able to pick up a signal in here. Had his killer taken it? But no, he wouldn't have had time before slamming the door on Sebastian Gilmore. Maybe it was in Gilmore's car or office.

Horton stood up, took a further swift look around and then stepped outside. Cantelli had the crowd huddled under the awning of a second warehouse watching the scene. As a police car swept into the yard, Horton was pleased to see it contained PC Seaton and WPC Somerfield. He gave instructions for Seaton to seal off the warehouse and stand guard over it, and Somerfield to go and relieve Cantelli.

Horton crossed to Sebastian's car, and tried the doors. They were locked. Taking the keys that he'd removed from Gilmore's pocket he pressed the zapper and the doors opened with a clunk. He poked inside the glove compartment. Just the usual paperwork: insurance, service documents. No mobile phone. Zapping the car locked he looked up to see Dennings arrive and, in the car beside him, Uckfield.

'What the devil's going on?' Uckfield demanded, climbing out and surveying the activity with an irritated frown.

Horton told him. Uckfield looked surprised, then incredulous, and finally very angry. After cursing vehemently, he said, 'I hope you've got a lead on this.'

Horton was very tempted to remark, 'It's not my case,' but instead said, 'No more than you or DI Dennings have.'

Uckfield glared at him, but Horton was immune to Uckfield's hostile stares, especially now he realized why Dennings had been appointed over him.

He dropped Gilmore's keys into a plastic evidence bag and pushed them into Dennings' hand. 'It's all yours, Tony. I've got enough outstanding cases in CID, which my boss wants solving . . . but there is one thing.' He turned to Uckfield and added, 'We need to know who that skeleton in the air-raid shelter is. This could be the result of someone seeking revenge for a relative or friend's death.'

Uckfield had thought the skeleton a distraction and now, holding Uckfield's glare, Horton saw his point had gone home.

'But why kill Anne Schofield?' Uckfield frowned, puzzled.

Yes, why? It was a flaw in his theory. Anne couldn't have had anything to do with the skeleton's death, and it didn't explain why the killer had also tried to roast him. The man in the air-raid shelter had died long after his mother had disappeared. Had the killer seen his name on the newspaper articles in Rowland Gilmore's study and assumed that his mother had been in on the murder? And, because he couldn't find Jennifer Horton, thought he'd take revenge on her son? It was a bit weak, but in a deranged mind it was possible.

When Horton didn't answer him, Uckfield continued. 'OK. Let's take a look at him.' He jerked his head at Dennings to follow. Over his shoulder to Horton he said, 'Call Dr Price and SOCO, and get some uniform back-up here.'

'Already done, sir,' Cantelli shouted back, and to reiterate his point another police vehicle on blue lights swept into the yard.

Horton turned to Cantelli. 'How's Selina?'

'Very angry. Blaming us for her father's death. I've left her with the personnel officer.'

Cantelli looked distant for a moment. Horton could see that this death and Selina's reaction had reminded him of his own bereavement. He had lost his usual bounce and wasn't even chewing his gum.

'Come on,' Horton said, 'there's someone I want to talk to before Dennings puts his oar in.'

With Gilmore dead, who did that leave as their killer? A relative of that skeleton as he'd suggested to Uckfield, or a hired killer, because Sebastian and the others had been, or were, involved in drug smuggling? If so, Horton reckoned they'd have little chance of catching him and his heart sank at that. He didn't fancy living with the prospect that his life might still be in danger, particularly if he pursued inquiries into his mother's disappearance. And then there was his future with Emma. Despite saying it wasn't his case, Horton knew he had to follow it through, either officially or unofficially, no matter what DCI Bliss might say.

In reception, Horton nodded at the worried looking security officer. He'd noticed the CCTV cameras on Saturday when they'd come here, and now he said, 'Do those run twenty-four hours?'

'Yes, sir.'

'Let us have all the recordings for last night, early this morning, and for last Wednesday, and Friday evening. I'd also like the ones at the entrance and any others you have on the yard. We'll pick them up on our way out.'

Horton wondered if they'd get anything from them, but it was worth checking. With Cantelli following he made for Janice Hassingham's office, knocked briefly and entered. She was at her desk but she didn't appear to be doing any work. Horton thought she looked unwell. She was pale and her eyes were ringed with fatigue.

'Is it true that Sebastian is dead?' she asked.

'Yes.'

She nodded sadly and waved them into seats across her desk.

'Were you working late last night?' Horton asked.

'Yes, but I didn't see anything or anyone. Seb returned from London at about four thirty. I know that because he came straight to my office to ask me about the accounts. It's our year end on thirty-first of December and there's always a lot to do this time of year. He stayed for about thirty minutes, whilst I ran through the final figures, which are showing a healthy profit. Then he returned to his office, or so I assumed. He wasn't in a very good mood, said the conference had been a complete waste of time organized and chaired by . . . well, incompetent people, although Seb was more coarse with his choice of language.'

Horton could imagine. 'Was he still here when you left?'

'Yes. His car was parked in its usual spot. I left here at eight o'clock, went straight home, had something to eat, watched TV and went to bed.'

And Horton guessed it was the same every night for Janice. 'Where is home?'

'I have an apartment in Admiralty Towers in Queens Street, not far from the harbour.'

Horton knew it. A whole rash of expensive and exclusive apartments had erupted on the site of the old brewery, cheek by jowl with council flats in one of the most deprived areas of Portsmouth — the one that Rowland Gilmore had administered over.

'Did you ever visit St Agnes's?' he asked casually.

She eyed him keenly. 'No. Wrong faith. I go to St John's Cathedral. But if you're asking did I ever see Rowland or come across him, then the answer is yes, very occasionally when I was walking to Mass or coming back from the shops. And before you ask, Inspector, no, we never spoke and I never so much as acknowledged him. Besides, I don't think he recognized me.'

'Why didn't you speak?'

She shrugged her shoulders. 'I didn't see any need to. Sebastian had nothing to do with his brother so I didn't think it was necessary or appropriate for me to strike up an acquaintance.'

Horton wondered if she blamed Rowland Gilmore for not saving her brother, and along with him Tom Brundall. Sebastian had been at the helm so perhaps he was absolved of any blame.

Horton left a short pause before asking the next question, a critical one. 'Ms Hassingham, when your brother was fishing with the Gilmores and Tom Brundall, did he ever say anything that made you think they might be doing something illegal?' He saw her stiffen.

'Of course not.'

Horton eyed her carefully. It appeared she was telling the truth. Her shock and surprise at his question seemed genuine.

'Did Sebastian see his brother, Rowland, after that encounter at the Town Camber?'

'He might have done. I don't know. I wonder what will happen now. I suppose Selina will take over the business.'

And how would Janice take that? From her frown, he guessed not well. They left her to her work. Horton noted that she didn't hurry along the corridor to comfort Selina.

'Sad woman,' Cantelli said when they were outside. 'It's as if you're staring at a world of missed opportunities and regrets when you look at her.'

And you were, Horton thought. 'Let's take a look in Sebastian's office.'

There was no police officer on the door and it wasn't locked. Dennings hadn't got round to that yet, which was rather remiss of him. He should at least have sent a uniformed officer up here to seal off the room. Maybe he thought they'd already covered that, Horton grudgingly admitted. He crossed to Sebastian's gigantic desk, whilst Cantelli rummaged around in the filing cabinets. 'What are we looking for?'

'You don't need me to tell you that. But if you come across . . .' Horton paused as he tried to pull open one of the desk drawers. It had got stuck on something, a piece of paper right at the back. He stretched in and released it and the drawer opened easily. It was an itemized telephone bill for the last month. Horton didn't expect to find the killer's phone number on it — Sebastian Gilmore wouldn't be that stupid — but it would certainly be worthwhile checking out these numbers and talking to Gilmore's contacts and friends. Maybe, Horton thought, scanning the numbers, they'd discover that Sebastian had spoken to his brother more recently than twelve years ago. They'd also need to check his landline. But it was Dennings' job to organize this. Horton had to get on with those CID cases as, no doubt, DCI Bliss would soon remind him.

'I wonder where Gilmore's mobile phone is. It wasn't on his body or in his car.'

'Perhaps his killer threw it into the fish tank,' Cantelli said, peering inside. 'There are some ugly looking blighters in here.'

'I don't expect they'd find you their pin-up of the month.'

That got a small smile from Cantelli.

'It's surprising what ends up in these things; drugs seem to be popular. The number of poor fish I've seen high.'

Finishing his search of the desk, Horton glanced out of the window as the SOCO van entered the yard. 'Get PC Johns, Barney. He can stand guard here.'

Horton continued his swift search whilst waiting for Johns. It revealed nothing. He left Johns with instructions not to admit anyone, and joined Cantelli who had collected the CCTV recordings from the security officer. At the station Cantelli took the tapes to the CID office to view while Horton gave Sebastian Gilmore's itemized telephone bill to Trueman. Any news on Peter Croxton?' Horton asked.

'Which one? We've found twelve so far.'

'Lucky his name wasn't Smith then. I'll be in my office if you get anything new.'

Horton was pleased to see that DCI Bliss wasn't around. He would dearly love to get a piece of evidence before Dennings. He hoped that one of the recordings might show someone entering that warehouse after Sebastian Gilmore, though he couldn't really believe the killer would be that stupid, or they'd be that lucky.

He groaned at the sight of his in-tray, which was overflowing onto his chair. There were pieces of paper with yellow post-it notes stuck on them, urging him to attend to this report, or review this file, or call someone back, but there was one file that caught his eye. Ignoring all the others he picked it up and sat down.

It was thicker than he had anticipated. He could hardly breathe through his anxiety of what he might be about to read on his mother and tried to steel his heart to repel the emotions that he felt sure were bound to assail him. Urging himself to consider this as just another missing persons case, and perhaps one which might provide him with some idea of what the Gilmores had been up to in 1977, he read on. Very soon, though, he found that his emotions were firmly in check and his police training had asserted itself. The investigation into Jennifer Horton's disappearance had been more thorough than he had expected.

A woman had formally reported Jennifer missing; she'd been listed as Horton's head teacher. He remembered her teasing the information out of him and went cold as he recalled that terrible day when he had eventually been taken from school by a social worker back to the flat and from there to a dismal house full of smells, other children and cold, tiny rooms. He shuddered and quickly turned his thoughts back to the file. There had followed a series of interviews with the people who had worked with Jennifer and her neighbours, including the lady that Horton had spoken to earlier at Jensen House, Mrs Cobden. There wasn't much more to add to the information that she'd already given him. Jennifer had left the flat at about one o'clock that day. She had been wearing her best clothes, and make-up, and was in good spirits. Mrs Cobden said she thought Jennifer was going to meet a man, though she had no real evidence to back that up.

Horton flicked through the reports; there were no interviews with Jennifer's friends. Why not? Didn't she have any?

And what about her family? Then his eye caught one report. No family. Both parents dead. Yet the report by a PC Stanley was inconclusive. It didn't say how her parents had died, when or where, and neither did it mention any relatives, save himself as next of kin.

His email alert told him that the press cuttings agency had come through with the articles on Gilmore. Reluctantly he pushed the file on his mother aside and scrolled down them, clicking on the headline of one or two, opening the file and skim reading the articles. He was disappointed to find no photograph of Warwick Hassingham. It seemed a waste of time, but he persisted.

It wasn't until he reached 1997 that he began to see a common factor. He sat up. With a racing heart he clicked back and then onwards again. Yes, several articles had been written by the same journalist: David Lynmor.

Onward Horton clicked and read, oblivious to the noises from outside his office. Then David Lynmor was no longer writing articles on the Gilmores. When did that happen? He checked back. The last one had been September 1997. Was that date significant?

Horton sat forward and steepled his fingers in thought, tapping them against his mouth. The timing was right for the skeleton in the air-raid shelter. But Lynmor could have changed jobs, or emigrated. He could have been run over by the number nine bus, joined a commune, or married an heiress, but Horton knew, by that feeling in his gut, that he hadn't done any of those things.

Lynmor had written extensively about the fishing industry and interviewed the Gilmores on several occasions — many more times, Horton guessed, than had finally appeared as articles in the newspaper and the fishing press. Perhaps he had become *too* curious? Had he discovered something that Sebastian Gilmore wanted kept quiet? Like drug smuggling? Was Lynmor's death, not Peter Croxton's, the secret that Tom Brundall had wanted to confess? He'd got the right theory, just the wrong dead man who had ended up a skeleton in the air-raid shelter.

Clearly, judging by one article Horton now read, David Lynmor had met Rowland Gilmore, because he'd written about the fisherman turned vicar. Had Lynmor discovered something that had made Rowland run to brother Sebastian who had summoned Tom Brundall? Had the three of them killed David Lynmor and stuffed his body in the air-raid shelter? And if so who were Lynmor's relatives?

Horton rose, his mind racing as he considered this new theory. It was possible. His phone rang and, irritated at being interrupted in his train of thought, Horton snatched it up.

'I've just got back from interviewing Russell Newton.'

It took Horton a moment to realize he was speaking to Inspector Guilbert from Guernsey. Now he gave him his full attention.

'He remembers the day on board his boat with Brundall quite well because their party was gate-crashed,' Guilbert continued.

Horton was ahead of him. 'Let me guess, by a journalist.'

'Yes, and a photographer who took that picture.'

'Of course.' Horton clicked his fingers. 'I knew there was something odd about that picture. Brundall isn't only looking surprised and shocked at having his photo taken, but he's not looking directly into camera, he's looking to the right of it, at the reporter.' And Horton wouldn't mind betting who that reporter was. 'Does Newton know the reporter's name?'

'No. The photographer was local though. I checked with the newspaper office. He was called Jacobs. He died in a car crash in August 1996, two weeks after that photograph was taken. His car veered off the road, went over the cliff and burst into flames. He'd been drinking heavily.'

'Or had drink poured down his throat,' added Horton.

'You think it's suspicious?' Guilbert asked, surprised.

'Oh, yes, highly suspicious. I think we've found his reporter friend dead in an air-raid shelter. He's been dead for some years.'

Guilbert gave a low whistle, then said, 'There's another thing. Newton says that after the incident he never saw Brundall again. He became more reclusive. Everything was done by phone, fax and latterly email or through Brundall's solicitor, Nigel Sherbourne. Does this help, Andy? Do you know who Nigel's killer is?'

'Not yet.' *But I will.*

He told Guilbert about Sebastian's death and his theory of the relative seeking revenge.

Guilbert said, 'Right, I'll start looking into Jacobs' death and re-interview Newton to see if I can get anything further from him. Keep me posted.'

'Likewise.'

Horton stuffed the file on Jennifer into the inside pocket of his leather jacket and hurried along to the incident room as Trueman came off the phone.

'I was just trying to get you. Marsden's found a link between Anne Schofield and Rowland Gilmore. They attended the same seminar in 1996. He's finding out if their acquaintance developed after that. And I've got some news about Peter Croxton.'

'Never mind about him,' Horton said excitedly, crossing to the crime board and staring again at the photograph of Brundall. Of course, he could now see clearly the line of Brundall's vision and it wasn't into camera. Lynmor had discovered the fishermen's secret, and had to be killed. Jacobs was murdered because Lynmor might have told him that secret. Taking up a pen Horton began to write the information Guilbert had given him on to the board saying, 'I think I've got an ID on the skeleton. He's—'

'Andy, I think you'll want to know about Croxton.'

Horton paused in mid scribble and turned. The intonation in Trueman's voice told him this was vital information.

Trueman said, 'Croxton doesn't exist. At least not the one who was involved in that marine incident. None of the Peter Croxton's alive or dead matches the age profile of the rescued yachtsman and neither has a Peter Croxton ever lived at that address in Guildford. He gave the coastguards a false name.'

Horton stared at Trueman, his mind racing with this new information. Croxton had disappeared quickly after the incident and hadn't shown for Warwick's funeral. Why? Because he didn't want anyone nosing into his business, or discovering who he really was. So was Warwick's death an accident or had Croxton and the others killed him and now Croxton, or whatever his real name was, had finally silenced the last of those who knew his identity: Sebastian Gilmore. Correction, the last but one. There was him. But he had no idea who Croxton really was. And how the devil were they going to find Croxton? The trail was as cold as that freezer he'd found Sebastian in.

'We'd better see if we can track down any of the coast guards who rescued Croxton to get a description,' Horton said, not very hopeful. He didn't blame Trueman for looking at him incredulously.

'Inspector,' a voice hailed Horton, 'Sergeant Cantelli's on the phone for you.'

Horton took the receiver, but before speaking into it said to Trueman, 'Also see if you can find a missing persons report for a David Lynmor. I believe he's the skeleton in the air-raid shelter. He was a journalist. Yes?'

'I think we've got something on the CCTV recordings that might just interest you,' Cantelli said.

TWENTY-ONE

'It was Walters who spotted it,' Cantelli said.

Horton hid his surprise. 'Glad to know you've earned your keep at last.'

Walters bit into his Mars bar as Cantelli said, 'This is the recording from yesterday evening at seven twenty-five. Sebastian is seen walking into the warehouse. It's taken from the camera in the yard. Nobody goes in after him but someone comes out half an hour later. See here.' Cantelli pointed at the screen and Horton was looking at a short, square-set man, wearing a cap pushed low over his head. He frowned, puzzled. Could this be Sebastian Gilmore's killer, Croxton or whatever his blessed name was, or was it a relative of their skeleton?

'Who goes into the warehouse before Sebastian?'

'Apart from the usual staff, Selina Gilmore and Janice Hassingham.'

And there was no reason why they shouldn't be there.

'I recognized Janice Hassingham,' Walters piped up, having finished his chocolate bar. 'She's on one of the recordings I checked earlier when I was looking for the muggers. She's walking up Queens Street.'

'She lives there, Walters.' Then Horton added sharply, 'That was Wednesday. What time?'

'About half past five.'

'That's early for a woman who usually works late at this time of the year, preparing the accounts,' Horton said thoughtfully.

'She could have had an appointment,' suggested Cantelli. 'Or decided to go Christmas shopping at Oyster Quays.'

Or she could have left early to go to a Cathedral service. There was nothing suspicious in her being in Queens Street, but Horton said, 'Get the recording, Walters, and check the exact time.'

Walters pulled himself up and crossed to his desk where he burrowed under his paperwork to find it. Turning to Cantelli, Horton said, 'Is she on the recording leaving her office at eight last night?'

Cantelli fast-forwarded it. 'There she is.' He pointed to a figure in a long raincoat heading towards the gates. Horton stared at her, feeling he'd just seen something important but couldn't place what it was. Sebastian's car was parked in front of the building.

Walters called out, 'Got it, guv.' He inserted the DVD into the disk drive on his computer, adding, 'I'm sure it's her. You can't mistake that coat, though you can't quite see her features even if I were to enhance it because of that stupid hat. But there's a better shot later.'

'Hat!' Horton felt a bolt of excitement shoot through him. That was it. He was beside Walters in a trice. 'Hurry up, man.'

Impatiently, Horton waited and finally Janice Hassingham came into view. Horton stood back from the screen with a smile. 'Recognize her, Cantelli?'

'Eh?'

Horton saw it was an effort for Cantelli to bring himself back to the case. 'She was at Horsea Marina the night Brundall was killed — the woman in the flowerpot-shaped hat. Janice Hassingham was there.'

'Perhaps she went for a meal,' Cantelli posed.

Horton scoffed. 'A likely story!'

'It's one she could tell though.'

Cantelli was right and Horton couldn't see her killing the man she had loved, or bashing Anne Schofield on the head and setting fire to her. Nor was she the person who had tried to kill him on his boat. She wasn't tall enough. She couldn't have killed Sherbourne either. Apart from the fact that she had to get to Guernsey, she wouldn't have been strong enough to lift a dead body and dump it in Sherbourne's office. But he was very curious to know why she had been at Horsea Marina the night of the fire and why she hadn't thought to mention it. His instinct was screaming at him that she knew something about these murders and he was going to determine what.

His phone was ringing. Heading for it, Horton tossed over his shoulder, 'Get her full address, Walters. Ask Seaton for it, he's at the scene of crime — but don't say why we want it.'

'I've got your missing man,' Trueman announced. 'David Lynmor, aged thirty-four, five feet eleven. He was a freelance journalist. His wife reported him missing on fifth of September 1998. She emigrated to Canada in 2004. There's a son.'

Horton had been right. This was their skeleton and he'd probably been killed by Brundall and the Gilmores and even this Peter Croxton. He gave a silent crow of victory. Maybe his revengeful relative theory was right after all.

'How old is the son?'

'Born in 1996.'

Horton felt the bitter taste of disappointment. The killer couldn't be a vengeful son then. 'Any other relatives?' he asked hopefully. Maybe Lynmor's brother had come seeking revenge and he was the man seen leaving Sebastian's warehouse last night.

'I haven't got the complete file, but there's none mentioned in the online report.'

Horton wasn't going to give up on that idea yet. 'Get the full details, Trueman, and ask the Canadian police to contact Lynmor's wife.' *Should he now say widow?* 'We'll be able to match DNA from the son to confirm it really is Lynmor.'

He put down the receiver and was about to call Uckfield when his mobile rang. He hoped it would be Frances Greywell but it was Charlotte Cantelli and she sounded worried.

'It's Barney . . .'

Horton peered through his blinds to see Cantelli hunched over his desk staring at the computer screen but Horton could tell that he wasn't really seeing it. He looked thinner, older and incredibly tired. He pushed his door to.

'Andy, I . . .' Her voice broke and she took a deep breath before continuing. 'I can't reach him. He's pushing me away. He won't even talk to his brother and sisters. He's gone into work because he didn't want to see them. We're all meeting up in half an hour's time to . . . you know, talk about Toni and sort out the funeral arrangements. I thought Barney would change his mind and come home. I know it will help him to start grieving. Andy, I thought you might . . . I know how much he admires and trusts you. Can you persuade him to come home?'

'Leave it with me, Charlotte. I'll get him there, even if I have to strap him to the back of the Harley.'

Horton beckoned to Cantelli to come into his office. Cantelli sat with a weariness that was far more than fatigue. It was as though the life had been sucked out of him leaving him a hulk of bones and flesh. His dark eyes had sunk further into their sockets. Horton knew that just telling Barney to go home wouldn't work. With Charlotte's sorrowful voice ringing in his ears, Horton swiftly brought Cantelli up to date with what Trueman had said about David Lynmor and Peter Croxton and explained his theories, ending with, 'So either Croxton is our killer, wiping out the witnesses to the murder of Warwick and the link with drug smuggling, or it's a relative of the journalist, David Lynmor, seeking revenge for his death. I think the former, because of his attempts to kill me, I can't see a relative of Lynmor's doing that, which means if Croxton believes I've somehow got some information on how my mother was involved with them then I'm

234

next on the hit list.' He could see that his final words had pierced Cantelli's veil of sorrow.

'Take some leave, go away until—'

'What? They catch Croxton? I might be on leave a long time. No, Barney, I'm not running away. I tried it several times when I was in those God awful kids' homes, until I finally realized that running away got me nowhere. I was still lonely. I've also tried to push the past away, but it's returned with a vengeance. I can't run away anymore and neither can you. Don't look so surprised, you know what I mean. You can't bury yourself in work, trying to pretend that you can cope with your loss. I know that's a bit like the pot calling the kettle black, me saying that, but believe me it doesn't work. I've had years of it. Your family needs you and you need them. You must grieve, not bottle things up. Talk about Toni, mourn together and celebrate his life.'

'I just thought being here . . . I can't . . .'

Horton sat forward and said softly but firmly, 'It's OK, Barney. Go home.'

After a moment, Cantelli pulled himself up and nodded sadly. Horton watched him go with a heavy heart. He needed a breath of fresh air. He said to Walters, 'I'm going to talk to Janet Hassingham.'

'Well, she's not at Gilmore's. Seaton said she left there an hour ago, but he gave me the number of her apartment.'

'Did she say where she was going?'

'Home. She couldn't work with all the distraction.' And that suited Horton fine, he thought, hurrying out of the station. As he made for Admiralty Towers he wondered if he should tell Uckfield or Dennings, but the thought of his mother made him hold back.

It was two thirty when he pulled into the car park at the back of the building, and before he could climb off the Harley, the rear door opened and Janice stepped out. From where he was parked he didn't think she could see him; she certainly gave no indication of it as she made for a small silver car in one of the bays. He froze as his copper's nose told him something wasn't right. In her left hand she was carrying a large briefcase, which looked as though it contained a laptop computer, and in her right she was wheeling a suitcase. Was she going away for the Christmas holidays? It was possible. Why then did Horton get the feeling that she was *running* away? Was that just his overripe imagination?

He thought about the sighting of her on the CCTV recording the night Rowland Gilmore had died and her appearance at Horsea Marina when Tom Brundall's boat had been set alight; had Janice Hassingham had a hand in their murders? She could have poisoned Rowland Gilmore and thrown a lighted match on to Brundall's boat. He frowned. There was something bugging him and then, with a shock, he realized what it was. Both Janice and Selina had entered the warehouse before Sebastian, but when had they come out again? Damn, he should have asked. It was a glaring oversight on his part. His head was too full of theories. If Cantelli had been firing on all cylinders he would have asked. There was no time to call in now because Janice was pulling out of the car park. Horton followed at a discreet distance. He was surprised when she turned right into Queens Street and headed towards the harbour, rather than left and out of the city.

Just past Oyster Quays she indicated right and after a short distance swung into the Wightlink Ferry car park. He pulled up on the opposite side of the road as she spoke to the man on the gate who directed her into one of the many already packed boarding lanes. She wouldn't get far on the Isle of Wight, he thought, unless she had a private aeroplane waiting for her at Bembridge or Sandown Airport to take her on somewhere. Or perhaps she was going to meet Croxton on a boat in one of the marinas there. That would certainly fit with his theory about Brundall and Sherbourne's killer travelling back and forth to Guernsey by boat. Maybe she was just spending the Christmas holiday on the Isle of Wight and he should let her go, but something told him he had to pursue her, even despite or perhaps because of a sense of excitement mixed with foreboding.

He craned his neck to see the electronic sign in front of the car park, which told him the next sailing was at three o'clock and it was already five minutes past three. The ferry was running late, probably because of the high winds and the sheer number of Christmas holiday passengers. He could see it now coming into the port and knew it had a twenty minute turnaround time to unload and load cars.

He watched Janice hurry across to the ticket office and then saw her re-emerge and climb into her car. He called Walters and asked him to check the CCTV recording for the times that Selina and Janice left the warehouse and call him back. Then he waited until the first cars started loading and swung into the car park. He didn't want to alert the staff to the fact that he was a police officer and on duty, so wearing his helmet he dashed into the ticket office, removing it once inside, and praying he'd get a ticket for the same ferry even though it was crowded. His luck was in. A few minutes later he was on board and they were pulling out of Portsmouth Harbour.

He found Janice in the main passenger lounge at the opposite end of the ship to the café. Taking care not to be seen by her he positioned himself at one of the tables where he was alone, keeping the back of her head in view, and when the safety announcement was over he called Trueman. For once he was grateful for the noise of the overexcited screaming children who were running up and down the aisles; they would drown out his voice.

'Is there an Isle of Wight number on Sebastian Gilmore's mobile phone bill? The code's 01983.'

'I'll check and call you back.'

Knowing that Janice couldn't get away on board the ferry, Horton waited until they were in the Solent and the crowd at the café had died down before fetching himself a bottle of water and some sandwiches. He wasn't sure when he'd next get the chance to eat. Janice was still there when he returned to the same table. The captain announced that the crossing would be slightly choppy, and a couple of car alarms were sounding off on the decks below as the ship began to roll a little.

He called Walters. 'Well?'

'I've looked until my eyes feel as though they're going to pop out of their sockets but I'm damned if I can see either of them leave that warehouse at any time. They could have slipped out at the same time as the forklift truck and been hidden behind it.'

That was a strong possibility. 'Check the recordings in the reception area and see if they re-entered the office block. And find out where Selina Gilmore is.'

Horton bit into his sandwich. So, the only person who came out after Sebastian Gilmore was the square-set man wearing a cap. Could this have been Selina? The build was wrong but she could have been padded out, and if she were wearing flat shoes instead of her usual high-heeled boots then the height wouldn't be far off. But why kill her father? Had Sebastian threatened to tell the police about his part in the killings and Selina thought it would ruin the business and her career?

Was this square-set man Janice Hassingham or a relative of Lynmor's? Perhaps it was an employee and perfectly innocent. Or it could be an employee with a grudge against Sebastian. Gilmore's death might have nothing to do with Brundall's and Rowland Gilmore's. But no, that couldn't be.

His mobile rang. It was Trueman. 'There's no Isle of Wight number on Gilmore's mobile account.'

Damn. Was this a wild goose chase? He rung off with a sinking heart. He was mightily glad he hadn't said anything to Uckfield. Best stay on the ferry as she docked at Fishbourne and then return to Portsmouth. He sat back feeling despondent. Munching his sandwiches, he ran through the facts. What was Selina's part in all this? Had she really gone to Tri Fare? Was that connection between Anne Schofield and Rowland Gilmore important? Was he completely hoisting up the wrong mainsail?

With Janice in sight, Horton had another thirty-five minutes on the ferry, so he delved into his jacket and took

238

out the somewhat crumpled file on his mother. He studied the statements taken from the casino staff.

There was nothing startling in them, just what a good worker Jennifer was and attractive. The punters loved her. Then one bright copper — thank the Lord for some intelligence in the force — had thought to ask if there had been any one punter in particular. There had been. Horton sat up. Hallelujah! But as he read on, his exhilaration turned to disappointment. The witness, Irene Ebury, couldn't recall his name and said that Jennifer had been very coy about him. Was this Irene Ebury still around? Could he find her? The address she had given no longer existed; those houses had been pulled down to make way for the continental ferry port.

He read on. Irene said that Jennifer had first started going out with this man about a year ago. Then he must have vanished from the scene because Jennifer had been mooching around with a face as long as a bloodhound's. Just before her disappearance, though, he must have returned because Jennifer brightened up. She hinted that she was going to chuck in the job, which of course had made the police think that she had run off with lover boy.

His heart gave a lurch at that. *Funny thing was though*, he read, *she kept singing that stupid song — you know the one that Marilyn Monroe sang in some film about diamonds?*

Horton felt as though he'd experienced an electric shock. Christ! How the memories flooded back. 'Diamonds are a girl's best friend'. Of course. This was it.

His mind whirred back down the years, his mother singing and dancing around the living room. Him smiling at her, happy because she was happy. She had taken his hands and spun him round, singing 'Diamonds are a girl's best friend'. Avidly he scoured the report.

"She nearly drove us all mad. I reckon lover boy decided to come back and she had to decide whether to go with him and ditch the kid, or stay behind and give up the boyfriend. Poor little bastard didn't stand a chance, and I mean the kid. I've never seen anyone so much in love as Jennifer was with this man. I don't blame her for being tempted but what mother could leave her own kid?"

Horton felt his breath coming quickly. Had this man, who Horton reckoned must be Croxton, returned to kill his mother? He felt cold, and hatred filled his veins. He had been right about smuggling, but wrong about the contraband. It wasn't drugs, it was diamonds. And his mother was dead.

His sandwich stayed half eaten on the table before him; the children's noisy squeals and car alarms faded as his mind raced through the facts. Jennifer had met Croxton a year before her disappearance. Warwick had been alive then. After the murder of Warwick Hassingham, Croxton had vanished from the scene because he didn't want the spotlight on him and his illegal business — diamond smuggling. He returned not because he was in love with Jennifer, no, Horton couldn't believe that of a ruthless man like Croxton, but because Jennifer had been bothering Sebastian Gilmore about where Croxton had gone, and why he had gone. Jennifer had become a liability. Horton tested his hypothesis. Croxton had returned to pick up with Jennifer, to lure her away and to kill her.

His heart hammered. He was convinced he was on the right track. According to what Janice Hassingham had said, Horton guessed that Jennifer had once been Warwick's girl, but Croxton had come along and swept her off her feet. Had Croxton killed Warwick because he was in love with Jennifer? Horton doubted it. Rather it was a case of Warwick wanting out of the diamond smuggling being organized by Croxton. They were all in on it, which is how they had made so much money, and somehow David Lynmor, the journalist, had discovered this, confronted Rowland with it, and had also challenged Brundall about it when he was on Russell Newton's boat in Guernsey. As a result, Lynmor had been lured to his death in Rowland's air-raid shelter and Jacobs, the Guernsey photographer, had met with a car accident. Horton suspected Sebastian Gilmore had still been involved in smuggling until his death and if he was about to confess all to the police then perhaps Selina Gilmore, who knew about the smuggling, didn't want it coming out. That would have been motive enough for her to kill her father. And if the square-set man was Selina then she would have entered the warehouse carrying something containing the disguise. He reached for his phone.

'Walters, did Selina go into the warehouse any time during the day carrying a case or carrier bag?'

'No.'

Could she have hidden it before yesterday?

Walters said, 'You wanted to know where she is. She's not at work or home. No one seems to know where she's gone.'

'Find her.' He was about to ring off when he said, 'Did Janice enter the warehouse carrying anything?'

'Only a briefcase.'

Hardly big enough then to carry an overcoat and hat. Then he reconsidered. There were all kinds of briefcases and accountants often used a special kind to carry large files. With a quickening pulse he said, 'Was it a large square one?'

'Yes.'

He rang off as the announcement came for the passengers to return to their cars. Now there was no question of his returning to Portsmouth. He had to stick with Janice Hassingham.

Horton disembarked before her and rode to the top of the exit road where he waited until he saw her car and then slipped into the traffic behind it. It was dark and raining heavily. Only the brightness of the Christmas lights on the houses he rode past illuminated the gloom of the December evening.

She turned right at the traffic lights and Horton, who knew the island well, having spent some time seconded here as a PC, thought she must be heading for Cowes, but she branched off and took the road to the capital of the island, Newport. There she made for Yarmouth.

He kept his distance but didn't let her tail lights out of his sight. She didn't seem to notice she was being followed.

Then she was through Yarmouth and heading for Freshwater Bay, where she turned off on to a country road. He hung further back, not wanting to alert her. The road twisted and turned. He eased the Harley round a bend in the country lane and found she'd disappeared.

He drew up. There was nothing but darkness. She couldn't have vanished into thin air. She must have turned off. Then he saw it. It was a track, which led up Tennyson Down. There was nowhere else she could have gone.

Slowly he set off after her. The road climbed towards the cliff top. Any further and he'd be over the edge. Then a tall hedgerow and gate came into view. Beyond it he could see a substantial modern house. Janice's car was on the driveway.

Horton took his mobile phone from his jacket pocket and once again called Trueman.

'Find out who owns Down House, just above Freshwater on Tennyson Down. Call me back as soon as you've got it. And hurry.'

Horton climbed off the Harley and kicked down the stand. The wind was roaring around him, bringing with it the taste of salt and sea spray. There was a light in the downstairs window to his left and another light upstairs. Even through the darkness he could see that the gardens were landscaped and the house, he guessed, must have at least seven bedrooms. It wouldn't come cheap. There was a large triple garage on the right. The doors were closed.

He waited impatiently for Trueman's call, wondering what was going on inside the house but not daring to get closer yet. His phone rang and he answered it almost instantly. But it wasn't Trueman. It was Dr Clayton.

'I can't talk now,' Horton said irritably. 'I'll call you back.'

'I thought you'd like to know what killed Rowland Gilmore,' Gaye responded crisply. Horton could tell he had offended her.

'I do. It's just I'm on surveillance.'

'Should have switched off your phone then. It was puffer-fish.' And she rang off.

Before he could even digest what she had said his phone rang again and this time it was Trueman.

'The house is owned by a James Rowthorpe.'

The name meant nothing to Horton but then Croxton would hardly have continued using that name. Perhaps Rowthorpe was Croxton's real name. He told Trueman to get all the information he could on him.

'Superintendent Uckfield wants to know what you're up to and DCI Bliss is asking where you are. What do you want me to tell them?'

'Tell the superintendent the truth. He can inform DCI Bliss, but for heaven's sake don't let Uckfield come charging in yet. Janice Hassingham might be here to spend Christmas with her lover and I'd look a damn fool with the Isle of Wight police swooping on us,' he answered, knowing that wasn't what he believed. 'Let me talk to her, then I'll call Uckfield.'

Horton switched off his mobile and stuffed it into his jacket pocket, wondering if he was also about to find Selina Gilmore inside. Leaving the Harley where it was, he pushed back the gate and went to meet his mother's killer: Peter Croxton.

TWENTY-TWO

The door opened before he got there, and a tallish man in his late fifties, with short, cropped grey hair, was standing on the threshold. He was expensively dressed in fawn casual trousers and a navy blue jumper. His eyes were vivid green and in a sharp-featured face that the neatly trimmed grey beard did little to disguise. Horton recognized him instantly. Here was the sharp-featured man he remembered from the Camber quayside, when he'd been a child there with his mother.

'Inspector Horton, come in.'

Horton wasn't surprised that he knew him. After all he had tried to kill him twice. He stepped inside feeling his body tense; it took an effort to keep his expression neutral. He felt a deep loathing and searing hatred for this man who had confined him to years of emptiness.

He followed Rowthorpe through an airy and spacious hall and into a cream and beige room on the left. It took a while for Horton to locate Janice Hassingham, because the room was immense, but he locked eyes on her as she sat on one of the three brown leather sofas that straddled a large fireplace. Behind her was a wall of glass that gave onto the grounds and, Horton guessed, would sport a spectacular view of the sea only it was too dark to make it out. The rain was lashing against the windows. There was no sign of Selina Gilmore.

Rowthorpe crossed the beech wood floor to the sofa where Janice was sitting and picked up a tumbler of amber liquid. Horton thought that he'd need a loudhailer to make conversation in a room this size as he followed him, and a compass to find your way around the house. He'd thought Sebastian Gilmore's house was a palace, but it was a mere shed compared to this. These men had made a mint out of their smuggling, and lives had been sacrificed because of their greed. Horton was determined to see that Croxton paid for it. He knew he too would suffer, because the truth about his mother would emerge, but maybe it was time for it all to come out, though he didn't know how Catherine would react to that. Fear gripped his heart at the thought that she might use it to prevent him from ever seeing Emma.

He stared down at Janice Hassingham and started violently. She was smiling and it transformed her face. She was no longer the dull, sad woman he and Cantelli had seen that morning in her office; years had sloughed off her and with it the heavy coarseness of her features. Her eyes were also vivid green, and her usual pallid complexion was flushed with exhilaration. The breath suddenly caught in Horton's throat. From the first time he'd set eyes on her at Horsea Marina he had known there was something familiar about her, but it had taken this transformation for him to understand why he'd had that feeling. Now he knew what had triggered the memory of the man on the Town Camber quayside. He also knew the true identity of the man standing beside her.

'You're Warwick Hassingham,' he said, staring at Croxton, whilst his brain raced to assimilate this latest revelation and put it in place with everything else he had learned.

'I haven't used that name for years. Drink, Inspector, or should I say, Andy? After all we're old friends.'

That last comment brought Horton up sharply. It made him sick with fury. Here was his mother's boyfriend and the man who had killed her. He wanted to hurl himself at Warwick

245

Hassingham and smash his face to a pulp. It took every ounce of his willpower not to do so and only the fact that he could see that was exactly what Hassingham wanted restrained Horton. They weren't alone in this house. Hassingham had protection. He spun round to see a man built like a brick outhouse, with shoulders bigger than DCI Dennings, standing in the doorway.

'My bodyguard, Trevor,' Warwick explained unnecessarily. Horton couldn't think of a more fitting job for eighteen stone of muscle. And he didn't fancy his chances against the shaven-headed muscle man. He turned his gaze back to Janice, who was looking smug; he'd get no help there.

'How long have you known that your brother was alive?' he addressed her sharply.

'Since I overheard Sebastian talking to Rowland on the telephone last Tuesday.'

'And that was why you were at the marina on Wednesday night? You went to see Tom.'

'Yes, I didn't know where he was until Rowley told me, but by then I was too late. He was already dead.'

'And how do you feel about your brother killing the only man you ever loved?' Horton said, watching her closely. Her eyes flicked to Warwick's.

'Sebastian killed Tom and that's why I had to kill him.'

'You locked him in the freezer.' So it *was* Janice.

'Yes.'

Then he recalled Sebastian's alibi. 'But Sebastian was at Tri Fare the night Brundall was killed.'

'The sales director lied. Seb asked him to. Selina went to Tri Fare alone. She lied to you too.'

Could Horton believe her? Her face was expressionless. Warwick was looking so sure of himself. Horton knew then that Warwick had killed Brundall and had spun his sister some claptrap about it being Sebastian. He'd got Janice to kill Sebastian for him. The evil bastard.

'Sit down,' Warwick commanded.

An arm shot out and Horton felt as though his shoulder had been trapped in a vice. He couldn't prevent a cry of agony escaping, as Muscles pushed him onto the sofa. Releasing him after a sign from Warwick, Horton rubbed his shoulder. Fuming with anger and smarting with pain, he said, 'Did you kill my mother?'

'Jennifer Horton's little boy a copper! It was a bit of a shock when Seb told me. It wasn't until Rowley returned to Portsmouth and made the connection that Seb realized who you were. I never thought you'd end up on the right side of the law. Just shows how wrong you can be about kids. It scared poor little Rowley almost shitless. Every day he lived in dread that you'd come knocking on his door to arrest him. He kept a very close eye on you.'

'You mean the newspapers.'

'You saw them?' Warwick glanced at his watch.

He knows I might have called for help and he wonders how long he's got. Horton wished now that he had done so, instead of telling Trueman to wait. His heart was thumping against his ribcage.

Warwick said, 'I managed to get rid of them after that woman vicar left for the church. I didn't expect the Church to put in a replacement so quickly and neither did Seb.'

'You killed Anne Schofield just because she'd seen those newspaper articles!' Horton cried, anger welling up in him.

'We couldn't take the risk. She said you'd already seen them.'

'So you frightened the poor woman into calling me, knowing that if she mentioned my mother I'd come running, and you thought you'd kill us both at the same time.'

'Pity you refused to die then, and on your boat. Although I thought I'd succeeded until Seb told me you'd been interviewing my sister. Still, third time lucky.'

Horton tried to ignore the threat, but he shuddered inside at the thought of the kind of end Hassingham had in store for him. It would probably be a house fire, if Hassingham ran true to form. And would Janice also be a victim? Horton guessed so, though Janice looked oblivious to the fact. Had Uckfield got enough information on James

Rowthorpe and this house to connect it with the murders and alert the island's police? Horton doubted it, and he was probably still waiting for that phone call from him, which unless he did something to get out of this, would never come.

Whilst trying to think of a diversion to distract Muscles' attention from him, he said, 'Which one of you killed David Lynmor, the skeleton in Rowland's air-raid shelter?' He'd scored a point by the look of surprise on Warwick's face. Only it was a hollow victory; Horton doubted he'd be allowed to live long enough to celebrate.

'Lynmor was a pest. He tracked Rowley to Wales and then to Portsmouth.'

'And then he found Brundall in Guernsey and grabbed a local photographer to gate-crash Newton's party. We haven't been as slow or dim as you think,' Horton sneered, 'and even if you kill me, which I take it you intend to do, then there'll be others after you.'

'I doubt that. I disappeared once, I can do it again.'

'It might not be so easy next time,' Horton threatened, but could see his words held no terror for Warwick Hassingham. This man probably had various escape routes and identities already mapped out. 'Who killed Lynmor and Jacobs?'

'I killed Jacobs and Sebastian dealt with Lynmor. He lured him to Rowley's house and stuffed his body in the air-raid shelter. He knew that Rowley would never go in there and find it. Rowley was cracking under the pressure. He was our weakest link. When he entered the church Seb wondered if he'd confess but Seb managed to persuade Rowley that the church would be more grateful for his money than his confession, and besides if he confessed that he was party to a million-pound diamond raid and a murder, then they wouldn't take him and Rowley couldn't cope with that, not after his wife and kid had died. It meant more to him than anything, and so he kept quiet. But Seb and I always kept an eye on him.'

And Rowland, a man of the church, had lived with that past all those years. How could he have been such a hypocrite?

'I see you disapprove,' Warwick continued. 'Rowley thought God had punished him by taking Teresa and Claire from him. Rowley tried to atone for his sins for the rest of his life, by living like a pauper and devoting himself to God and his parishioners.'

'Until Brundall showed up on Tuesday wanting to confess,' Horton snapped, but his mind had picked up on something Warwick Hassingham had said. The four fishermen had killed Croxton, or whatever his real name was, and had claimed it was Warwick's body. Why? He'd been right about the diamonds but it wasn't smuggling. Warwick had said 'a diamond raid', which meant a robbery.

He had to get Warwick to tell him about it, not that it would do him much good if he was dead, but he was still alive and he would fight with all the strength and guile he had to keep it that way.

Warwick crossed the room and poured himself another drink. 'Unfortunately, Brundall had developed a conscience as well as cancer.'

'And that was when Sebastian came scurrying across to Cowes to meet up with you so that you could plan his death.'

'I told him to loosen the gas cooker pipe on his return and then later that evening throw a lighted match on to Brundall's boat.'

Horton dashed a glance at Janice. Her hands were in her lap and her body erect as she sat on the edge of the sofa. Her eyes followed her brother. Yet, Horton was curious, her expression had changed; she was no longer smiling and there was something sharp and dangerous behind her eyes.

Then Horton saw quite clearly what had happened. 'You've got that wrong,' he said with an edge of steel to his voice. 'You came back with Sebastian on his boat on Wednesday morning, only no one saw you. You stayed below deck whilst the boat went through the lock. Sebastian left for his office and then for Tri Fare as he told us. Only you told your sister that the sales director at Tri Fare had lied, as had Selina. It was you who went to meet Tom

Brundall on board his boat. And you who loosened the gas cooker piper and then left. You saw Nigel Sherbourne arrive. You guessed what Brundall was going to do, or maybe he told you. Here was a man who was dying; perhaps he didn't care if you killed him. Maybe he wanted you to kill him and by doing so we would start an investigation and the truth would come out. That was Brundall's confession, only he couldn't have envisaged you'd kill Sherbourne, his Guernsey solicitor.'

Horton could see that Hassingham didn't like this very much. Horton was very close to the truth. He risked another glance at Janice; she was so tense that Horton thought she might snap in half.

He paused. 'Later that evening you threw the match on to the boat and left Horsea Marina to come back here, but not on Sebastian's boat because it didn't leave the marina. How did you get here, and how did you get to Guernsey and back? Do you keep a boat in Cowes Marina or Yarmouth?'

Warwick said, 'Are you sure you don't want a drink, Andy?'

Horton flinched at the use of his name. His mind spun down the years when he'd heard this man speak to him. He felt physically sick. Warwick must have seen the torment in his eyes.

'You always were a bright kid, Andy. Bit of a pain in the arse sometimes, but I could always get rid of you with money to buy an ice cream or go to the pictures, whilst Jennifer and I . . .'

Horton leapt up and was halfway across the room before Muscles fell on him like a starving tiger and nearly ripped his arms from their sockets.

Warwick waited a moment, watching Horton's grimace of pain, before he said, 'Let him go.'

Horton collapsed on the floor trying to ease the pain in his arms and shoulders without betraying how much it hurt. His eyes flicked to Janice and what he saw shocked him. Quickly he looked away, not wishing to draw Hassingham's attention to his sister's expression of loathing. No, it was more than that. It was a fury that exceeded even his. Horton felt hope. But what chance would he and a middle-aged woman stand against Muscles and Warwick Hassingham? Warwick was older than Horton and not nearly as fit. Horton knew he'd get the better of him, but he doubted he'd stand a chance against the Jolly Green Giant.

Janice rose. 'I'm hungry. I'll make some sandwiches.'

'We haven't got much time. We'll be leaving in five minutes.'

'We can take some with us.'

As she left the room, Warwick said, 'It'll give the sad bitch something to do.'

'What are you going to do with her?'

'What do you think?'

'She's your sister, for God's sake.'

Warwick shrugged and Horton saw the evil that had driven this man to kill, cheat and lie. He shuddered to think what his mother had suffered at his hands, and prayed her death had been swift. He silently vowed that before he died he would make Warwick Hassingham pay in some way for what he had done.

Steeling himself to control his feelings, he said, 'So you all got rich on the proceeds of this diamond raid.'

'Yes. And we wouldn't have done if it hadn't been for Jennifer. I see that shocks you. Jennifer was very beautiful; she met Peter Croxton in the casino. He fell for her in a big way and couldn't resist a bit of pillow talk.'

'Which you encouraged,' Horton said with bitterness. Warwick wouldn't have let his mother live with that knowledge.

'He told her he was about to undertake the biggest diamond robbery in history and that he would buy her all the diamonds she wanted.'

'And she told you.' Horton drew himself up. He heard the implications of Warwick's words about his mother's sexual habits. Warwick Hassingham had been nothing more than a bloody pimp, using his mother's infatuation of him to extract valuable information from Croxton.

'Croxton was a con artist and a very good one. He'd already set up the false identity of James Rowthorpe. I simply took it over when he died. We were very alike and that's what gave me the idea in the first place, though it was Jennifer who first pointed out the likeness to me.'

Horton felt a pang of sympathy for his mother and he was shocked by the emotion. It was as if the picture of her he'd been looking at for years had suddenly and sharply come into focus. And it wasn't how he had imagined it. For once he put himself in her shoes and imagined her as a victim and not his cruel, heartless mother.

He said, 'So Croxton pulled off a big jewellery heist.'

'Hatton Garden. He got away with millions,' Warwick said boastfully, as though it had been his robbery. Horton saw that the temptation to tell him was too big to resist.

Warwick topped up his drink. 'He was an importer and exporter of diamonds so he knew his way around. He wasn't called Croxton there. He used a dual identity. Everyone at Hatton Garden knew him as Philip Crane. Then on the fifteenth of August 1977 he simply entered the vaults and emptied them, got away with diamonds, jewellery and cash worth over £1.5 million. No one noticed they'd gone until Monday morning; by then it was too late. Most of the people whose safety deposit boxes were stolen never came forward because they didn't want anyone to know what they had in them. They were either the proceeds of crime or tax evasion. It was clever and simple.'

'Croxton drove down from London that night,' Warwick said. 'He'd hired a motorboat and arranged for Jennifer to meet him, only she didn't turn up. We did.' Had his mother known what was going to happen? He didn't like to think so. That would make her an accessory to robbery and murder. How could he live with that if it came out? And it would. His mother's past would be emblazoned across every newspaper and television screen in the country when or if Warwick

Hassingham came to trial. Even if his mother's part in this was innocent there would be enough mud thrown for it to stick. Horton saw slipping from him both his career and his daughter; the two things he valued above all else in the world, and he shuddered at the memory of being so utterly and completely alone once again. He wasn't sure he could bear it. But what could he do — kill this evil bastard sitting arrogantly before him, with that smug grin on his sharp pointed face and wickedness glowing from his green eyes? It went against everything he believed in and yet . . .

Janice reappeared with a shrink-wrapped packet of sandwiches and some on a plate. She set them down on a table between her and Warwick.

'Thought you might like some now,' she said. 'Before we get going.'

Hassingham took one, smiling sycophantically at her. With his mouth full he said, 'I took the motorboat out with Croxton on board, dead by then, of course. The others met me off the Isle of Wight. We scuttled the boat, staged the accident and called the coastguards. I became Croxton and poor Warwick Hassingham perished overboard in a heroic rescue.'

Janice's hands were grasped so tightly in her lap that her knuckles were white. The hatred in her eyes shook Horton. How could Warwick not see it? But then he was so sure of himself that he wouldn't have noticed it if she had spat daggers at him. And even if she had done, Warwick wouldn't have cared. This was a man who had manipulated and destroyed so many people and got away with it that he thought he was invincible.

Horton could see that she hadn't been fooled by her brother's lies; she knew that Sebastian hadn't killed Tom Brundall, because she had seen her brother kill him. She'd been there. Rowland had told her where to find Tom; that was what she had said. And even through the pain in his shoulders, his feelings of hatred and panic that this man was about to destroy his life, as he had destroyed his mother's, Horton was making connections. He was grappling to arrange the facts, and one leapt out at him. Janice had been walking down Queens Street to the vicarage to find out where Tom was staying and then to kill Rowland, because in that overheard conversation between the brothers she had discovered that Warwick hadn't perished in the sea after all but was alive, fit and wealthy. But why had she killed Rowland and Sebastian Gilmore?

Warwick was saying, 'I discovered I had a talent for selling diamonds and getting people to do what I wanted. I've made a good living from it.'

Horton brought his attention back to Warwick whilst his mind raced with thoughts. 'You threw Croxton's body into the sea, dressing it with your rings, and by the time he was washed up, he was unrecognizable. There was no DNA test in those days so how did you get away with the dental records matching up?'

'I switched them. Jennifer found out who Croxton's dentist was, then I stole my records from my dentist and substituted them. It was quite simple.'

Had his mother known about the switch? He wanted to believe she was an innocent victim in all this, but his copper's brain was telling him something different and it made him sick to his stomach.

'And Sebastian did the odd smuggling of diamonds for you.'

That got a reaction from Janice. 'I don't believe it!'

Warwick turned his patronizing and pitying gaze on his sister. Her head came up and she glared at him.

'How do you think he could afford to live like he did?' Warwick said, reaching for another sandwich. Horton wondered if Selina knew this. With his mouth full, Warwick said, 'We'd better get moving.'

There was only one track out of here; otherwise it was over the cliff and into the sea. But again Warwick thwarted him.

Stuffing the rest of the sandwich in his mouth, he said, 'Trevor has many talents, and one of them is piloting a helicopter.'

Trevor grabbed Horton and pulled him up as though he was a rag doll. So that was how Warwick got to Guernsey to kill Sherbourne and back again. After killing Brundall, he must have caught the Fast Cat or Hovercraft back to the Isle of Wight where Terry was waiting with the helicopter, only there had been some delay in getting to Sherbourne before he'd left for his client on Thursday morning.

As Trevor hauled Horton to the door, Horton said to Janice, 'You don't think your brother's going to take you with him? You're a liability like me. You know too much. Once outside he'll kill us both, or maybe Trevor will kill you and Warwick me.'

She dashed hateful eyes at Warwick and in them Horton saw a glimmer of triumph as the final pieces of the puzzle fell into place. His heart lurched. He knew what she had done, but he still didn't know why. He tried to recall how long it had taken Rowland Gilmore to die of poison, for Horton was certain that Janice was killing her brother the same way she had killed Rowland Gilmore — with pufferfish poison in the sandwiches. When would it take effect? Should he tell Warwick? Horton needed time to think, but that was a luxury he didn't have as Trevor manhandled him along the path and onto the sodden grass, the icy rain beating into his face. Janice and Warwick were in front of them, their bodies leaning into the bitterly cold wind, Warwick with his hand firmly on his sister's arm. If Horton did nothing, then surely he was as guilty of murder as Janice would be? Yet if Warwick died then the facts about his mother's past need never come out. But if he let Warwick die, Janice and Trevor had heard what Warwick had said about Jennifer Horton, and so what was he going to do: kill them as well? Hardly.

The helicopter suddenly loomed out at them from the dark. Horton could hear the waves crashing onto the rocks below the cliff face and wondered if that was where they would find his battered and broken body. With his heart pounding he shouted above the roar of the wind. 'Will you push Janice out over the sea, Warwick, or is that pleasure reserved for me?'

Warwick spun round and a slight nod of his head warned Horton what was about to happen. In that split second he tensed his stomach before a fist crashed into it. The breath expelled from his body like a balloon being punctured with a pin and he doubled over in agony. Muscles hauled him up and dragged him along. Even in his pain and discomfort Horton was wrestling with his conscience. Time was running out for three of them. They were beside the helicopter and Warwick was showing no signs of the poison taking effect. Janice looked confident though. Taking a breath, Horton knew what he had to do.

'She's poisoned you, Warwick, just as she poisoned Rowley. It was in the sandwiches. If you don't get help now, you'll die like Rowley did.'

Warwick smiled, but as he turned to his sister and saw the triumphant grin of hatred on her face the smile died on his lips.

Horton pressed home his advantage. 'Call for the ambulance or get Trevor to fly you to a hospital. There might still be time.'

Warwick grabbed Janice by her arms. His mouth opened but no sound came from it. Janice stared at her brother. 'It's too late, Warwick. You won't get out of this one. You ruined my life and you ruined Mum's. You let her believe her beloved son was dead. She died because of your stupid filthy greed. You're evil, wicked and I hope you rot in hell,' she screeched above the wind.

Horton swiftly turned to Trevor, who still had a grip like iron on him. 'For God's sake let me go. I might be able to help him.'

'You're going to die, Warwick,' Janice roared as he suddenly let go of her, and gasping for breath, he sank to his knees. Trevor loosened his grip on Horton to step forward and help Warwick. It had been the moment Horton had been waiting for. With lightning speed he brought his knee up hard into Muscles' groin and felt the impact with his balls. Screaming in agony and holding on to his crotch, Trevor buckled over. Horton brought his fist up, ramming it as hard as he could into his jaw and forcing the man down like a sack of lead. Horton raced over and grabbed Warwick who was struggling to breathe and beginning to convulse. Janice was watching him, smiling.

Horton could see he hadn't got long. There was nothing he could do to save him. He didn't have a moment to lose. He had never pleaded in his life, but there was a first time for everything.

'What did you do with her, Warwick?' he said, reaching for his phone. 'For God's sake tell me what you did with my mother's body.'

Warwick opened his mouth. He struggled to speak. His face was contorted with pain. Horton bent low over him. 'Just tell me, did you kill her? Nod or shake your head.'

Horton could hardly bear to see the suffering and horror in Hassingham's eyes. He told himself he was looking into the eyes of a ruthless killer and an evil manipulator of people. 'Did you kill her?' Horton repeated.

Hassingham shook his head.

'Did any of the others kill her?'

Hassingham was convulsing. He didn't have long to live.

'Did they kill Jennifer?' Horton shouted above the roar of the wind, grabbing Hassingham by his jacket lapels. Finally, just when Horton thought it was going to be too late, Hassingham shook his head. Horton looked into his terrified eyes and saw he was telling the truth.

He lowered Hassingham's inert body to the ground, letting out a breath, feeling the tension drain from him. Unexpectedly he was swamped with an emotion so strong that it made him feel sick. Was she still alive today? Could he find her? Did he want to?

Then some instinct warned him of danger; he was caught off guard but managed to dodge to the side. He was too late though to fend off the violent blow, and it struck him on the side of his head. He slumped forward. He felt the phone being snatched from his hand. Through the shooting pain and his blurred vision he looked up to see Trevor running towards the helicopter. It spluttered into life, and shakily Horton pulled himself up. The ground spun and he staggered around, trying desperately to clear his head and focus on what was happening.

Horton had no idea where his phone was, probably on the cliffs below. He had to get back to the house and alert the authorities. Then he looked round for Janice and realized she'd gone. His eyes scoured the dark night until he saw her some distance ahead, running along the cliff edge. What the hell was she doing? Where did she think she was running to? He felt the blast of air as the helicopter lifted off.

'Janice,' he shouted. She was perilously close to the cliff edge, but his warning was drowned by the wind and the roaring of the helicopter.

Suddenly the helicopter was almost on top of him and Horton flattened himself into the sodden earth. As it swept past him, Horton stumbled up. Christ, it was heading for Janice. Horton sprinted after her. Again he cried a warning but it was too late. He watched helpless as the helicopter lurched downwards. Janice gave a cry and staggered back, her foot slipped and scrambled for some firm foothold, then she was gone.

Horton swore and with his head throbbing he increased his speed. The helicopter hovered a moment then swiftly turned and disappeared over the sea and into the night.

Breathless, Horton reached the cliff top where he thought Janice had gone over. Was she dead, smashed to pieces on the rocks below?

The rain suddenly stopped and the moon appeared from out of the scudding clouds. Buffeted by the icy wind, Horton peered over the cliff edge. Cupping his hands around his mouth he called her name and strained his ears listening for her cry. Nothing. She must have gone. But no, there was a faint call.

'Janice!' he roared again.

Another feeble cry in response. It was coming from his right. He edged along the cliff cautiously; he wasn't certain how solid the earth was beneath him, and he didn't want to go over.

Then he saw her. She was lying on a narrow ledge with her hands grasping a small tree trunk whose roots had already lifted from the soil, her legs and feet were dangling perilously over the edge. Horton scoured the cliff face. Could he get down?

'I'll get help.' But it was a long way back to the house.

She screamed as the trunk gave way a little. The earth crashed down below her and splashed into the sea. Shit, one more like that and she'd go. He had no time to lose. If he could just get down to the narrow ledge above her and grab hold of her. It was stupid to try and he knew it. Every instinct was warning him against it, but when had he ever listened to them?

Gingerly, he edged his way down, his feet seeking a foothold. Every now and then he sent earth tumbling down to the rocks below. The sea seemed to be licking its lips in anticipation of receiving them. He could see flecks of white spray crashing on to the rocks. Slowly, he eased his way towards her, talking gently, urging her to hold on. He could see her pale terrified face. His breathing was laboured; his head was pounding, his body screaming with tension. At last he was on a ledge above her.

'I can't hold on much longer,' she cried fearfully.

'I'm nearly there.'

The tree trunk shifted again and she screamed. He could see that she had only one hand holding on to it now the other was swinging over the edge of the cliff, dangling like her body. There was only one tree root left and when that went . . . Horton stretched out a hand, but knew it was pointless. He was still too far away from her.

'Hear my confession,' she cried. 'I overheard Seb talking to Rowley on the telephone saying that Tom was back in Portsmouth and wanting to confess that Warwick had never died, but a man called Croxton had. All those years and I thought Warwick dead. His supposed death killed our mother. *He* killed her. He made her suffer terribly. She died of a broken heart.'

The tree trunk gave again. The earth sprayed down and made her cough. Her face was etched with pain and hatred as she continued. 'After I saw Warwick at the marina I got a copy of Seb's mobile phone bills and called his numbers until on Monday I recognized Warwick's voice. I told him Seb was going to tell you everything and that I would kill Seb in exchange for money and the chance to start a new life. I told him I was sick of being a drudge. Warwick agreed and told me where to come. I knew he would try to kill me, which is why I brought the poison with me.'

Her pale face was contorted with the pain of holding on.

'I'll get closer,' Horton cried urgently.

'No. Don't risk your life. I didn't intend you to come here. I wanted them to pay for what they did to Mum. I've seen justice done. I'll be with her now.'

The trunk snapped like the sound of a hundred canons roaring in his ears. Janice screamed. Horton reached out. It was useless. He snatched his head away not wanting to see her body bounce against the cliff and smash on to the rocks below. His heart ached, his head throbbed and his ears rang with Janice Hassingham's last words and the sound of her screams long after they died.

TWENTY-THREE

He wasn't sure how long he lay on the narrow ledge, feeling numb. Maybe he would have stayed there for ever if it hadn't been for the sound of a helicopter and a powerful white light beaming out of the sky like something out of *Close Encounters*.

Someone was calling his name and the beam of light fell on him. Minutes later he found himself at the top of the cliff, thanking his rescuers. There seemed to be an awful lot of people and a great deal of activity, including the setting down of the police helicopter. A bulky figure in a big camel overcoat climbed out. 'Strange time of night to go rock climbing, Inspector,' Uckfield yelled, drawing level with him. 'What happened? Who's the man in the field?'

'Warwick Hassingham.' He saw Uckfield's surprise. As they returned to the house, Horton explained what had happened, leaving out all reference to his mother. Those who had known about Jennifer's part in the robbery and the marine incident were dead; everyone that was except Trevor, and how much did he know? More than the confession he'd heard tonight from Warwick?

Three police cars were parked outside the house and Horton watched the SOCO van pull into the driveway. He rubbed a hand across his eyes. The investigation into the deaths of Brundall, the Gilmores, Sherbourne and Anne Schofield was over, but the one into Warwick Hassingham and his past was only just beginning. And there was that missing persons file on his mother, which miraculously still nestled in his pocket against his chest.

He said, 'Janice Hassingham poisoned her brother and Rowland Gilmore.'

'Dr Clayton called me after she spoke to you,' Uckfield interrupted. 'She said that the poisonous parts of a puffer-fish — the liver, ovaries and roe — had probably been put in a sandwich.' Horton recalled the fish tank in Sebastian Gilmore's office and Cantelli saying something about some funny-looking blighters in it. 'Apparently this poison is almost impossible to detect and paralysis can set in within ten minutes or can be delayed for up to four hours; after that death within one to two hours.'

Did that mean that Hassingham was still alive, wondered Horton, seeing the coastguard helicopter sweep overhead? It was probably transporting Hassingham to the hospital. If he were alive, then it wouldn't be for long.

'Gilmore's paralysis took longer to take effect than Warwick's,' Horton said. 'I watched Warwick eat the sandwiches she made. Within fifteen minutes he couldn't speak.' Janice had saved his life.

Uckfield said, 'Next time you fancy going off like Indiana Jones, bloody well let me know.'

'Worried the helicopter's blown your budget for the month,' Horton said sarcastically.

'Yes, and you can damn well pay for it.'

Horton managed a smile.

Uckfield said, 'We found Selina Gilmore. She's staying with a friend. Do you think she knows about the diamond smuggling?'

'I wouldn't mind betting so.'

'I'll bring her in for questioning. Do you want to come back with us on the chopper?'

'No. I'll go by boat. I've got the Harley.'

262

'Are you fit enough to ride it?'

'Of course I am.'

'Then you're fit enough to come into work in the morning and make out your report.'

'No. Not tomorrow.' He saw Uckfield eye him curiously. There would be no spending the day with Emma, not now, but there would be in the future and soon. He was determined. And now that the threat to his life was lifted there was no reason for Catherine to prevent him.

'I'm going sailing,' Horton said firmly. He needed to get the stench of Warwick Hassingham out of his nostrils, and the taste of death from his mouth. Battling with the elements would totally occupy his mind on the day he should have been spending with Emma. 'I'll do it Christmas Day.'

Uckfield looked about to say something then changed his mind. Horton watched him stride back towards the house. He turned and made his way to the Harley. His head was reeling with thoughts, only this time they weren't of Emma but of his mother. Neither Hassingham nor the others had killed Jennifer, so who did? Or perhaps she was still alive. Why did she disappear on her birthday? Did she leave him to go with a lover? Did she simply not want the responsibility of bringing up a child? Mrs Cobden, his ex-neighbour, had said that Jennifer was happy. That was hardly the mood of a mother walking out on her child. Would he go in search of her?

He pulled on his helmet. This case had lifted the lid on his past and had let fly all kinds of thoughts, emotions and memories. And painful as these were he knew there was only one answer to that question. He throttled back the bike and headed for the ferry and home.

THE END

ALSO BY PAULINE ROWSON

THE SOLENT MURDER MYSTERIES
Book 1: THE PORTSMOUTH MURDERS
Book 2: THE LANGSTONE HARBOUR MURDERS
Book 3: THE HORSEA MARINA MURDERS

Thank you for reading this book.

If you enjoyed it please leave feedback on Amazon or Goodreads, and if there is anything we missed or you have a question about, then please get in touch. We appreciate you choosing our book.

Founded in 2014 in Shoreditch, London, we at Joffe Books pride ourselves on our history of innovative publishing. We were thrilled to be shortlisted for Independent Publisher of the Year at the British Book Awards.

www.joffebooks.com

We're very grateful to eagle-eyed readers who take the time to contact us. Please send any errors you find to corrections@joffebooks.com. We'll get them fixed ASAP.

CPSIA information can be obtained
at www.ICGtesting.com
Printed in the USA
LVHW032323110423
744123LV00013B/238